THE
COCKTAIL
CLUB

THE
COCKTAIL
CLUB

PAT TUCKER

SBI

STREBOR BOOKS

NEW YORK LONDON TORONTO SYDNEY

Strebor Books
P.O. Box 6505
Largo, MD 20792
http://www.streborbooks.com

ISBN 978-1-59309-481-2
ISBN 978-1-4516-9848-0 (ebook)
LCCN 2014931192

First Strebor Books trade paperback edition August 2014

Cover design: www.mariondesigns.com
Cover photograph: © Keith Saunders/Keith Saunders Photos
Cocktail photo: © Africa Studio/Shutterstock.com

10 9 8 7 6 5 4 3 2 1

Manufactured in the United States of America

For information regarding special discounts for bulk purchases,
please contact Simon & Schuster Special Sales at 1-866-506-1949
or business@simonandschuster.com

The Simon & Schuster Speakers Bureau can bring authors to your live event.
For more information or to book an event, contact the Simon & Schuster Speakers
Bureau at 1-866-248-3049 or visit our website at www.simonspeakers.com.

ACKNOWLEDGMENTS

I thank God for the endless blessings bestowed upon me. All of the love I can muster up to my patient and wonderful mother, and lifelong cheerleader, Deborah Tucker Bodden; and the very best sister a woman could have, Denise Braxton; my gorgeous, patient, and loving husband, Coach Wilson, thanks for your love and support.

My handsome younger brother, Irvin Kelvin Seguro, and Amber; the two best uncles in the world, Robert and Vaughn Belzonie; aunts, Regina, and Shelia; my loving and supportive family in Belize, Aunt Flo, Aunt Elaine, Therese, my cousins, Patrick, Marsha, and Cassandra, and the rest of my cousins, nephews, nieces, and my entire supportive family, including my awesome older brother, Carlton Anthony Tucker.

We don't share the same blood, but I love them like sisters: Monica Hodge, Miranda Moore, Nikki Brock, Karen Williams, Jeness Sherell, Gloria Shannon, Keywanne Hawkins, Desiree Clement, Yolanda Jones, and the rest of those exquisite ladies of Sigma Gamma Rho Sorority Inc. and especially all of my sisters of Gamma Phi Sigma here in Houston, TX.

I'm blessed to be surrounded by friends who accept me just the way I am. ReShonda Tate Billingsley, thanks for your constant support, listening ear, and unwavering faith in my work. Victoria Christopher Murray, your kindness, giving heart, and willingness to help others are the truth!

Alisha Yvonne, I appreciate your help with this story! Many, many thanks to Yolanda L. Gore, for helping to keep me on track, Markisha Sampson, LTC Logan, Ron Reynolds, my KPFT Family, Marlo Blue.

Special thanks to my agent, Sara, and a world of gratitude to my Strebor family, the dynamic duo Zane and Charmaine, for having faith in my work. Special thanks to the publicity Queens led by Yona Deshommes at Atria/Simon & Schuster who help spread the word about my work. JeCaryous Johnson, I look forward to our new adventure!

But as always, I've saved the very highest praise for last, _____ (your name goes there!) Yes, you, the reader! I know you are overwhelmed by choices, and that's what makes your selection of my work such a humbling experience. I will never take your support for granted. I'm so honored to have your support. There were so many book clubs that picked up *Daddy by Default*, *Football Widows* (which is being made into a movie), *Party Girl*, *Daddy's Maybe*, and *A Social Affair*, I wanted to honor some of you with a special shout-out: The bible of AFAM Lit: Black Expressions book club! Johnnie Mosely and the rest of the wonderful men who make up Memphis' Renaissance Men's book club, Sisters are Reading Too (They have been with me from day 1!!) Special thanks to Divas Read2, Happy Hour, Cush City, Girlfriends, Inc., Drama Queens, Mugna Suma, First Wives, Brand Nu Day, Go On Girl, TX 1, As the Page Turns, APOO, Urban Reviews, OOSA, Mahogany Expressions, Black Diamonds, BragAbout Books, Spirit of Sisterhood, and so many more. I appreciate you all!

Also Huge thanks to all of the media outlets that welcomed me on the airwaves to discuss my work: "Inside her Story" with Jacque Reed, on the "Tom Joyner Morning Show," Yahoo Shine, Hello Beautiful, Essence.com, the *Huffington Post-Houston Chronicle—*

Guest Blog, Author Tuesday's presents, Northparan.com, The Book Depository.com, *Black Pearls* magazine, S&S Tipsonlifeandlove. com, nextreads.com, *The Dallas Morning News*.com, Interview— KFDM-CBS Beaumont, TX, 3 Chicks on Lit, Clear Channel Radio News & Comm. Affairs, KIX 96 FM, KARK TV Little Rock, AR, KPRC NBC, Houston Beyond Headlines, Artist First Radio show, The Mother Love Radio Show, It's Well Blog Talk Radio March.

If I forgot anyone, and I'm sure I have, always, charge it to my head and not my heart. Please drop me a line at pattuckerbooks@ gmail.com. I'd love to hear from you, and I answer all emails.

Connect with me on Facebook, and follow me on Twitter @ authorpattucker—I follow back!

Warmly,

Pat

BEFORE
HAPPY
HOUR

PETA

My life would be much better if I wasn't screwing two men at the same damn time. I've known the root of my problem from day one, but why I couldn't do right was beyond me. At times, I said to hell with it all, and allowed the chips to fall where they may.

Lover Number One, Gordon Smith, was worse than a ticking time bomb. Despite this major character flaw, he did it for me. My attraction to him made no sense, but it was what I had to work with. So I handled him with extra care. His crazy behind might have gone postal at any moment. I kept that in mind while we talked on my cell phone.

"I'm finally about to get in the tub," I said. The drinks I'd had with dinner earlier helped to relax me a little, but the bath would finish the job. Between work and everything else, my day had been incredibly busy.

"Oooh, maybe I should come right over," Gordon responded.

His copper-colored skin was soft to the touch despite its hard, muscular appearance. He had the dreamiest, light-brown eyes, and a sexy smile with the cutest, little gap between his two front teeth.

Gordon was real cool, but we weren't *that* cool. We were more than friends with benefits, but we were far from serious on my part. I ignored his comment about coming over, and dipped my free hand into the water to gauge the temperature.

The water felt good, nearly the perfect amount of heat, but not too hot. I could still sit in the tub comfortably.

After the stressful day I'd had with my mobile boutique customers, I craved relaxation like I needed the air I breathed. I had worked hard to create the perfect setting to unwind in at home. My bathroom walls were painted maroon, so when I dimmed the soft, yellow lights, there was the right hint of darkness.

A soothing fragrance floated through the air from two massive lavender and vanilla-scented candles that flickered in the corners near the French double doors. Sensuous sounds from some of my favorite slow songs were programmed to repeat on my iPod. The setting was ideal for a quiet night of relaxation.

"Peta, you still there?"

"Oh, yeah, uh-huh."

"How come you didn't say nothing when I offered to come through? I could help wash your back." He chuckled.

His offer made me a little uncomfortable. Gordon realized I wasn't alone, and he should've known better. When I couldn't stand the silence that hung between us, I spoke up.

"Look, Gee, you know we're good and all, but my daughter is here. I don't allow strange men to run in and out of my house when she's home."

Gordon sucked his teeth. I predicted that would set him off a little, but I didn't care. He shouldn't have gone there.

"Oh, so now I'm some *strange* man?" he huffed.

"You know what I'm saying."

Our conversation had gone in a direction that I didn't need. I rolled my eyes, and braced myself for the fallout.

"Nah, I don't, Peta. All I know is, anytime I talk about us hooking up or gettin' closer, you find some excuse why we can't. At least not until you feel like blessing me with some of your precious time. That ain't even cool."

I tried to ignore his complaint, but I should've known he was gonna press the issue. He should've taken my explanation and left it alone. But no, he couldn't do that.

"What do you want me to do? I'm not one of those women who introduces her kid to every Tom, Dick, and Harry." I dropped my robe from my shoulders.

"Oh, snap! Now I'm some Tom, Dick, and Harry? Damn, that's real cold, Peta. Real cold. But, I feel ya, though," he said.

I rolled my eyes at his theatrics. A fight was the very last thing I needed. It was best to hold my tongue, and let him have his say. My bathwater was almost ready. I had half a bottle of wine, and a good book on standby. Drama was definitely not on the menu for me tonight.

"Gordon, all I'm saying—"

"Oh, I hear what you sayin', ma. Don't trip!" he yelled before I could explain myself. "You ain't gotta clean nothin' up for me. I'm a man, baby! But on the real, though. We been at this for what, nearly a year now? And I'm still not good enough to meet your shorty? Hell, that's telling me exactly what I need to know."

By "been at this for nearly a year," he meant an occasional dinner here or there, and of course, the booty call that came in really handy for me. I felt that our arrangement worked. "Gordon, we don't have to make this into a big thing."

He ranted on like he hadn't heard a word I'd said. He was on autopilot, and there was no way to stop him.

"Peep this, Peta, I'm real clear now. It's me, but I'm good now. All this damn time, this body's been on reserve, and you basically ain't had no plans for no damn future with me. That's *my* bad, though, ma."

When Gordon got worked up, he slid back into his street lingo, and I couldn't reason with him. Once he took that turn, nothing good would come from the conversation. I didn't get a chance to respond to his claims. Suddenly, something else had grabbed my attention. I was no longer alone. I stooped down, and grabbed my robe.

"I know you ain't got no fool up in this house with my daughter up in here."

My eyes nearly popped from their sockets at the sound of the intrusion from Lover Number Two.

"Whoa! Hold up a sec. Is that your baby daddy?" Gordon yelled in my ear. "Oh, now I see what's really going on!"

I hated when people called Kyle my "baby daddy." I didn't get knocked up after we hooked up or anything like that. Kyle Nixon was my ex-husband. I was married to him for more than five years, so there was a difference. Much to my astonishment, he was in my bathroom, in the flesh. Shock numbed me from head to toe. I felt my spine tighten, as recognition slowly etched into Kyle's features.

His mouth hung wide open, and his eyes danced frantically around my empty bathroom. His stare settled on me, as I used the robe to cover my nakedness.

"Uh-oh. I thought, ummm—" he stammered and stumbled back slightly.

"What the hell are you doing in my house?" I screamed. I pulled the phone back to my ear. "Hey, listen. I need to run. I'll call you back." I didn't wait for Gordon to respond. I ended the call, and turned my wrath on Kyle's simple behind. He stood in front of me, looking like a complete ass.

Kyle wasn't a bad-looking man. Actually, he was quite handsome. The problem was he knew it. He had flawless, walnut-colored skin.

His large, dark, expressive eyes were outlined with the thickest, longest eyelashes ever. As if that weren't enough, he had a sharp, chiseled jawline with a cleft in his chin. Kyle's body was also very nice to boot.

"You are trespassing! You ain't got no right bombarding your way into my damn house like you paying bills up in here!"

"Peta, all that is uncalled for. I don't want no men hanging around my daughter, that's all. I heard voices up in here, and I didn't know what was what. You can't fault a brotha for looking out for what's his," he yelled back at me.

I was so fed up with Kyle and his bogus excuses. He popped up at my house whenever the feeling hit him. It didn't matter how much I cursed or threatened him, my words seemed to bounce right off of him. He still did whatever the hell he wanted.

If the sex between us wasn't hotter now than when we were married, I might've been moved to change the locks. Instead, I convinced myself that he needed access to help look after his daughter.

"Mom, why you fussing at Dad? I asked him to come over." Our daughter, Kendal, stood in the dimly lit doorway, rubbing her eyes with the backs of her hands.

"Sweetpea, it's late. What are you still doing up? You got school in the morning," My tone softened instantly when I spoke to my daughter. There had never been a cross word between us. She was a great twelve-year-old, and gave me no trouble whatsoever.

Regardless of how I felt about Kyle, I never spoke badly about him in front of, or to, our daughter.

"I had a bad dream, and I called Dad. You were tired and trying to relax in your bath. I didn't wanna bother you. Now you guys are fighting all loud and stuff. And it's all my fault!" She pouted.

I released a trapped breath. The frightened look she'd worn so many times made me feel guilty that I had gone off on Kyle. Even though he was wrong, it was painfully clear that our daughter still suffered from our divorce. It made me sick how he babied her, but I decided to let their relationship evolve in its own way.

"Honey, it's not your fault; it's mine," Kyle explained. "I thought someone was in here trying to do something to your mom, and I kinda pushed my way in. I only did it to make sure she wasn't being hurt or anything like that."

He made me want to throw up. I rolled my eyes at his explanation, but our daughter seemed to eat it up. The love in her eyes as she dreamily gazed at him sent a pang of jealousy through my heart, but it was short-lived. It was quickly replaced by the rage that I still felt toward Kyle.

"See, Mom, Dad was only trying to look out for you like he used to do when we lived together. You know, like a real family."

Kyle's jaw tensed, and I fought the strong urge to sock him right in it.

I exhaled and ignored him.

"Okay, sweetie. Please go back to bed. I didn't mean to wake you with all the yelling and fussing."

Kendal smiled faintly. "Daddy, are you still gonna come up and lay with me for a little while? Huh?"

"Of course, Princess," Kyle said.

Her face lit up with relief. I watched as my ex guided her out of the bathroom. I was still pissed, but I had to let it go if I wanted to reclaim the serenity he had disrupted.

I rolled my eyes and muttered, "Uuugghh, what's taking Happy Hour Thursdays so damn long to get here?"

2

DARBY

I rolled my eyes toward the vaulted ceiling as I listened to the angry voices on the phone. My heart raced, thinking about the words these shallow heifers were throwing my way.

"So, Kelly, you, Renee, and Callie thought this phone call was a good idea?" I hissed.

Kelly and the other ladies were members of a neighborhood playgroup. They lived in another subdivision close by, but we committed to meeting up so our children could play and hang out at least once a week. At first, I thought the call was about next week's play date. But, I quickly learned that this was their idea of an intervention of sorts. I listened to each woman plead her case. And the case was against me.

"For Christ's sake, Darby. You pull out your flask on the playground!" Kelly said.

Wishing I had it at that moment, I didn't respond. I wanted to tell her that my flask and I were the least of her concerns.

"I'm sorry, but is that against the law, or just against your rules?"

"We're not saying the kids can't play together. We simply don't think it's wise for you to come to the playground, if you can't leave the booze at home," Renee said.

What these women didn't know was that I was just about as tired of them as they were of me. The reason I needed my "mommy juice" was because their simple conversations bored me to tears. If I didn't have the flask, they wouldn't want me present.

"Okay, fine, I won't bring my juice to the playground." I swallowed the sour taste in my mouth. I needed a drink now. We made plans for the next meeting and wrapped up the group call. I sighed and fell back onto my bed.

When the phone rang again, I thought twice before picking it up. But once I realized it was my girl, Felicia Cole, I answered right away.

"Hey girl, hold on a minute," I said.

Before I could get into the conversation, turmoil began to brew on the other side of my bedroom door. I was already on edge from the phone call with Kelly and her drinking police.

I closed my eyes and tried to wait for the noise to boil over, but my thoughts traveled elsewhere.

Andrea Yates and Susan Smith were mothers who had killed their kids. And while I would never do it, these were the times that made me feel like I could halfway understand what had pushed them over the edge.

When I couldn't take it anymore, I finally hung up the phone with Felicia. The noise outside my door seemed to get louder and louder, until I could hardly hear myself think. I was pissed that I couldn't even talk on the phone in peace.

I closed my eyes, and prayed my husband, Kevin, would handle things. I was not about to go out there.

"Ma! Kevin's not doing what Daddy said," my six-year-old son, Taylor, cried. His voice brought me back to the madness that was my life. Screaming kids, a lazy, penny-pinching husband, crazy family members, a secret relationship that some might consider beyond taboo, and not enough liquor to make them all go away. That was basically my life.

I squeezed my eyes shut, and prayed that I'd suddenly develop the super power to vanish into thin air. I had been tucked away in my room, and wanted to kick myself. I should have had the foresight to bring a little taste in with me. My purse was either in my car or in the kitchen. So that meant I was dry and completely sober.

"You stupid! Why you always gotta tattle?" Kevin Jr., my eight-year-old, screamed at his younger brother.

It would be only moments before the fight spilled into my room, and really drove me nuts. I already felt like yanking out my own damn hair. My eyes focused on the digital clock on my nightstand. I had no idea what was taking eight-thirty, the kids' bedtime during the week, so long to get here.

Should I go or should I stay? I didn't want to get in the middle of their squabble, but I also didn't need it to escalate. If those little nuccas started throwing blows, one of them would end up hurt, and that would make matters worse for me.

"Ma! Kevin said a bad word!"

"No, I didn't! Liar!"

The next thing I heard were footsteps stomping toward my bedroom door. Suddenly, without a knock or a warning, the door flew open and the boys stood in my doorway, yelling and screaming in each other's faces.

"You did! Ma and Daddy said you don't call nobody stupid! That makes it a bad word and you know it! Stupid!" Taylor yelled.

"You stupid!" Kevin Jr. screamed back at his younger brother.

"No! You stupid!"

I exhaled, got up from the edge of my bed, and stood between the boys.

"Where is your dad?" I asked. I was exasperated, and completely exhausted.

I had fixed lunches, cooked dinner, divided dessert, supervised baths, and thought I was finally about to relax. I tried to take advantage of the last minutes before their bedtime, when the boys usually watched TV. I didn't expect to have to referee a squabble. To make matters worse, my husband was nowhere to be found.

"Daddy had to go to the store, and he told Kevin to put on his pjs and go to bed," Taylor said. His bony, little finger stabbed the air in his brother's direction.

There was no way my husband had gone to the store. Hell would have to freeze over three times before he'd step foot in a grocery store, and I preferred it that way. When I found out the only reason he bought two-ply toilet tissue or paper towels was so he could try to separate the roll and have twice as much, I was glad to keep him out of the stores.

My husband was a senior chemical engineer for British Petroleum, where he made very good money. The problem was he was a major tightwad, and unless it was absolutely necessary, he wouldn't spend a dime. He believed money was made to be saved and tried to keep me on a tight financial leash.

"That ain't what he said! He said put on our pjs and be ready for bed when he comes back!" Kevin Jr. retorted.

My youngest snatched his arms up across his chest, and stood with a menacing scowl across his face.

My husband made me sick when he slipped out, without as much as a whistle to let me know I'd be alone with the boys. We lived in a sprawling, thirty-five-hundred-square foot, four-bedroom house, yet when the boys fought, it might as well have been smaller than a six-hundred-square-foot efficiency.

"You two need to go to your rooms right now," I said to them. They still had a good hour before bedtime, but I couldn't take the quarreling anymore.

They began to cry. Dammit, I wanted to cry, too. I was tired. The glass of wine that usually took me through the evening had worn off long ago. I felt irritated and alone.

"But Daddy said we didn't have to go until he got back! That's not fair! See what you did, stupid!" Kevin Jr. screamed at his brother before he stomped away.

Taylor stood there, tears gushing down his cheeks. I silently cursed my husband, and tried to console my son. When I reached for him, he jerked away and left me standing there. I threw my hands up in disgust.

I grabbed my cell phone and called my husband.

"Why didn't you say you were leaving?" I asked, the moment he answered.

"Oh, my bad! Sorry, babe. Bruce needed me to help him move a new workstation for his garage. I meant to tell you, but I had forgotten all about it, so when he called, I kinda jumped up and ran out. My bad."

"Yeah, well, the boys are up in here going at each other's throats, and I had no idea you had even left."

Since they were in their rooms, I eased into the kitchen, and opened the pantry door as I talked to Kevin. I tried not to look at his collection of fast-food ketchup packets that he kept in a large freezer bag. I hated when he used them to refill the ketchup bottle. Some habits never died, and if he thought it could save a buck, my husband would give it a try.

I reached to an upper shelf, and grabbed the tall, tin container that held spaghetti. As I listened to Kevin's half-ass excuses, I removed the lid, and pulled out the slim bottle. I poured a little more than a shot of the coconut-flavored Cîroc vodka into one of my fancy glasses, and added a splash of cranberry juice. I put the vodka back inside the container, and stepped back into the pantry. I moved the bags of flour and sugar, and the box of bread crumbs aside, and put the tin can into its spot near the back of the shelf.

I hid my stash. I didn't need to listen to my husband complain about my drinking or the fact that my drink of choice was too expensive. Knowing him, he'd find a way to calculate the cost of each ounce.

I remember I had given up alcohol before. Something had clicked in my head years ago, when I found out that my twin sister, Darlene, had been killed by a drunk driver. Chandler Buckingham had been arrested three different times before for DWI.

After that, I couldn't stomach the smell of alcohol. But once I fell off the wagon, I couldn't comprehend how I had gone dry for even one day. I remember the moment that I laid eyes on Chandler. I instantly came up with a plan. I was going to make him pay; make him feel a fraction of the pain he had caused my family and me.

"Yeah, babe, my bad. Tell them boys I said to behave," my husband said, like that would make everything better.

I could tell he was completely distracted. My frustration meant nothing to him as usual. His mantra was that since I stayed at home, anything that happened involving the home was my responsibility.

"Yeah, okay. When are you coming back?" I was beyond irritated.

"I'm gonna be at least thirty more minutes," he said. That really pissed me off.

"If you knew you were gonna be gone that long..." I stopped myself before I finished the complaint. "Okay, whatever." *What was the point?*

I closed the pantry door, and moved closer to my drink on the counter. When the call ended, I placed the phone down. I didn't want to linger on thoughts of how much my husband irritated me at times.

"To hell with it all!"

I brought the glass to my lips, and swallowed the drink in one big gulp. I exhaled, rinsed the glass, and put it in the dish rack to dry. The liquor hadn't worked that quickly, but instantly, I felt better. I was about to turn to my other guilty pleasure, but couldn't. There was no way I'd be able to focus on an Internet chat when my kids were still up.

When my cell phone rang, I thought it was my husband calling back. It turned out to be the children's school.

"I need to speak with the parent of Kevin Jaxon," a woman said. She hadn't even said hello. Her voice was cold, rushed, and unfriendly.

"Uh, hello to you, too. This is Darby Jaxon, Kevin's mother," I said.

"Yes, Mrs. Jaxon, I'm so sorry. I absolutely hate making these kinds of calls, but Principal Johnson is very concerned about Kevin's recent behavior. We are all baffled, because…well, Kevin is usually a good student, so I talked with one of our counselors before I even called you."

My heart dropped to my toes like I was on one of those cheap carnival rides.

"Excuse me? *Kevin?* What's the problem?"

"Did Kevin bring the note home?" she asked.

"No, Kevin didn't bring home a note."

"I wanted you to call me before we had you meet with Mr. Johnson. When we didn't hear back from you last night, and Kevin wouldn't answer questions about the note earlier today, I decided to call. The bottom line is, Kevin's been extremely distracted and disruptive lately, and we wanted to know if there are any changes going on at home that we should be made aware of."

"Changes? Like what kind of changes?"

"Well, when we see such a sudden and dramatic change in be-

havior, it's often a sign that they're acting out as a result of something happening in the home."

Of course, blame the parents.

"What exactly is Kevin doing? " I asked. I grabbed the glass from
the dish rack, put it back on the counter, and moved back toward
the pantry.

3

IVEE

I f you ain't got no job, you can't tell me a damn thing about what's going on with mine. I hated when Darby felt like she was an expert in all things related to other people's lives. When she got like that, I simply changed the subject as I had done moments earlier.

"So anyway, girl, what you fixing for dinner tonight?" I asked as I maneuvered my car over to the turning lane. Rush-hour traffic was always a beast. I stopped at the light behind the vehicle in front of me, and listened as her voice floated through my car's speaker system.

"Don't you hate the fact that we always have to be the ones who worry about what everybody is gonna eat?" Darby said. "It's like, what would they do if we went on strike? I could see Kevin's butt now." She laughed. "He'd probably have the kids recycling plastic ware, paper plates, and using old pickle and jelly jars for drinking glasses."

"I don't see how you live with that man."

"Oh, I put my foot down. There's some stuff I won't cut corners on, in order for him to save a buck. Seriously, the boys would really be in trouble if I weren't the one in charge of feeding them. But sometimes it wears me out."

"Umph, I feel you. It irks me to no end, too," I said. The light changed, and traffic began to move again. "You think I wanna stop at the grocery store when every other working person is gonna be up in there making a mad dash for the only two registers they'll have open?"

"Better you than me." Darby chuckled. "But seriously, your husband should be glad he's getting a home-cooked meal. I stopped at Pizza Hut, and that's what we had for dinner tonight."

I wondered whether I should point out the craziness in what Darby had said, considering she stayed at home all day. If anybody would cook every day, wouldn't it be her? *Hell, I have my own issues,* I reminded myself, and pulled into the grocery store's parking lot. The sight of the rows and rows of parked cars forced me to exhale a frustrated breath.

"Not a single parking spot," I muttered. "Great!"

"Yeah, see, that's what I'm talking about. Who wants to be out in all that madness?"

I could clearly hear the clinking sound of ice cubes dancing around in liquid through the phone as Darby spoke. I instantly got jealous. She was enjoying a cocktail while I was fighting traffic.

"Look, girl, let me go so I can try to get in and out."

"All right, chile, call me later," she sang.

Luckily for me, once inside, the grocery store wasn't as bad as I'd expected. On top of that, the store had a chef who demonstrated quick and easy meals, so I was able to snag a great recipe idea from him. I quickly snatched up all the ingredients, and made my way to the register to check out.

Once I got home, I was surprised that my husband hadn't made it in yet. I walked straight into the kitchen, and began to rinse the large prawns I'd bought for dinner. The meal was simple—a shrimp and garlic pasta dish.

Nearly thirty minutes later, I heard keys at the door, and Zion's baritone voice floated into the foyer. I heard him before I saw him. Zion's deep voice ran all through me, and I flinched slightly. Everything was in order, but he would be able to find something that could've been improved upon. That was his way.

He spoke on his cell phone as he walked in, and I was glad for the temporary distraction.

"I'll check the blueprints in about an hour," I heard him say.

My eyes glanced around the kitchen. I was nearly finished with dinner, and the mess had been kept to a minimum.

"Zy?" I called out when I didn't hear his voice anymore.

"Sure smells good in here," Zion said as he eased up behind me. My husband's skin was the color of blackberries. He was a large, broad-shouldered, square-faced man with intense features. His hair was styled into a skillfully lined fade that matched his neatly groomed facial hair—a slight beard and matching goatee.

I felt his warm breath on the back of my neck, and that gave me pause. I inhaled through my nose, held it in for a few seconds, then exhaled when he moved away from me. My mind danced with thoughts of what he'd scrutinize next. It was simply a matter of time.

"What got into you today?" he asked. "I expected to be eating out of a bag or a Styrofoam container as usual."

I took in the comment, and prepared to fire back at him, but by then, he had turned his focus to the mail he held in his hands. If he would've glanced my way, he might have noticed that my eyes had narrowed into slits.

At that moment, I chose to avoid the fight. I exhaled again, and added the finishing touches to our meal. There was no need to respond to his comment.

Zion turned, and walked toward the back of the house. "Oh, I'm gonna eat in the office," he said over his shoulder.

I could've pointed out how I rushed to the grocery store, and fought traffic to make sure he had a cooked meal, and he decided to eat in isolation? But, that would've been pointless.

As I prepared the tray, I told myself it was no big deal. Over the years, we had gone from passionate kisses and loving words each time we parted, to barely being affectionate toward one another. But it was what it was, and I had grown accustomed to what we'd become.

When we first married six years ago, you couldn't tell me we'd be reduced to one of *those* couples. But our busy schedules forced us to behave more like roommates instead of man and wife.

I fixed our plates, put his on the serving tray along with a cold beer, and walked toward his office. He was on the phone when I walked in, so I knew to be quiet.

He tapped my behind on my way out, and I swatted at his hand. That was his way of saying thanks for the service I had provided.

Before I got to my own food, I walked into the bedroom and changed out of my work clothes. Once I was comfortable, I went back to the living room and ate dinner alone. As I finished, my cell phone rang.

It was my assistant, Jessica Sanchez. She was an older, Mexican woman who treated us all like her children.

"Hi, Jessica," I answered.

"Oh, Miss Ivee, I don't mean to bother you at home, but that client of yours, you know, the cheap, grumpy one? He says he needs to meet first thing in the morning." Her voice was laced with worry.

"Thanks for the call, Jess, but you can schedule him for Thursday afternoon."

"Thursday? He was cussing up a storm, Miss Ivee, and I'm afraid that he may—"

"He'll be fine, Jessica. Trust me."

Zion walked by with his tray, and gave me a thumbs-up with a smile. My guess was that he had enjoyed dinner.

I ended the call with Jessica, and decided not to think about the client. He always had an issue or a problem. I hated when work seeped into my time at home. My work was the major contention with Zion and me, and the last thing I wanted to do was give him a reason to provide his unsolicited career advice.

Hours later, as I got out of the shower, Zion startled me.

"I didn't hear you come in," I said.

"How could you? The water was running."

I had a towel wrapped around my body, and used another to dry the edges of my hair that had gotten wet.

Zion cocked his head, and looked at me like he was perplexed. "You know, that meal got me thinking," he said. "This ain't what you wanna hear, but I still think if you worked for yourself, our lives would be a whole helluva lot better."

"Working for yourself isn't as easy as you think," I said.

"Didn't that one friend of yours go out on her own?"

Felicia was the friend he referred to. We both used to work for Geneva JoHarris, who owned the firm where I still currently worked. Felicia had decided to start her own business. To me, she worked harder now than she did when we worked together. But, it would've been pointless to tell Zion that.

I didn't want to remove the towel that was wrapped around my body. I wasn't in the mood for his analysis. If a home-cooked dinner made him reevaluate my career, I could only imagine what he'd have for me after seeing me naked. I instantly thought that he could've waited to start with this. I hated when he wanted to talk about my job. He was starting to sound like a broken record.

"You already know it's not time for me to venture out on my own," I said. I didn't even try to remove the sarcasm.

"I'll bet JoHarris heard that a lot before she took the plunge," he said. The moment he learned that Geneva had stepped out on faith and started her own firm years ago, he'd determined that I was underemployed by working for her and not myself.

There would've been no use in pointing out the stark differences between my boss and me. This was not a new conversation for us, and it never ended well.

We both stood and looked at each other as if we weren't sure what to do next. I tried to avoid looking him directly in the eyes. I loved my husband very much, but I often had mixed emotions about him. Over the years, it seemed as if it became harder and harder for him to say anything nice to me. He was the only person alive who ever bullied me and got away with it, and I felt myself grow nervous in his presence most times.

"I'm gonna help put lotion on your back," he suggested.

That was his way of telling me he wanted sex.

"Oh, thanks, but I got it." That was my way of telling him no.

"C'mon here, Ivee, I'm your husband." He reached for me. "You act like I haven't seen everything you got already."

Before I could suck in my gut, he grabbed my towel, and it fell to the floor when I tried to step back.

I stood frozen.

"Has it been that long since I've seen my wife naked? You look like you've picked up a few pounds," Zion said.

The words flowed from his mouth naturally.

4

PETA

When more than an hour had passed and I hadn't received a response, I knew what I had to do. I hated having to kiss up to Gordon, but being lonely and horny was a bitch. Kyle had taken Kendal for the night since she had an early morning field trip, and it was his turn to chaperone. That meant I was as free as a horny *Home Alone* teenager whose parents were out of town. I was about to hang up the phone when he answered.

"Oh, hey what's up?" Gordon said.

He didn't sound like he was still pissed about the other day with Kyle, but still I decided to tread lightly.

"Yo', I got that pic you sent me. That was on point!" The tone in his voice was friendly and cool, which I liked.

"Good. I'm glad you like it. It was sorta like a peace offering," I said cautiously.

"Hmm, well, whatever it was, it was all good. So, what's up? You free tonight or what?" he asked.

That was music to my ears. Between the issues with work, and whatever the hell Kyle was up to, I needed some one-on-one adult distraction. Gordon could handle that with no problem whatsoever.

"It depends on what you have in mind," I teased.

"Well, that picture you sent told me exactly what you have in mind, so what's up? You ain't into teasing, now are you?"

"No, nothing like that at all. I thought you'd like to see the new line of pearls I ordered for the boutiques," I joked. I had taken a topless picture with strands of pearls strategically placed around my neck, and sent it to Gordon's phone.

"Shiiiit! I don't give a damn about some pearls. Those beautiful-ass titties you got told a different story," he joked.

"Oh, yeah? What did they say?"

"They said, 'Can you come and handle a situation over here?'"

"Oh, is that what they said?"

"Damn straight!"

"Umph, you may have been reading a lot into a simple picture," I told him.

"C'mon now, girl. That picture said everything you expected it to say. And I ain't for all this bull right now. You wasting precious time."

Gordon seemed rushed, and that wasn't the mood I was in. I wanted to play a little. We both knew how the night would end.

"Oh, really? How you figure?"

"Peta, soon you gon' be whining about having to get home to your kid and all that so, what's up? We gon' do this or what?"

"Well, I'm kind of hungry," I said.

"Okay, so you basically saying I gotta wine and dine you before I can hit that."

"Gee!" I squealed.

"See, you playing and shit, and I'm trying to tell you let's make this happen! What time you gotta be back at the house tonight anyway?"

"I got a free pass, alllll niiiight long," I sang.

"Whhhhaaaat?! You doin' it like *that* tonight?"

"You tell me," I said.

"Well, listen. I could eat a lil' somethin' myself, and then maybe we can order some food!"

"Boy, you so nasty!" I joked, loving every minute of our back-and-forth tease.

"That's exactly how you like me." He laughed sexily.

"So, for real, what are we gonna do? You wanna meet somewhere? You said you're hungry, too. What kind of food you in the mood for?"

"Oh, you said food, right?" he asked.

We laughed at that.

About an hour later, I found a parking spot, and eased out of the car. Gordon had already texted me that he had arrived at the restaurant. We were at Pappadeaux Seafood Kitchen in the Fountains, located off of Highway 59, in Stafford.

The moment I hit the door, it was sheer chaos. The place was packed. Music, laughter, and loud chatter seemed to compete for attention. I was so glad Gordon was being escorted to a table the moment I walked in, since usually the restaurant wouldn't seat you until your entire party arrived.

He turned and smiled. "Oh, good. You're here."

I squeezed by a throng of people who stood near the hostess' podium at the front door, with drinks in hand. I pecked Gordon on the lips. He smelled great, and looked good in a pair of dark, designer jeans, loafers, and a painter's button-down shirt that fit his body extra nicely.

As we followed the hostess to the table, I noticed a few heads turn to look at us. Gordon and I looked good together, but I wasn't ready for anything hot and serious.

We were seated near the back of the restaurant in somewhat of a quiet area, and that was cool with me. Once we were left alone,

Gordon smiled. I fought the urge to jump across the table, and shove my tongue down his throat.

"What made you reach out tonight?" he asked.

I gave him a half shrug, and picked up my menu. I wasn't sure what I craved more—the tantalizing seafood entrees or him. I told myself to chill out. No one liked a thirsty chick, regardless of how mutual the attraction.

"I ain't tryin' to start nothing, but maaaan, it pisses me off when you hang out with your baby daddy," Gordon said. He hadn't looked up from the menu.

There he goes with that again. That term *baby daddy* made my skin crawl and my blood boil every time I heard it. I told myself that now wasn't the best time to point out to Gordon that he really didn't have a right to be mad about who I chose to spend time with. He and I were cool, but we weren't making-future-plans-cool. Since I wanted to end the night in his bed, I held that thought.

"My ex-husband wants to make sure he's a dominant figure in our daughter's life. Sometimes the way he goes about it isn't the best, but I had a little talk with him. All I can do is hope he will respect the boundaries I set for him."

Gordon looked up at me. He smiled, and gave a little chuckle while his mouth stayed closed.

I shrugged.

"Babe, all you gotta do is say the word, and I can make the message real clear to him, if you know what I mean."

I had no idea what he meant by that, but the focused look in his eyes sent a chill up my spine. Despite that, my other body parts that needed his attention later forced me to ignore whatever his comment might have suggested.

"You ready to order?" I asked.

A young and handsome Mexican waiter bounced over.

"Hi, I'm Eric, and I'll be taking care of you tonight." He flicked two paper drink coasters from his apron and placed them on the table. "Can I get you started with cocktails from our full-service—"

"I'll have a Swamp Thing," I blurted out before he could finish.

Gordon's eyes widened in delight. "Add a Long Island Iced Tea for me."

We flirted with our eyes and feet under the table. I was glad to be with him, and wanted to get to the best part. We kept the conversation light and flirty, which meant we'd avoid an argument or disagreement.

Dinner was fast and great, but nearly thirty minutes later, dessert promised to be even better.

My head still swirled a little from the strong drinks I'd had back at the restaurant, and each time I licked Gordon's perfect, chocolate nipples, I swore they tasted like hints of the hurricane and margarita mixture I'd sucked down earlier.

His body was magnificent. As I spread my legs to allow him entry, I clutched on to his ripped biceps, and relished in the sheer bliss that he'd deliver.

Gordon lowered his head, and planted a wet, sloppy kiss over my mouth as he entered me.

5

DARBY

I hated when Kevin pulled this kind of mess. It wasn't enough that I had to break him out of adding water to milk and juices to make them stretch, but his obsession with hoarding money was too much. I sat at the ATM machine, fuming.

How could there not be enough money for me to withdraw forty damn dollars? It didn't help that I had just ended a screaming match with my brother, Roger, who insisted that I had betrayed my family, and therefore, I needed to make myself available for the unannounced visit that my mother and aunt were trying to execute. There was no doubt that I was in a hot, funky mood.

Their antics reminded me of when we were little. Roger, the youngest, was always in the middle of any brewing mess. Darlene and I were the epitome of twins. We finished each other's sentences, dressed alike, and even felt each other's emotions. We were closer than anyone could imagine. When she was killed, my life changed forever. Since her death, nearly eighteen years ago, our entire family had fallen apart. I was no longer close with my mom, my aunt, or Roger, who used to lovingly call me "Sissy."

Most of us had moved on, but my mother didn't want to let go of Darlene. Out of all of us, I was messed up the most over Darlene's death. I still missed her like she had died a few seconds ago, but my sister would've wanted us all to live; not mourn her the way my mom had.

While I'd made an effort to move on with my life, I vowed that I would do whatever it took to avenge her death. I became obsessed with getting next to the man who had killed her. Chandler would feel my pain, even if I died making sure he did. I would get next to him, gain his trust, and set him up. I had it all planned. I was going to plant two kilos of cocaine in his house, and then call the police. His fancy lawyer would not be able to get him out of that one.

Roger told me that he felt trapped in the middle of a major family feud. If he would stop trying to force reconciliation, he wouldn't feel that way. As I told him, if he was going to turn my entire family against me, maybe we weren't as close as I thought we were in the first place.

When a horn honked behind me, I realized that I was blocking the ATM. After I exhaled, I dipped my card back into the machine, and pressed the option to read the balance. When I saw the numbers that appeared across the screen, I wanted to strangle my penny-pinching husband. There was $39.89 in the account.

Suddenly, that fool's words ran through my mind as if he'd spoken them seconds ago. *"Hey, I put some money in the account."*

"For Christ's sake! What in the hell is wrong with him?"

Instead of taking my frustration out on the machine, I whipped my car out of the bank's parking lot, and headed to the Walgreens across the street. I stormed inside, bought a pack of gum for thirty-five cents, and then requested thirty-nine dollars back in cash.

"You want thirty-nine dollars?" the pimple-faced cashier asked.

"Yes!" I snapped.

"Oh, okay. Just checking to make sure it was the right amount."

A slow-burning anger took hold of me as he counted out my tens, fives, and four one-dollar bills. I strode out of the store's automatic doors on fire.

"Ma'am," the cashier called after me.

I almost didn't turn around until I heard him yell, "Your gum! You forgot your gum!"

Everyone thought my life was a fairytale since my husband insisted that he didn't want me to work outside the home. If they only knew the shit I had to deal with in exchange for that so-called luxury.

With the money clutched tightly in my hand, I climbed back into my car, and headed toward my son's school. Since Kevin was the sole breadwinner in the family, nearly everything else fell on my shoulders. He may have been a chemical engineer, but I was the domestic engineer, and my job was far more stressful!

When the school called about my son's sudden change in behavior, there was no question about who would go up there and meet with the principal.

My mind was still stuck on my husband's cheap, frugal behind when I realized that I needed to get it together before the meeting. Sitting outside of the school, I tried to put my mind in the right state. I dug into my purse, and pulled out the small, rhinestone-encrusted flask. I removed the lid, and took a couple of swigs.

Next, I checked my lipstick in the rearview mirror, and then I popped a peppermint into my mouth. I sucked on the candy really hard, chewed it up, and popped another one in.

Once I felt I was good to go, I got out of the car, and walked into the cool building.

The front office was decorated like a living room with two large, plush sofas. There was a coffee table, two small bookshelves, and a flat screen TV that hung in a corner. I turned to my right, and spoke to the lady who sat at the desk.

"I'm Darby Jaxon, and I have an appointment with Principal Johnson."

"Oh, yes, Mrs. Jaxon, he's expecting you. Right this way." The secretary stood and walked to meet me at the doorway. She escorted me behind the half-swinging door and down a carpeted hallway.

When she knocked at the door, my stomach did an awkward somersault. I never liked the principal's office, and all these years later, nothing had changed.

"Who is it?" a male voice asked from behind the closed door.

"Mr. Johnson, Mrs. Jaxon is here to see you."

"Oh, yes!" I heard movement, and soon the door swung open. "Thank you, Linda," Mr. Johnson said as he looked at me.

Linda nodded slightly, and turned to leave.

"Mrs. Jaxon, thank you so much for taking the time to meet with me. Please have a seat."

Principal Johnson was a fortyish-year-old man with a slicked-back mane of thick, jet-black waves. He towered over my petite frame, and didn't take his seat until I sat.

"Well, it's not like I had a choice," I said.

His office was neat and homey. There was a large, wooden desk, and two wooden file cabinets to the left. A tall, leafy tree stood in the opposite corner, along with an oval-shaped table surrounded by several chairs. The lighting in the room was far too soft for my taste, but I could feel the mood he tried to set with the faint jazz that played in the background. He even had curtains at his windows.

It was hard to believe that the idea of a visit with the principal struck such dread into my heart, yet the thought of my kid in trouble frightened me even more.

"Are you okay, Mrs. Jaxon? Can I offer you some coffee or water?" he asked.

A flood of adrenaline rushed through me as I wiped a bead of sweat from my forehead. I didn't like the idea of him and his colleagues talking about my family, and that was probably exactly what they had done.

"Oh, no, I'm fine, but thank you. Now about Kevin Jr."

"Yes, well, as my secretary told you, this is most unusual. I've been an educator for more than thirty years, and I can read children pretty well. Here lately, he's seemed very hostile. He's on edge quite a bit, and it's almost as if something drastic has happened. So, naturally, we try to reach out to mom and dad to see if there are any significant changes at home?"

I scoffed inwardly. The hairs on my neck bristled on end as I listened to the man describe a stranger. It took a moment for me to grasp that there was a question in his statement.

"Oh, nothing has changed at home," I said quickly, realizing how long the pause had been. He eyed me skeptically.

"We often see this sudden change when parents talk of divorce, or if a close relative dies suddenly." He tried to lead me into a confession. I had nothing for him.

I sat erect in the chair, my hands folded in my lap as he described a couple of other possible scenarios that could explain the change in my son's behavior. Still, I felt lost. At home, Kevin Jr. seemed normal. I would notice the so-called change if it was as drastic as the principal described.

Then, as if he had read my mind, he asked, "By chance, have you noticed any changes at home?"

"Nothing. This is all so strange to me."

"Well, we finally called when Kevin told Lucas that he'd slap the piss out of him the other day," Principal Johnson said.

"Lucas Stevens?" My eyebrows probably touched my hairline.

Lucas lived a few houses down, and the boys played together often, or at least they used to. I knew where my son had heard those words, and I prayed the principal didn't question their origin, although I feared he already knew.

"So, again, this is completely unlike Kevin. We are at a loss."

The two swigs in the parking lot had definitely not been enough. *I should've drained the flask*, I thought as I stared blankly at Principal Johnson. I wasn't sure what he wanted me to say.

After a few additional moments of awkward and uncomfortable silence between us, he asked, "You do stay at home? I mean, you don't work outside the home, correct?"

It might have been the way he asked. I was instantly irritated.

"That is correct."

It never failed. Everyone thought *that* was supposed to make such an incredible difference. Right off the bat, I knew where his mind was. Of course *my* kid couldn't act up. My perfectly manicured lawn, and leisure-by-day, laid-back lifestyle didn't allow for such an abnormality.

After all, I did stay at home! What in the hell was I doing with all of my free time? Was I too busy consuming bonbons and being pampered to notice that my perfect, suburban kid was morphing into a thug? He probably thought I had a gardener whose bedroom privileges blinded me to the chaos that had been brewing in my own damn house.

Being under the principal's scrutiny was no fun at all. I really needed to have a talk with my child, and then enjoy a stiff drink.

6

IVEE

My focus centered on the hairline crack that created a zig-zag pattern on the wall near the clock. I was determined not to check the time again. It seemed as if the hands had started to taunt me long ago. *Could they move any slower? Had they gone a few seconds backward?* I sighed. When thoughts of what I would've rather been doing flashed through my mind, I shook them off. I shifted in the chair that was too hard for comfort, stifled another yawn with a forced, fake smile, and tried not to make my eye roll too obvious.

Yes, I was bored, and beyond tired of work. I had to be present at my last meeting of the day. Or at least I thought I had to be there. It was clear that my client was in a mood, as Jessica had already warned. On top of that, I realized he was angry that I'd made him wait an entire day for the meeting. As I sat across from him, allowing his words to sink in, I wondered when the integrity in business had vanished. I had totally missed the memo on the new wave of business people.

Carson Liam was a middle-aged man who ran his family's business. He could pass for much older with his potbelly and receding hairline that looked more like a greasy mop of salt-and-pepper strands. The blemishes and age spots that marked his face did very little for his appearance. With the dark, drab colors he always wore, he looked just as miserable as he probably was.

"You see here, Ivee, these figures are for the three-week period following the media campaign you designed specifically for us," Carson said.

My eyes followed his raggedy finger, with dirt-encrusted nail beds that had probably never seen a manicure, and took in the numbers he pointed out in an effort to make me seem incompetent. I forced myself to focus on his fingers. His teeth, covered in what looked like a yellow blanket, made my skin crawl.

"Yes, Mr. Liam. I see," I responded dryly.

"Well, what's concerning to us is that there was virtually no increase whatsoever. None! Now, we've done newspaper before, and that worked out pretty good for us."

What savvy businessperson relies only on newspaper for advertising? An old man with old ways equals failure.

"Mr. Liam, it's like I told you before. We don't guarantee any kind of immediate increase in sales, and honestly, a few weeks into a campaign isn't really a true representation of the impact of your reach."

He chuckled.

"These things take time."

"Now, see, all that fancy talk right there—that's what got us into this situation in the first place. I guess I'm not as sophisticated as all the other slick Wall Street types you're probably used to, but my Main Street mentality tells me that what we were doing before probably worked better for us anyway."

His bushy, black and gray eyebrows jumped.

"Back when my grandpop started this business…," he continued.

I listened as the miser tried to blame his mom and pop shop's declining sales on the multimedia package I had convinced him to invest in. The real problem was that Mr. Liam was accustomed to doing business a certain way, and was reluctant to change. When he did finally agree to give change a chance, it hadn't worked fast enough for him, so he wanted someone to blame.

What he didn't understand was, that as close as we were to the end of my workday, I was not in the mood to listen to how ineffective I was at my job.

"What exactly are you trying to say?" I asked.

"Straight shooter," he quipped. He cupped his hands and rubbed them together. "You say we need to hang in there for what, a good six months?"

"Yes, that's the length of the contract you signed," I reminded him.

"Yeah, yeah, about that." He broke out into a round of hacking coughs that sounded as if he might pull up a lung. He began waving his hand toward me as if to say he'd be fine.

I hadn't moved a muscle. I needed him to spit it out, and get back to the business at hand. He doubled over, cleared his throat loudly, and composed himself. His eyes were filled with water when he finally whipped his head upward.

"Whoa!" he exclaimed. Now he spoke as if bile was still caught in his throat. An offer of a glass of water would've been the polite thing to do, but he had pushed me to the brink already. The niceties were a thing of the past.

Once he fully caught his breath, his dark, beady eyes focused in on me. "Ah, what I'm trying to say is, we think a few weeks is good enough. And we wanted to know who we need to talk to about maybe prorating the remaining months in this here contract."

His straight face left me at a loss for words.

All I could do was exhale a hot and exhausted breath.

His cell phone rang, and I was relieved when he raised that rusty index finger to silence me before I could speak again.

"Hold on a sec," he said and rose from his chair. "I gotta take this. Hope you don't mind."

"Not at all," I said.

He mumbled into the phone, and eased out of the conference room door.

I needed liquid therapy like nobody's business. This man had me wound so tightly. I had to remind myself that he was a client, and his business was still very needed. I sat alone for about ten minutes before it dawned on me that he was still in the hall talking on his cell phone.

A few minutes were excusable for an urgent call, but ten minutes and counting was downright disrespectful. I turned in my chair to see if he was near wrapping up, but it was hard to determine. As far as looks could tell, he didn't appear pressed.

His massive frame leaned against the wall, and there was no sign of stress across his face as he grinned and talked into the phone.

I had a standing Thursday appointment, and Mr. Liam was not about to make me late. For his sake and mine, I began to gather my documents, powered off my iPad, and rose to leave.

By the time I finished, Mr. Liam still stood in the same spot. It was obvious he was in no hurry to get back to our conversation. I treaded my way toward him, prepared to stand my ground.

As I approached him from behind, it sounded as if his call was more pleasure than business. I tapped him lightly on his shoulder. "I have another appointment; fifteen minutes was all the time I had. Please call my assistant tomorrow, so we can schedule another meeting for next week."

"W-w-what the hell?"

"Yeah, you've been out here for fifteen minutes. My next appointment can't wait. We'll pick up where we left off on Monday or Tuesday," I said as I passed him.

"But I was hoping we could get the ball rolling on the refund before then," he stammered.

I stopped, pivoted, and looked him dead in his eyes. "Oh, there'll be no refund. We can discuss rearranging some spots, and making adjustments to the schedule, but the contract is clear. Please see page thirteen, the fine print under Section C."

He stared at me, seemingly unable to speak as his mouth fell open. I kept moving.

"We'll chat later. I didn't mean to pull you away from your call." I turned and wiggled my fingers in the air.

If he had a response, I didn't hear it. I had already slipped out of the door, and made a beeline for my car. The meeting with Mr. Liam helped me to realize that I needed to readjust my schedule on Thursdays. I would have to limit client meetings to the mornings, and end my day with paperwork.

I didn't like to feel rushed as I made my way to my standing, weekly appointment.

Despite how hard I tried, the vision of Mr. Liam's stingy behind pointing to those dismal figures was imprinted on my memory, and that frustrated me. My reputation was directly tied to my work. As a media consultant, everything I did spoke to my credibility, and my ability to make things happen for my clients.

I worked at a firm that contracted media-related services for businesses. In most cases, the business either didn't want, or need, an in-house department to handle media placement, advertising, or anything related to the press. As a senior partner at the firm, I served as a spokesperson, a buyer, and a media liaison for my clients.

I turned on Elgin, and rode Westheimer Road down to Kirby Street. That much-needed liquid therapy was a good parking spot away. A whirlwind of adrenaline pumped through my veins as I swung my car into the parking garage attached to the building that housed Eddie V's Prime Seafood Restaurant.

HAPPY
HOUR

7

DARBY

The moment I swung my car into a parking space, Roger's number popped up on my cell phone's screen. Instead of the green button, I hit the red one to decline, and climbed out of the car. I wasn't in the mood for any of his nonsense.

My plan was to sit in the car, and text with my friend as I waited, but Roger's call had thrown me off. Suddenly, I needed the numbness that only a good, strong drink could provide.

I speed-walked from the parking garage to the restaurant, and decided to leave all my issues behind. I pulled the glass door open and stepped inside. I enjoyed absolutely everything about happy hour—the incredible aromas of all the fun foods that were torture to my waistline, the loud and giddy laughter, and the awesome eye candy. But the very best part had to be the time with my girls. It had quickly become the highlight of my week.

The hostesses at the front desk greeted me with smile as I damned near skipped past them and over to the bar area. Yes, I loved happy hour.

Of course, I drank pretty much every day, but nothing compared to the colorful, delicious cocktails with my girls. My time at home all day, taking care of the kids and my husband, who behaved like another kid, really made me appreciate my alone, adult time with my friends. After my recent stint in the principal's office, and the intervention phone call from the playground moms, I couldn't get liquor in me fast enough!

We had been cuttin' up, laughing, and carrying on when the waitress approached. I hardly paid her any attention. I hadn't asked for anything else.

"Ummm, where did this come from?" I asked as she placed a drink down in front of me.

The laughter and conversation stopped immediately. All eyes shifted in my direction. First, they looked down at the drink, and then back up at me. We hadn't ordered another round yet.

The waitress turned to her left, and looked toward the end of the bar. "The nice gentleman there in the plaid shirt sent it over for you," she said, then smiled.

I looked over her shoulder at him, and flashed a quick smile. I mouthed the words "Thank You," and listened as my girls teased me.

"Damn, it's like *that*, Darby?" Ivee chided.

"Yeah, it's something about those wedding rings," Peta said. "My single behind hardly ever gets a drink sent over, but you and Ivee," she joked. "Y'all are like man magnets!"

I watched as high-fives went around the table. We busted up with laughter again. The drinks flowed, and we enjoyed the sights and sounds. Every so often, I noticed the man in the plaid shirt as he glanced in our direction, but he kept his distance.

I had ignored three calls from home already, and when the fourth one came, I started to get concerned. What if I ignored the wrong call, and something serious had happened? I tried to focus on the story Ivee was telling about her cheap client at work, but I couldn't concentrate.

Kevin wasn't always bad. Unlike most husbands, he didn't really have a problem when I hung out, and that made me wonder whether it could've been something serious.

Guilt forced me to leave the table and step outside of the bar.

"It's home. I need to take this." I waved the cell phone as I walked away. "I'll be right back," I said over my shoulder.

"One damn night! One night! That's all we ask! One friggin' night!" Ivee yelled toward my back.

Everyone began to laugh. We often talked about our husbands, and how they behaved the moment we had something to do that didn't involve or include them. The strong, independent men suddenly became worse than needy toddlers.

In the beginning, Kevin would call constantly when he couldn't find a certain toy, or remember where he put the checkbook. As time passed, he got used to it. And once I heard other people's horror stories, all in all, Kevin wasn't that bad. I took Ivee's jokes in stride. As far as husbands went, Kevin could've been a lot worse. I had grown accustomed to his neediness.

Once outside, I redialed the house number. I didn't panic right away when there was no answer. I took a deep breath, and blocked out the sounds of laughter and fun that poured from the inside of the bar each time the doors opened. I dialed the house again.

"Hello?"

My heart nearly stopped when there was finally an answer.

"Uh, hello?" I greeted my mother-in-law, Madelyn, and wondered what in the hell was going on. I adored Kevin's mother, but with hearing loss in one ear, she could barely hear. She also could hardly move around, and our kids were too much for her to handle alone.

"Oh, hey, honey. Kevin didn't tell me who gets what medicine, and I'm all confused," she shouted.

"Um. Excuse me?" I pulled a finger up to plug my free ear. It was hard to hear her, despite her shouting.

"Medicine for the kids. I don't know who gets what, and you and Kevin wouldn't answer your phones. He's off at Bruce's."

"Okay, Madelyn, okay, it's just Kevin Jr. He's the only one who should get the medicine, and he needs five milligrams. It's the first line you see on the small, clear cup," I said.

"Huh?"

I was so pissed at Kevin. He never told me he had plans. He could've waited to go to Bruce's house. Once I slowly repeated my instructions, Madelyn put me on hold. When she returned, she confirmed that she'd poured out the right amount of medicine for my son. I spoke briefly to the kids, and thanked her for calling.

By the time I made it back into the bar, I felt like I had just arrived. My buzz was a thing of the past.

8

PETA

After the day I'd had, happy hour couldn't have come fast enough! It all started at eight-thirty in the morning. I was about to leave Gordon's house for a meeting with a new shoe distributor when my cell phone rang. It was Cecily Palmer, one of my drivers.

"Hey, Miss Peta," Cecily sang into my ear.

Cecily was a good find. She always dressed well, and enjoyed talking to the clients about the latest fashion trends. She wanted to be a fashion designer, and was honest during her interview when she told me she wanted to own a boutique one day. I loved her honesty and her style.

All of the drivers were able to wear the items that we sold. They were like walking billboards for the boutique. When I first branched out, one of my main concerns was how to prevent the staff from stealing. I decided the best way to avoid that was to let them have first dibs on what they wanted. The staff bought everything at incredible discounts. They paid five dollars for tops, ten dollars for pants and skirts, and twelve dollars for shoes. Since I bought my products from China at wholesale prices, I wasn't taking a serious loss.

We ordered items in small quantities, so that helped to move product quickly. Women liked the idea that we never exceeded twenty-one of the same item, per truck. They knew that meant they had to buy fast, or miss out. I made sure that I only picked the most unique items, and some of the best feedback we received was that our clients often stood out in a crowd. Business was growing, but I hadn't turned a profit yet. I was able to pay my employees and myself a small salary. So my ex-husband's money helped to take care of my daughter while I tried to build the business.

"Hey yourself, Cecily. What's up?"

She sighed hard and loud in my ear. "I was on my way to my route, and I blew a mickey fickin' tire! The only reason I'm calling you is because I was supposed to deliver something like seven orders this morning, and I've been waiting on triple-A for nearly an hour already. I dunno how long this thing is gonna take." She sighed again.

I glanced down at the clock, and I wanted to cry. I'd have to reschedule the meeting again.

"Where are you?" I asked.

"Fifty-Nine and Kirby," she said.

"Oh, wow! It's going take me some time to get to you," I told her.

"I know, Miss Peta, I know. I'm so sorry. I only called because I didn't want the clients getting all worked up. You know how they get when their stuff comes in," she said.

"Oh, yes. No, you did the right thing by calling me. I agree we don't need them waiting for their stuff any longer than they have to."

In my head, I rearranged my morning, but decided to hold off on moving my lunch appointment back.

"I need to make a few calls. I'll head your way shortly," I said.

"Okay, and, Miss Peta, I'm sorry again."

"No, no, not your fault. I'm glad you called. We'll get it together."

Early morning traffic in Houston, from any direction, was a

nightmare. For that reason alone, I set all of my meetings at ten in the morning. I figured there was no point in wasting good gas and time sitting in traffic.

Kendal was already on her school field trip, and as I headed out on I-10, I wanted so badly to crawl back into Gordon's bed, but duty called. Traffic moved slower than I walked. My blood boiled instantly. Since I was stuck in traffic anyway, I needed to handle some business. I dialed Cecily again.

"Hi, Miss Peta, AAA still isn't here," she reported. I heard the disappointment in her voice.

"Oh, that's fine. I figured since I was sitting in traffic, I may as well do something. If we have any special orders, please text them to my phone. Also, the seven clients who are waiting on their orders, please call them, and let them know I will be making the deliveries."

After I called Cecily, I returned other calls, and made voice notes of special orders that needed to be placed. I finally got to Cecily. As soon as we'd finished loading the orders in my car, the AAA vehicle pulled up.

"Ain't that some mickey fickin' luck for ya?" Cecily said.

I shook my head. "That's the way it works."

"Okay, Miss Peta, all except one of these are already paid for, and most of the deliveries are going to Chevron's headquarters. They are on Louisiana Street downtown." She gave me a slip with a name and phone number written on it.

"Theresa will come down and meet you; she'll sign for everything, and make sure her coworkers get their orders."

"Oh, that's good. So after that, I stop at the radio station in Montrose, and the preschool across the street from there?" I confirmed.

"Yup, that's it."

"Okay, this isn't so bad after all."

Hours later, I sat and waited for my lunch appointment to arrive. I felt like I still had tons to do. The meeting with a shoe distributor was rescheduled for the following week, but lunch was with a hair distributor who wanted to supply my fleet.

By the time lunch was over, I was off to my next appointment. My cell phone rang the moment I got behind the wheel. It was Kyle. If I ignored his call, he'd simply call back until I answered.

"Hello?" I tried to sound rushed. I hoped he'd take the hint and not hold me long.

"Peta, ummm, listen. I need to talk to you about something,"

"Okay, you've got ten minutes," I said.

"No, that's not what I'm saying. I mean this evening, or tonight, after work."

"Kyle, it's Thursday. I'm not free. Let's set something up for next week."

He huffed loudly.

"Look, Peta, this is real important to me. It can't wait 'til next week. I don't understand why we can't meet when I get out of here today."

I wanted to say, *"Because my life no longer revolves around you, and I really don't give a good goddamn about what's important to you."* Instead, I kept it cool. "Kyle, if we can't meet next week, I don't know what to tell you. I have plans this evening, then I'm booked solid tomorrow, and I refuse to entertain the thought of this weekend."

"Damn, Peta, can you stop for a second and hear me out? I really need to talk to you," he said.

My next appointment called.

"Kyle, I need to go. If you can't do next week, I can't help you!"

Before he could say another word, I clicked over and took the next call.

9

IVEE

I stood, raised my glass, and cleared my throat.

"Okay, y'all know what time it is!" I spoke loud enough so everyone at our table could hear my voice over the noise.

We were a regular fixture among the mixed crowd of sexy, sleek, urban professionals at Eddie V's. There, you could see almost anyone—bankers, couples on dates, or groups, like us, meeting after work.

If I had to guess, I'd say the crowd's ages ranged from late twenties to early forties, but it wasn't the type of crowd that made you feel left out if you were younger or older. The doors opened at four in the afternoon, and usually by the time we arrived, the bustling sounds of chatter and laughter already filled the air.

Felicia picked up her glass, and extended it forward. Her signature drink was the Lemon Drop martini, with colored sugar at the base and around the rim. Belvedere was her vice.

Darby liked sipping on the Porn Star. I never saw her actually eat the blue cheese stuffed olives, but that was her drink. If I wasn't mistaken, she preferred Grey Goose.

"Oh, hell naw. I know good and well you all ain't starting without me!" Peta screamed as she squeezed through a group of men to rush up to our table.

She flung her designer hobo onto the back of the chair, and grabbed the only glass that still sat on the table. She preferred the

Cosmopolitan, and she'd take any kind of vodka—Skyy, Tito's, Cîroc, to the bottom-of-the-barrel house brand.

Regardless of what everyone ended up drinking as the night wore on, we all started with our infamous double shot of Patrón. And the only rule was, no sipping allowed.

The V Lounge was a cozy and elegant space on the opposite side of the restaurant's elegant dining room. Its tables and booths, only steps away from the bar, were perfect. The horseshoe-shaped bar was ideal for people watching, but we had outgrown that space, and made our weekly home at Table Number Three.

We held court at our table, located at the left end of the bar where the soft and seductive lighting created a perfect setting for our favorite time of day, happy hour. That was where we handled the business—dishing the dirt, getting the latest scoop, and of course, catching up on the drama that was each other's lives, every week.

"Peta, you know the drill," I said. "It goes *doooownn* every Thursday at six-thirty, right here. Rain or shine, with or without you!"

"Well, I ain't missed a gathering yet, and I don't plan to either. So where were we, and what did I miss?" Peta asked.

"We were just getting started, so you're right on time," Felicia said.

With our shot glasses hoisted in the air, I began our mantra.

In unison, we all shouted:

"Up to it! Down to it! We do it because we're used to it! Fuck those that don't do it! Now let's get fucked up!"

As if on cue, everyone took their drinks to the head at the same time, and slammed the glasses down when they finished. The liquid burned as it blazed a fiery trail down my throat. I winced, swallowed hard, and blinked my watering eyes.

"Whew! That was niiiice," I said.

We all started cracking up, and the laughter didn't stop until the waitress walked over and interrupted us. She skillfully balanced everyone's drink of choice on her tray.

"Hey, ladies, how's everyone doing at Table Number Three this evening?"

"It's all good over here," Peta said.

"I'll drink to that!" Darby said.

We were cracking up again.

The waitress laughed, too, as she placed each glass in front of its rightful drinker, and then smiled. "Can I get anything else for you, ladies?"

"We'll take two jumbo lump crab cakes," I said.

"Oh, and two orders of your pot stickers and the shrimp cocktail," Darby added.

Nothing went better with happy hour than great food and even better conversation.

"Okay, coming right up. I'll be back soon." The waitress turned and walked away.

"Let's drink to bastards who try to make our jobs that much harder for no damn good reason at all," I said.

We touched glasses, and each took a sip.

"Oh, I got one, I got one," Darby interrupted. "Let's drink to the judgmental mothers at play dates who act like they don't understand when mommies need their own time out," she continued.

"Hell, I'll drink to that," I added.

"Oh, and this round is on me," a deep, sexy voice declared. It sounded like he was in my ear. When I turned and saw the twinkle in his hazel, bedroom eyes, all I could do was pray for strength.

I knew right off the bat, a willing, sexy man, and too much good liquor on a Thursday night, could only lead to trouble.

AFTER
HAPPY
HOUR

10

DARBY

I swear, I'm good. I texted into the phone.

U sure? No way I'd let you be out there like that.

Seriously! Jus' pulled in my subdivision. I'm good. Promise. But sweet that ur worried.

I texted him back quickly, and dropped the phone. I was out of order on so many levels—tipsy, texting, and buzz driving. I had already sent him a few bare-breasted selfie messages from the bathroom before I left happy hour.

"Oh, Lord, please help me!" I said aloud.

U see your house yet?

Yup, told you, I'm good. Now let me go. chat 2morrow.

I erased the text messages, made sure the phone was tucked into my purse, and got out of the car. I stumbled into the house quietly and fumbled with, but finally locked, the door behind me. I kicked off my sky-high heeled shoes, and allowed my bare feet to bask in the feel of the soft carpet.

The cool texture felt good against the soles of my feet. I smelled like an alcohol distillery.

The girls and I had a blast, and somehow I managed to make it home earlier than ever. Usually, I was down for whatever on Thursday nights, especially since, unlike the other ladies, I didn't have to punch anyone's time clock the next day. Once I got Kevin and the boys out the door, I could crawl back in bed and sleep it off.

"Damn!" I stumbled over a toy that was in the middle of the floor. Lord forbid my husband might clean up behind the kids, and himself, on my one night of freedom each week. His mama didn't teach him a damn thing except how to not spend money! I reached down for the toy, and nearly passed out when my husband bolted upright from the couch like a jack-in-the-box.

"You in early. What happened?" he asked. He rubbed at his eyes like Kevin Jr. did when he was sleepy.

"You scared the crap out of me!" I screamed.

"Sorry, babe, but you know I can't sleep good when you're out painting the town with the Rat Pack," he said groggily.

Kevin worked quite a bit, but on Thursday nights, regardless of when I came in, he was ready to play. At first, he used to whine and complain about me hanging out with my girls, but after a while, he seemed to get the hang of it. He must've realized that most times I came home tipsy and horny. Every once in a while, he'd act up. I figured it was to let me know he wasn't completely on board with the idea, but for the most part, he went with the flow. I felt like if I had to put up with him, his ketchup refills, and jelly jars, he could indulge my one vice.

"I'll wait for you upstairs," he said, and yawned.

I held the toy in my hand, and watched as he yawned again, grabbed his pillow, and stalked up the stairs. I wanted to ask him where he had been, and why his mother needed to watch the kids earlier, but I wanted another sip more than his answer. So I let him go up.

"Okay, I'll be up in a few minutes."

The minute he was gone, I rushed around picking up the toys and clothes that were scattered all over the family room. When everything was in its place, I grabbed my purse, and pulled out the little rhinestone-encrusted flask that I carried at all times.

I unscrewed the top, and took a couple of swigs. It didn't matter that the liquid burned as it slid down my throat. I had a two-drink limit while out with the ladies when we only did happy hour, and not a club or a lounge afterward. So I always had a nightcap when I came home.

I usually took my time with the nightcap. Kevin would wake the moment I crawled into bed, so I never felt rushed. He was lucky we called it an early night. Usually I didn't come in until close to two or three o'clock in the morning. He knew not to complain since, as a stay-at-home mom, my life resembled more of a maid's than a wife's.

It was a far cry from the image most people had of the extravagant home with a lakeside pool, nestled inside a prestigious hillside golf course.

Once he left the next morning, I'd meet with my neighbor Carla, who lived three houses down. I'd be able to dish about Kelly and the other playground moms. I'd also have to discuss her business. Carla had been on me to team up with her, and I was reluctant to at first, but I needed to rethink that.

The way Kevin was tight with money made me feel like a kid who had an allowance that was never enough. Of course, I kept a secret stash, but even that was limited, mainly due to my weekly happy hours. I liked to buy a few rounds, hating to feel like a charity case where the other girls had to get me all the damn time.

I shook the flask, and decided I'd had about three good swigs left before bed. Suddenly, a thought crossed my mind. I eased up from the sofa, and crept upstairs.

My mother-in-law was fast asleep in the guest bedroom. I checked in on the boys who were both knocked out, and then I tiptoed down the hall toward the master bedroom.

I eased up to the door, which was open, and stood for a second. Once I heard the rhythm of Kevin's snores, I turned around, and headed back downstairs.

Even though everyone was fast asleep, I still didn't trust using the computer in the family room. I pulled out my iPhone. Roger had called thirteen times, and left several messages. I was not in the mood, so I sent the customary text message to make sure the coast was clear. I turned the ringer off on my phone and waited.

The flask was fuller than I thought. After a few swigs, it dawned on me that my wait was quite long. In the meantime, my mind danced with thoughts of the money I could make with Carla if we played our cards right. For me, that money would mean a kind of freedom I'd never know under Kevin's penny-pinching behind.

Just when I was about to give up the wait and go upstairs to bed, my phone lit up as it vibrated. I was overjoyed by the simple message.

'Sup?

Just got in. what u about to get into?

Nada.

C'mon! Ur gonna do something/some1 LOL.

U got jokes.

Sometimes. Life a'int always serious.

Maybe not 4U.

U in a mood?

Nah nothin' like that. Jus' sayin'.

Ok well didn't want nothing. Just letting u know I made it in safe.

Cool but kinda late for nothing.

Like that sometimes.

Bet that.

GN.

K. don't hurt nobody.

Can't make any promises on that.

Bet that.

When I saw the smiley face, I felt better about the exchange. Our exchanges were always quick and brief, but still they brought me joy, and I couldn't explain it. I drained my flask, got up from the sofa, and stretched.

I hoped Kevin wasn't too out of it. I needed a serious, toe-curling orgasm, and I didn't want the kind that my battery-operated friends produced.

11

PETA

I had done some dumb things, but driving while I was tipsy was one of the dumbest. I wasn't drunk-drunk, but I felt *real* nice. I was probably less than one drink away from a bad situation if I had been pulled over by the cops. As I drove, all of the lights seemed blurry. I could read the street signs as long as I was right up on them. That was not cool, and I knew it.

When I finally turned the corner to enter my subdivision, I let out a huge sigh of relief. Usually, after happy hour, we'd go to another spot like Sugarhill or Club 21. That second spot gave us time to work off the alcohol, but that didn't happen tonight.

I was right on the edge. I felt good, more than a little tipsy. One more drink would've done the trick. That's why I'd have another taste once I made it to the privacy of my own house, but first, I had to make it there in one piece.

Once I got in the car, I had rolled down all of the windows so that the alcohol fumes from my breath wouldn't make me feel sick. The breeze also helped me to sober up as I drove. I even sang along with the songs on the radio.

"I've got to ease up a bit on Thursdays, especially when the party ends at happy hour," I muttered to myself as I turned onto my cul-de-sac. Relief washed over me. I was home, safely.

I hiccupped hard and loud as I turned the car onto my street. I brought it to a sudden, but careful, stop right before I swung into my driveway to find Kyle's car parked there.

"What in the hell?"

Visions of the last knockdown, drag-out verbal brawl with Kyle came to mind. He was pissed merely because I chose to go to happy hour, instead of having what he considered an important discussion. As I eyed his car, it pissed me off even more. I had told him time and time again not to pull into my driveway when I wasn't home.

He knew damn well that he had no parking privileges, but he simply didn't want to listen. If he thought discussing his important issue tonight was a good idea, I had news for him. I cursed as I threw the car into reverse, and backed up. I had to settle for a spot on the street. Now, I was really pissed. My high-heeled shoes were never made for actual walking, especially while drunk.

After I parked, I rolled up the windows, and turned off the car. I sat for a moment, trying to get my mind right. My heart raced as anger burned deep inside me. I was in no mood for the fight I realized awaited me.

I didn't understand how Kyle could spend so much time at our house without his woman having a fit. If he had focused on home like this while we were married, maybe we'd still be together. The thought sent a shiver down my spine, and shook me to my core.

I grabbed my purse, and fumbled my way out of the car. When I hiccupped again, I nearly lost my balance. I dropped back against the car, and swallowed the bile that threatened to come up. The cool, fresh air felt good, but it reminded me of how much I had overdone it. After a few minutes, I found my balance and attempted to make my way up the shrub-lined walkway that led to my front door.

On Thursdays, Kendal knew to leave the porch light on. I generally came home tipsy, and would struggle to find the right key in the dark. I was disgusted when I staggered to the door, and realized it was pitch dark.

"Shit!"

I stumbled a bit as I pulled my bag open, and rummaged through all of the junk inside. It was hard since I couldn't see a damn thing!

"Shoot, dammit! Hate big purses! Where are the doggone keys?"

There was no question. I was pissy-assed drunk, and mad as hell. I couldn't find the damn keys!

I felt like crying until my front door suddenly creaked open.

"This shit has got to stop!" Kyle whispered angrily, through gritted teeth. The low, sensual sound made my insides tingle. Instead of allowing me inside, he squeezed through the opening, stepped outside, and pulled the door closed behind him. "Do you realize how drunk you are?"

I wanted to say, *"Yeah, mofo, what do you think I was doing at the door? Playing with myself? Of course I was drunk, but your bitchin' is about to mess up my high."* Instead, I held my tongue, and thought before I spoke.

"Ain't nobody drunk!" I said.

Unfortunately for me, my denial sounded more intoxicated than I actually felt. I quickly pulled my hand up to my lips, but that did nothing to stop another hiccup. Kyle grasped my arm, and pulled me close.

"What kind of example you setting for our daughter? You leave her every week to go get drunk and rowdy with your trampy girls! I'm tryna tell yo' ass that ain't a good look."

Even though he hadn't raised his voice, the heat of his breath assaulted my face, and his sharp words cut deep. I wanted to reach out, and slap the shit out of him, but I'd probably lose my balance and wind up on the ground.

"You don't own me; you can't tell me what the f-f-fuck to do anymore!" It was a weak comeback, but it was the best I could do.

"I don't want to own you! My daughter is looking at you to teach her how to become a woman, and the shit you showing her right now is foul!"

His face was so close to mine that I smelled the mint from his breath. I shuddered at the thought of what mine must've smelled like.

"You drinking and driving and shit! What if you were pulled over?"

I stared at him, and cocked an eyebrow.

"I ain't drunk!" I tried to jerk away from him, but lost my balance, slipped, and nearly fell. Kyle grabbed me. And maybe it was the way he clutched me even closer, but something in me stirred again.

He had to have felt it, too. The next thing I knew, his mouth cupped mine, and our tongues began a vigorous wrestling match. My heart raced. I couldn't get enough of his taste, so I sucked and sapped like his mouth held the key to all of my problems.

We kissed and sucked. He reached behind his back, and opened the front door. We stumbled into the house, and picked up right where we'd left off.

This time, I didn't want to pull back from the kiss. I didn't want him to see the lust that burned in my eyes. That was the thing about Thursday nights. When I got drunk, and sometimes even just tipsy, I'd get horny as hell. Sure, I had done some questionable things, and all of it could be blamed on the alcohol. It made everything feel that much better.

Kyle pulled away, and eyed me for a second. I felt so naked as his eyes bore into me. I didn't know if the look on his face was regret, disgust, or plain lust.

"Listen, Kyle—" I was breathless.

"Shhh!" He put a thick, sausage-like finger to his lips. Then he pointed toward the ceiling, indicating that Kendal was asleep in her bedroom upstairs. We needed to be quiet.

"C'mon," I whispered.

"Where're we going?"

"Follow me." I stepped out of one shoe, then eased off the other as I led him toward the hallway. I opened the door, and tugged him in by the arm.

"In the damn bathroom?" he asked.

"Shhh!"

Once inside, I kissed him more aggressively, and yanked at my top. The moment I pulled out my left breast, he pounced like a magnet drawn to metal. When he reached down and tugged, seemingly about to unbuckle his pants, I raised my hand to stop him.

"Leave 'em on," I whispered, and grinned wickedly.

"W-w-what?"

I grabbed his waist and pulled him closer. My heart raced with anticipation as I unzipped his fly, and dug in to feel his stiffness. His dick felt magnificent. It was warm and hard as it throbbed in my hand. It was as if it had a mind of its own. "Here. Sit on the toilet. You got a condom?"

Kyle could've been a magician. Out of nowhere, a gold and black Magnum wrapper appeared. That, plus no mention of whatever the hell he wanted to discuss earlier, and I was in heaven.

12

"I am such a filthy slut!" I declared, and cracked up with laughter into the phone. My head still hurt a little from cocktails the night before, but it was nothing major. When we went hard on Thursday nights, I usually worked from home the following day. Last night was minor compared to the way we usually got down, but I needed to play it safe anyway.

"What did you do? And when did you do it? We wrapped up early last night," Peta reminded me.

"Well, let's just say it ain't always how much time you've got, but how wisely you use it. Last night was a perfect example of maximizing limited time to the fullest."

"Umph, well, I don't want a damn summary. I want details, so get to dishing," Peta said.

Before I could start the story, my other line rang. I rolled my eyes, and sighed heavily. It was the office. I had already told Jessica that I would be working from home, so I didn't understand why anyone would call me.

After about the third ring, I told Peta we'd have to catch up later.

"Girl, it's work, but I'm gonna get with you. Maybe we can do lunch or something like that. I gotta take this call."

"Ivee Henderson," I greeted. I did nothing to hide my irritation until the voice rang out in my ear.

"Ivee, this is Geneva JoHarris."

My motor skills and reflexes weren't as sharp as they normally were. That quickly changed. At the sound of her voice, my spine instantly stiffened. Without even trying, my body snapped to full attention.

"Uh, Geneva? Hi, how can I help you?" I hoped my voice sounded professional enough. Instantly, my eyes scanned the room for any files that were near.

"I understand you are working from home today, but I need a face-to-face. If you'd like, we can meet at a restaurant," she offered.

Geneva was fearless. In the male dominated field of media consulting, she had built both a solid and ruthless reputation. She was known for doing anything necessary to get the job done. Rumor around the office was that she had breastfed a client's infant once, in order to close a deal. When the client brought his screaming kid to a board meeting, nothing would shut the kid up. Each time the father started to say something, he'd stop midsentence to try and stuff the pacifier in the baby's mouth.

According to legend, right after they'd negotiated the terms and length of the contract, the kid's cries filled the room. Geneva snatched the baby, walked outside, and moments later, he was quiet. She and her team left with a signed contract in hand, and the father's complete support. Later, when asked how she had quieted the child, Geneva turned and said he was a breastfed baby, and that a bottle or pacifier wouldn't do.

No one had the heart to ever ask her about that, but that urban legend floated around the industry, and spoke volumes about her dogged determination when it came to closing deals.

Before I could answer the question, Geneva had spoken.

"I'll see you in my office in thirty," she said.

My mind began to race with all sorts of wild thoughts. Was it

Carson Liam's account? Had I missed anything pending? I rushed to get ready, but all sorts of worst-case scenarios ran through my mind.

Despite feeling severely hung over, I hauled ass, got dressed, and rushed to the office. The moment I got there, I was ushered into Geneva's sprawling office.

Sitting with my back to the door, I didn't even need to turn around to tell she had entered. Her scent always announced her arrival.

Geneva was a tall, statuesque powerhouse. Her mere presence commanded attention everywhere she went. She was one of those women who always looked her very best. Her copper-hued skin looked like she had just received a facial. Her shoulder-length, brunette hair was always slick and in place. Her birth certificate might have put her at sixty-five, but her body, her passion, and poise could rival any forty-year-old.

"Don't get up," she said, as she walked in.

The white, jewel-embedded pencil skirt she wore fit as if it was made specifically for her thin frame. She had on a matching silk top trimmed in black, and a pair of sky-high Michael Kors, pointy-toed pumps.

"Geneva." I rose ever so slightly.

She waved her arms, and dismissed my greeting as she moved behind her desk. Geneva always looked so fresh and easy breezy that she could lure you into a false sense of comfort. I knew better. I understood the unspoken seriousness of being summoned to her office.

Despite how much her Russian, red-matte lips smiled, it was always high-stakes poker with her, and that smile could lead to the kiss of death. When the smile vanished, and her pretty features twisted into a frown, I braced myself for the worst.

"Oooh, a little too much Belvedere last night?" She giggled.

If my skin were pale, I would've turned several shades of crimson right where I sat. I was more than a little embarrassed.

"That obvious?" I asked sheepishly. I wanted to say, *"You wouldn't have been assaulted by my fumes had you left me to my work at home."*

"It's seeping through your pores," she joked. "A woman after my own heart." She reached for a thick folder, and dropped it onto her desk.

She had not called me in to discuss my drink of choice, but I couldn't rush her, despite how badly I wanted to.

"Carson Liam is making some serious allegations of negligence on your part. He's demanding a meeting, and I need to know what I'm walking into Monday morning."

Negligence. I allowed her words to roll around in my head before I responded, but the main one that stuck, cut deep.

"Geneva, Carson is impatient. He doesn't understand that any campaign needs time. He wants instant returns."

She stopped what she was doing, and eyed me closely.

"Ivee, you are very talented and more than capable. I am not going to lecture you about how to do your job, but the bottom line is, we are here to give the clients what they want, and that isn't necessarily what they need."

I was even more vexed with Carson. He had basically put me on Geneva's radar unnecessarily. While I was confident my work more than spoke for itself, I enjoyed being complaint free. When a client complained, regardless of who was right, it cast a negative shadow. I'd seen it happen with others, and we all talked about it. When someone received that mark, it seemed to hang around forever. Whispers around the office about who had a client switched to another colleague was a sure sign that one shouldn't expect any kind of bonus or pay increase.

Geneva and I talked, and although she kept it lighthearted, I didn't trust the false sense of security she tried to shower on me.

By the time I left her office, I felt like the kid who had been silently reprimanded by parents who had unrealistic standards.

As I walked into the elevator, I murmured to myself, "Well, if that bitch thinks I'm gonna sit and wait on her to strike, she's got another thing coming."

13

PETA

I made it a priority to have dinner with Kendal at least three or four times a week. The boutiques kept me busy, and I loved it. However, it was easy to fall into the trap where my focus was solely on work. And as a single parent, I couldn't afford to neglect my girl.

Gordon and I texted back and forth, but I didn't call him. I had plans. After dinner, Kendal and I popped in a movie. I listened as my daughter rambled on about which of her classmates were no longer friends, and who said what about whom.

"So, Mom, Heather was like, you can't be friends with me if you're gonna be friends with Leslie. And, like you will not believe, Shelly totally said she was not gonna talk to Leslie anymore!"

"Wait. Right there in class?" I asked.

Kendal's eyes grew to the size of saucers. A massive grin spread across her face. That was when her dimples really set in, and she reminded me so much of her father. I shook that thought from my mind, and focused on our conversation. It may have been mind-numbing to me, but the middle school drama seemed crucial to her. I walked back to the sofa, and got comfortable again.

"So, lemme get this straight." I grabbed a fist full of popcorn, and prepared to stuff my mouth. "You're telling me that Shelly stopped talking to Leslie right there on the spot because Heather told her to?"

My daughter slapped her palms against her thighs and nodded. "Mom, it was totally wild! I was like, this is totally not happening! And right there, right in front of everyone, too."

"What were you doing when all of this was going on?" I asked.

"Mom, I sat there with my mouth like super wide open. I couldn't believe it." My daughter sipped from her soda. "I felt like totally bad for Leslie. I mean, she's a mean girl, too, but remember like just yesterday she was like BFFs with Heather and Shelly."

"What would you have done if Heather had said that to you?"

My daughter gave me a cockeyed look; then she smirked.

"C'mon, Mom! You know those girls don't like me, and besides, I'm a leader. I ain't no follower. I woulda told Heather, 'You might think you're all that, but you don't tell me what to do!'"

I smiled at her.

That's my girl, I thought. We eased into our comfortable spots on the sofa, cuddled, and watched our movie.

Nearly two hours later, the vibration from my cell phone woke me up. Kendal had curled into a ball near the foot of the sofa.

When I saw Kyle's number on my screen, I was tempted to ignore his call, but he'd simply call back. I got up from the sofa, and ran my finger across the screen to accept his call.

"Hello?" I whispered.

"Damn, Peta, why's the deadbolt on?" Kyle's irritated voice asked.

I whipped my head in the direction of the front door. I nearly lost my breath when I saw his shadow on the other side of the door's glass panel.

Once I made certain my daughter was asleep, I got up, and made my way to the front door. I tried to calm myself before I came face-to-face with him. He had been a complete ass since I didn't drop everything I was doing and make time for his emergency.

At the door, I took a deep breath, and tried to calm down. I unlocked the deadbolt, and cracked the door open.

"Kyle, what's going on? You've been blowing me up, and now you're here. What gives? You didn't even bother to call before you popped up. I could've had company!"

"Yeah, yeah, sorry about that. But, Peta, I really wanted to talk to you about what happened after happy hour."

I was a bit caught off-guard, but my shock didn't last long. Images from the other night flashed through my mind in bits and pieces. I hadn't noticed it before, but when he moved forward, and I saw a massive blue bottle he clutched in his hand. He eyed me like a lost puppy.

"I was thinking we could have a nightcap and talk, you know, about the other night," he said. "I can't seem to get ten minutes of your time."

Despite how hard I tried not to smile, I couldn't resist. Kyle had brought my friend, Skyy, and he knew that would definitely win him major points with me. It also told me that he was up to something. I wasn't sure what he wanted, but his tactic told me it was gonna be something serious.

I glanced over my shoulder when I thought I heard my daughter stir. When I looked back, I realized that Kyle's eyes had followed my gaze. He looked good.

"She ain't sick or nothing, is she?" he asked.

There weren't many things I admired about Kyle, but the unshakable love he always showed for his daughter made my heart soften.

I frowned. "No, she's fine. We fell asleep watching a movie. Since she's asleep in the family room, you're gonna have to be real quiet," I whispered.

I stepped aside, and Kyle entered the house. He handed me the bottle of liquor. I accepted it, and walked toward the kitchen.

I sighed.

He gently picked Kendal up, and took her upstairs to her bedroom. I wanted to tell him to stop treating her like such a baby, but I held my tongue. When he came downstairs, I had two drinks waiting. At first, we sat quietly and enjoyed our drinks. That was when I realized how tired I was. Still, somehow, he convinced me to play strip poker.

By the time we finished the fourth round, I was two hands away from being as naked as the day I was born.

I stopped making drinks after the second round, and Kyle took over.

I smacked my lips after I took a sip from the drink Kyle made.

"Damn, did you put any juice in here?" I balked.

"Oh, I know you're not complaining. I'll bet if we were at happy hour, you'd be singing my praises!" Kyle joked. "You and your girls would be tryin' to tip me, and y'all would be begging me to keep 'em coming."

I felt it. I was good and gone. Kyle could've probably gotten any and everything he wanted out of me at that moment.

And I'd learn soon enough, that was exactly what he had planned.

14

DARBY

The gloomy and ominous clouds that hung overhead should've been an indication that misery was nipping at my heels, but my mind was preoccupied. It had been that way since the call from Roger, nearly an hour ago. Now, as I walked back from the mailbox, I thought about the conversation I'd had with him.

"Aunt Saundra is here. Mom wants you to come over to the house," he had said.

I rolled my eyes, and released a deep breath. Strained couldn't begin to describe my relationship with my mother and the rest of my once close-knit family. I never thought I'd see the day when I'd ignore my mother's calls, and basically alienate myself and my kids from the close clan, however that's exactly what had happened over the last few years.

So when my brother called to tell me that I was being summoned home, I wasn't the least bit motivated to make a move. He knew I wasn't going anywhere near those judgmental hypocrites.

"How could you?" I asked.

"How could I what?" he asked, feigning innocence.

Something in his voice told me he had revealed my secret, and now he was trying to set me up for one of my family's infamous interventions. Well, I didn't need a damn intervention. I knew exactly what I was doing, and my plan was going to be far more effective than theirs. I was still committed to getting revenge for Darlene. A plea deal had ended their crusade, but mine was still ongoing.

"You said something, didn't you?" I barked into the phone.

"Darby, why are you tripping? Mama and Aunt Saundra say they haven't seen the kids in almost three years. We need to come together as a family, and work this thing out. Besides, what's wrong is wrong, and you know it, too."

"You told them, didn't you?" I asked again.

When he didn't answer my question right away, he didn't have to say anything else. His silence told me everything he couldn't bring himself to say. I was beyond mad. It was really by sheer accident that Roger had even discovered my plan, and there was still a part of me that hadn't come completely clean. When I realized that he had found out, I quickly tried to lie my way out of it.

I still remember the day. I was so preoccupied on the computer that I didn't even notice that Roger had walked into my house. I'd signed for a package, and Carla came in at the same time. When she left, she obviously didn't lock the door.

"Is that who I think it is?" Roger had asked over my shoulder.

Startled, I jumped at the sound of his voice. "I didn't hear you come in."

"Your neighbor was leaving when I came in," he said.

"Oh." I tried to log off the Facebook chat, but the look on his face told me he had already seen the picture of Chandler.

"What are you doing on his page?"

"I was keeping up with him, that's all," I stammered. I had done more than kept up with him. Over the years, I had frequently passed by his family's business and, a few times, I had even followed him. When I thought enough time had passed, I searched for him on social media sites. When I first reached out to him, I thought for sure it was a long shot. But, he stunned me with a quick response, and we'd been communicating ever since. My mind left the past, and returned to the phone call at hand.

"Goodbye, Roger. Don't call back," I warned.

"Darby! Wait—"

Once I ended the call, I glanced up at the clock, and began to calculate my time. I didn't have enough time to go by there, but I could get in a quick chat and some sexting. Carla and I were supposed to hook up to talk about some more business details. I figured as long as that happened before the kids got off the school bus at four-fifteen, I'd be good.

After I double-checked and made sure the doors were locked, I walked into the home office and locked that door, too. I logged on to the computer, and signed into my Facebook account.

Since I didn't find what I needed, I picked up my cell phone, and sent a text message. Only a few minutes passed, but it felt so much longer. When the phone vibrated, I grabbed it, and smiled as I looked down at the message.

Moments later, my fingers trembled as I signed back into my account, and began a chat.

Why you keep reaching out to me?

What kind of question is that? I was glad he couldn't sense my attitude through the computer.

I jus' wanna know what u want from me?

Initially, I thought he couldn't possibly remember who I was. Not only did he remember me, but I think a part of him wanted to prove to me that he was not a cold-blooded monster. Sure, he had avoided jail for his crime, but I believed the accident that killed Darlene had changed his life, too.

I stared at the screen, and thought about that question. I wasn't sure what I wanted. I didn't understand why the question was necessary. My eyes focused on the screen again when I saw a series of question marks pop up.

What makes you think i want something from you?

Ppl usually do.

Maybe i'm different.

Bs. But if that's how you wanna play this thing. Cool w me!

Do it! The voice in my head taunted me. I wanted to. I desperately wanted to ask the question, but I couldn't bring myself to do it. I stared at the screen again. My brother's words echoed through my mind.

"...*what's wrong is wrong and you know it, too...*"

I shook his words from my mind and focused on the text message.

TTYL.

I erased the letters and retyped them again, but I didn't send the message.

'Sup?

My eyes focused in on the new question. I quickly hit the *Send* button, and logged off. I didn't realize I had started crying until tears fell onto my lap and wet my skin. It seemed like knowing I had shed tears opened up the floodgates, and the waterworks began with full force. I got up, and rushed to the refrigerator. I wiped my cheeks, and opened the door to grab a bottle of wine.

The sadness didn't last long. It would pass. It always did. As a matter-of-fact, by the time I finished the first glass of wine, I felt better. That was a good thing, too, because my cell phone rang. It was Carla.

"Darby, when do your kids come home?" she asked.

"Well, hello to you, too, Carla," I said.

"Girl, you know I'm not always for the pleasantries. Now, how long before your kids come home?"

I glanced at the clock, and tried to refocus my attention to the business at hand. "We have about a solid hour. How much do we need to cover?"

"Ummm, we can get it all worked out. We need to set up a time to meet with everyone, and go over some of the changes you want to put in place."

"Okay, you coming over here, or am I coming to you?"

"I can come there. I'll be there in ten minutes."

I poured some more wine, and finished it off in three, big gulps before the doorbell rang. I rinsed the glass, and placed it back in the dish rack.

"Coming!" I yelled as I darted toward the front door.

"Whew! What you do, brush your teeth with liquor?" Carla asked as I opened the door, and she passed me.

"No! I had a glass of wine."

"In the middle of the afternoon?" she asked, an eyebrow raised. She had some nerve. I tossed a hand to my hip, and gave her a look.

"I got an excuse. I'm usually working early, so I gotta start early," Carla said, as she sashayed into my breakfast area.

By the time I got back to the kitchen, she had an empty glass in front of her.

"Okay, where's the drank? Don't be shy now. It's time to share."

Since we didn't have much time, I opened the refrigerator, and removed the bottle. As I poured our drinks, Carla looked at me like she was trying to figure something out.

"What?" I asked.

"How come you don't work?" she asked.

I paused before I put the cork back into the bottle.

"It's obvious we've got enough working girls on the roster. Besides, someone's gotta be the brains behind this operation."

Carla cracked up at that one.

"I didn't mean in the business of socializing with married men, silly," she said jokingly. Carla winked, then sipped from her glass.

"Oh, Kevin and I agreed, I'd stay home and take care of the kids while he worked," I said.

"Well, maybe your husband should stay his ass at home, and let you bring home the bacon. Besides, if you went to work, you'd realize how much you're missing out on."

I hoped Carla wasn't about to become one of those people. Most were obsessed with the fact that I didn't work outside the home, and I couldn't understand why it was such a rare thing.

The problem was, it was hard to decipher who was intrigued by it, and who harbored deep-rooted jealousy.

I downed my drink, and then poured myself another one. I couldn't believe this bitch. Here she was screwing married men on their lunch breaks, but she was worried about me not having a job outside the home. I was ready to pour another drink when the question popped into my head.

Did I really need money that badly? The answer would come a lot faster than I expected.

15

PETA

I was highly pissed, but I had to choose my words carefully. Of the four drivers I had, only one was a problem. Beverly Hicks was a ticking time bomb, and she could explode at any moment. I had to handle her very carefully.

"No, no, that's not where Truck Three is supposed to go!"

I screamed, and caught myself before things spiraled out of control. It was simple. Boutique on Wheels had four trucks. Their schedules were pretty much routine. We hit the downtown business district, the oil and gas campuses in Katy, The Woodlands, and Sugar Land. We might have parked in various locations, but the cities and truck assignments never changed. It was best to keep the drivers, who doubled as fashion consultants, in their respective neighborhoods. The clients knew them, and they knew the clients. The rapport between them helped sales immensely.

"Beverly, I'm looking at the schedule, and I don't understand why you would think you were supposed to be in Sugar Land today. I've had a dozen calls already!"

"Well, you screaming at me ain't gonna get me where I need to be no faster," she snapped.

My mobile boutique business, specialized in unique fashion, accessories, and shoes. We brought inventory directly to the consumers. We catered to the busy-on-the-go professionals, and as a complete one-stop-shop, business was good. In addition to our inventory, we also had catalogs for specialty orders.

I inhaled deeply, and tried to calm my nerves and my anger. As CEO, I knew how hard it was to replace drivers, and that was the last thing I wanted to do. Beverly had her faults, but she had a knack for sales. She knew fashion, and the customers loved her. Nevertheless she was directionally challenged.

"All I know is, in the meeting on Monday night, you kept talking about Sugar Land. I figured that's where you wanted me."

"Beverly, your truck is north side, Sugar Land is south side. Listen, we need to fix this 'cause I've got clients in The Woodlands who are waiting for their orders."

Beverly huffed. "Well, traffic has already started to pick up. Ain't no way I'm gonna make it there before close of business today."

I could hear the frustration building in her voice, and I didn't want to do anything to add to it. A squabble with her was not the way to go.

Beverly was completely correct, and there was nothing I could do to change the fact. I squeezed my eyes shut and tried again to calm myself. I couldn't stay mad at her. She was a crucial part of my business.

"So, what you want me to do?" Beverly asked after a long and awkward silence between us.

"Lemme think," I said.

The problem was, the trucks had specific permits. It wasn't illegal to move them around, but if an officer wanted to be difficult, he could ticket us when we were in a new location.

"Hey, Bev, give me a little time. Lemme see if I can reroute you. In the meantime, you can hold tight until I radio back to you."

"Well, I'm gonna go grab me some lunch," she said.

I didn't bother with a response. Beverly knew damn well she needed to be north of the city, but I didn't have the time or energy to fight.

Once I hung up with her, I dialed Sandy to make sure she was where she was supposed to be.

"Boutiques on Wheels, Sugar Land," Sandy's cheerful voice answered. Sandy Newton was an older retiree. She didn't act her age and was a complete people person. She enjoyed driving the custom RV that housed our boutiques and loved her job.

"Hey, Sandy, it's Peta, calling to see how everything's going today," I said.

"Oh, it's well over here, darlin'. Things have slowed a bit, but lunchtime was sheer bananas, and I loved it! Now listen here, buttercup. We don't restock 'til Friday, but I'm running real low on merchandise, so we may need to bring me in tonight."

"Tonight?"

"We can hold out 'til Friday if we have to, but our lingerie stock is almost zilch. The maxi dresses are all gone, and those cute nude sling backs—those cuties sold out before lunch," Sandy reported.

"Sandy, you're awesome! Our clients always call to tell me how you help them piece outfits together, and I don't say it enough, but your idea to have bottomless mimosas was nothing less than genius!"

"Oh, boss, you don't have to thank me. It's me who should be thanking you. Thanks to you, I'm out and about again, meeting new people and having the time of my life in retirement. You're so smart, and before long, this business will be all over the country."

Sandy had lots of spunk. Her short, bleached-blonde hair was spiked on top, and she always wore bright colors. She may have been a retiree, but she moved better than most thirty-year-olds I knew.

"I'm not sure about that, but for now, let's cover the greater Houston area, and I'll be happy."

"Well, like I said, I really need more inventory. Friday is pay day, buttercup. We should be fully stocked 'cause the business park off Dairy Ashford asked if we could spend the entire day there."

"Oh, wow! That's great news," I said.

"That's what I said. Cha-ching! So that's why I'm telling you we need to be ready for that mad rush."

Secretly, I wished Beverly, Farah, and Cecily could all be more like Sandy. She always had great ideas about ways to improve business, and she had a very pleasant disposition. She looked at the job as a privilege versus what it really was—her helping me tremendously.

"Okay, lemme see what I can do. I'll call you back before close of business today."

Hours later, I drove toward the George R. Brown Convention Center to meet Beverly. After I made sure all of the other trucks and drivers were okay, I rerouted Beverly to the convention center. Since there was an educator's conference going on, I figured I needed to be there to help her out.

I parked and made my way over to the RV where a long line snaked around the front of the vehicle. That was a great sign.

"Excuse me," I said to two women who stood at the front of the line. They tossed me a dirty look as I squeezed by and entered the RV.

"Hey, Bev!" I yelled over the voices and chatter.

"Boss lady, everything okay?"

Beverly assisted a woman near the fitting room as several others looked on. The custom RV was outfitted with two sofas and racks of dresses and tops. There were custom shelves that displayed shoes. We had two transparent dressers with photos of lingerie pieces displayed on the front panels. Soft music flowed through speakers, and the women who sat and waited sipped on cold beverages.

A tiny, crystal chandelier hung from the ceiling, and added soft, yellow lighting that helped perfect the customers' images in the mirrors. The carpets were a bold royal blue and purple and the furniture was trimmed in the same colors.

Beverly did a great job of keeping the atmosphere lively.

"Okay, ladies, who can I help next?" I asked.

"Oh, I need to pay for these shoes," a petite redhead said as she popped up from a chair.

I took the box from her, scanned it, and accepted her credit card.

My cell phone chirped, announcing a text message. I finished up the sale, then took a peek.

Whassup?

It was Gordon. Before I could respond, I turned around, and another customer stood balancing an armful of merchandise.

I made a mental note to hire an assistant for Beverly.

16

DARBY

I enjoyed this time of morning most. All was quiet and calm. The house was so silent, I could hear my appliances as they hummed, and even that never disrupted the serenity. It was right after the kids were tucked away in school, the hubby was at the office, and I was in my zone.

The View had just come on when a thunderous knock at my front door pulled my attention away from the screen. I growled, irritated. I hated when the phone rang, or when people popped up during my shows.

Who the hell could that be and what's on fire?

I turned toward the sound of the knocking, but couldn't get up fast enough. The knocking got louder. "Darby! You there? OH MY GOD! Please open up!"

The knocking became more frantic. It sounded like there was some kicking thrown in, too. I dropped the remote and bolted from the sofa.

I rushed to the door, pulled back the curtain, and could hardly believe what I saw. Red, puffy, raccoon eyes stared back at me. I took in the trail of running mascara mixed with tears that stained her cheeks. Her lipstick was smudged along the side of her jaw, and her wild hair was all over her head.

Carla looked frantic, disheveled, and like she had run for dear life.

Heat climbed my neck and face as I snatched the door open, and she scrambled to get inside. I helped her up as she struggled to catch her breath. I couldn't figure out what was more stunning, her wardrobe, or her appearance. She looked a hot, funky mess! I hadn't seen her for a few days.

She wore a corset, a garter belt, fishnet stockings, and the whole nine. The flimsy see-through robe she had on covered nothing at all. I couldn't believe she had run out of her house looking the way she did.

"Hurry, lock the door! Oh God, Darby! I hope they didn't see where I went!" She spoke in shaky fits and forced her words out. "Oh my God!" She trembled.

"Whoa! ...Who in the hell are you running from?" I pulled back the blinds to peek outside.

"No! Move away from the window!" Carla shrieked. The child looked like she'd seen a ghost or had been chased by one.

"I'm calling the cops! What in the hell is going on?"

My nerves were bad. I walked toward the back of my house with her hot on my heels. I didn't understand why she had run to my house. I didn't need anybody bringing drama to my doorstep.

"What in the hell is going on?" I asked again. I tried to calm her while I went for the phone.

"Darby, please don't call no cops. Please. Let's be real quiet. She didn't see me. They don't know where I went. Let's chill out for a sec," she begged.

"She? They? Who are you talking about?"

I didn't have to wait too long for the answer. A loud, crashing noise turned both of our attention toward the foyer. I rushed back to the front.

"Oh, hell naw!" I screamed. "What the hell is really going on?"

That crashing noise was my front door, which now hung on its hinges.

"Oh, shit! Oh my God!" Carla cried. "Bitch, you're crazy! You need to leave. We called the police!" Carla said to the woman who stood near the damage.

"You wanna screw around with married men? What kind of tramp sleeps with a bunch of married men?" the woman asked.

"Why did you kick down *my* damn front door?" I asked, flabber-gasted.

"Look, lady. My issue is not with you. It's with your trampy friend here. Shove her ass out here, and we're done with you."

"Yeah, push the trick out here," another voice said. That's when I realized she wasn't alone.

"Look at my damn door. What in the hell is your problem?" I said to the first woman.

She stood on my doorstep, dressed in what looked like army fatigues. Her sidekick was dressed all in black, and leaned up against a massive, barrel-looking object. I figured that was what they'd used to demolish my front door.

"Who's gonna pay for this damage?"

"Make *her* ass pay! You can't stay here forever," the woman said to Carla.

Carla was careful to keep her distance. When she spoke, she did so from behind me.

"I told you, I'm not having an affair with your husband. I told you that already!" Carla yelled.

"Bitch, why is he pulling up to your house every Tuesday at ten in the morning, if y'all not fuckin'?" the woman asked.

"Look, I don't care who is fucking whom! What I wanna know is who's gonna fix my damn front door? I ain't got nothing to do with none of this, and somebody'd better be talking about picking up the tab for the damage to my property."

"You know what, if you don't push her ass on out here, you may have to eat that. I'm trying to tell you, our issue ain't with you, but you seem like you wanna stick your neck out for her," the woman said.

"Carla, go to the back. I'm not about to stand here and negotiate with these thugs. I don't care what in the hell she did, you had no business breaking down my front door."

"Go in and snatch her ass out," the woman's friend suggested. "I ain't trying to go to jail over this trick."

"Nah, girl, we need her to come out on her own. You know how it goes in Texas. Ain't nobody shooting me, talking about protecting their castle," the first woman said.

I was glad she knew better than to step over my threshold, but that didn't make me feel any better about the damage to my front door. I stepped back and grabbed the cordless phone.

"Somebody's gonna pay for the damage to my property, that's all I know."

The woman and her friend exchanged knowing glances, but neither seemed pressed about my threat to call the police. I didn't really want to call the law. I didn't need them all up in our business, but I needed to put the fear of God in Rambo and her partner.

After I grabbed the phone, I dialed 9-1-1.

"Nine-one-one, what is your emergency?"

When the dispatcher answered, I spoke like I was on a mission. "Yes, someone kicked in my front door," I said.

"This shit ain't over, Carla," the woman spat.

Her friend picked up the massive tool she had brought, and they high-tailed it off my porch.

"You done fucked with the wrong one! Believe that!" the other woman yelled.

I walked outside and tried to get their license plate number, but they were parked too far away. I was more than pissed when I walked back into my house.

The dispatcher told me an officer was on the way, and asked whether I was in any danger. I was grateful it was a weekday morning, and most of my neighbors were at work.

"Carla, the cops are on the way. You should go find something else to put on!" I yelled.

She had come out of hiding, but her eyes wandered around like she wasn't sure if the women were really gone.

"I told you not to call the cops. You know I got you for the door. Now we're gonna have to be answering all kinds of questions and shit," Carla said.

"Listen, if we're gonna do this, we're gonna do it right. I keep telling you, when you go dumpster diving, you find nothing, but trash."

Carla listened to me like she'd heard it all before, and none of it had sunk in.

"So, are you telling me you're gonna be a full-blown partner?" she asked.

"In order for me to sign on to what you got going, we need to make a whole helluva lot of changes."

The truth was, I probably needed Carla's business more than she needed me. I was sick of being on a kid's allowance. My husband feared I'd send us to the poorhouse.

"Okay, Darby, I'm good with some changes. And I may not be the best businesswoman ever, but you gotta give credit where credit is due. How else can you pull in a few grand a month, be your own boss, and *sleep in* every damn day of the week?"

"A few grand a month?" I repeated.

"H-h-hello?" she said.

A knock at the door pulled my attention away from our conversation.

"Girl, this stuff is like literally stealing candy from babies," Carla said as she slipped up the stairs.

I went to meet with the officers as the figures she mentioned flew around in my mind. That kind of money was definitely worth the risk, or so I thought.

17

"Mama, that lady called you again," Kendal said the moment I walked into the house the other day.

"What woman?" I asked.

"Pamela Evans."

My mama didn't raise no fool. Pamela Evans had been on my bad side since she called awhile back and bombarded me with a million questions about how I do what I do.

In my line of work, it was rare that potential clients insisted on a face-to-face consultation like she had. They usually wanted to see the truck, so they could browse the inventory. But not her. She wanted to meet specifically with me, and that had been the second thing I hated about her. When she showed up at my office, I realized I had nearly forgotten about our appointment. I had a good mind to cancel on her, but thought better of it and decided to go through with the meeting.

She had rubbed me the wrong way from jump, and in person, she had managed to irritate me even more. Pamela was in my space for less than fifteen minutes, and almost immediately, I hadn't dug her vibe. It wasn't the way she took in my dark purple walls, or the way she gazed at the two-tier antique French gold and crystal chandelier that hung prominently in the center of my office. It was more than that.

I was accustomed to intriguing stares once people stepped into my office, but that's what it was—*my* space. The furniture, the pearl white, shag carpeting, and the glass desk were all designed to suit *my* taste.

"Hmmm, I really like it in here, Peta," she had said. But her tone told another story. A fake, frozen smile hovered on her lips as she looked around and scrutinized my pictures.

"Paris, Brazil, wow! Where was this one taken?" she asked.

I glanced over and said, "Oh, that's Belize. I go there a few times a year to decompress."

"Oooh, Beeelize!" She complimented me, but her pretty features twisted into a frown. "I really, really like your style."

I moved closer to my desk and took a seat as she finished looking around. Even after she claimed her seat, her eyes wandered around some more. I noticed she had already slipped her gaze down to my designer shoes. It was slight, and hardly noticeable, but I caught the way her eyebrow twitched as she took inventory. I didn't care. I made no excuses for living well, and taking good care of my daughter and me.

"Are those Jimmy Choos?" she asked.

"They are." I pointed my toe and flexed my foot for her to get a better look.

"Yeah, real nice. Sooo, I'm tryna get this straight," Pamela said. "You're not a designer, like you don't have a degree in business, but basically that's exactly what you're doing," she insisted.

Obviously, Pamela hadn't done her homework. If she had, she would've realized that having a degree in business was not a requirement or prerequisite for success in business. I had grown bored with her and the one-sided interview she conducted.

Pamela was very pretty. She was a former NFL cheerleader, and she'd kept herself up fairly well. But her vibe told me she was up to something. I had been at this long enough to be able to discern when someone was serious about doing business with me, or if they were fishing for information. Pamela Evans was on a major fishing expedition. The only reason I entertained her was because I wanted to know why she had chosen me.

She quickly corrected herself. "Well, I guess I should let you tell me what it is that you do."

"That's the odd thing," I said. "I'm confused. Are you trying to decide whether you need to buy into a company, or are you trying to shop?"

"I guess I'm intrigued, and well, a friend of mine found a unique wrap dress, and she told me she got it from your place. I'm looking for the right kind of distribution."

I felt like I had already given her enough information. As much as we had talked already, she knew whether she wanted to distribute her product through my fleet.

"I'm trying to figure out how you were able to secure the clients and your prime locations. And, do you mind me asking what kind of money you make? By the looks of things, it seems like you make a pretty good living," she said. That series of questions gave her another chance to look around my space again.

"Pamela, I have a standing appointment on Thursday evenings." I glanced at my watch, although I didn't need to see the time to know I had had enough of her. "And I need to prepare for it."

"Oh? I thought we'd have more time. I have so many more questions."

"Well, we've spent enough time to last the equivalent of at least ten sessions. You understand that I can't run a business this way. I hope you reach your decision soon, and I'll follow up with you at a later date." I stood.

That must've made her feel compelled to follow suit. She popped up as if the chair had suddenly caught fire and burned her behind.

"Oh, yeah. I totally understand. I'm glad you were able to meet with me, and I do appreciate your time. I think what you do is so fascinating," she said as she used her palms to smooth out the skirt she wore.

"Okay, well, I hope the information helps and you find what you're looking for." I moved toward the door, and she followed.

She moved slowly as if she was reluctant to leave. She eased past me, and I smiled until I closed the door behind her.

Once she was gone, I returned to my desk, and tried to figure out what she might've been up to, and what it might have to do with me. Initially, she passed herself off as a person who had a series of high end designer T-shirts that she wanted me to help distribute, but the more I talked to her, the more it felt like she was trying to use me as some kind of guinea pig.

"Oh well, in another hour or so, Pamela and whatever she's trying to do will be nothing more than a faint memory," I said aloud.

I called down to the parking service. "Hi, this is Peta. Please bring my car around. I'll be leaving in about fifteen minutes."

"Sure thing. We'll have it ready," the parking attendant replied.

As I rode down on the elevator, I thought about the stressful past few days I'd had. Thursdays had quickly become my favorite day of the week, and I could hardly wait to dish some of the dirt that weighed me down.

18

DARBY

"You need to do what you need to do until tomorrow morning. I can't talk to you about this right now!" I screamed into the phone.

"Darby, where have you been? I've been calling you since about six o'clock, and now it's almost eleven!" Carla screamed back at me.

At that moment, I noticed my husband's number pop up on call waiting.

"Look, I go to happy hour every Thursday with my girls, and right now, you're messing with my buzz. I need to talk to you in the morning," I said as I drove west on I-10, the Katy Freeway. I had just passed Highway 6, and was headed home when I got Carla's call, and she was working my very last nerve. When Carla had something to say, it was like her ears shut down and she couldn't hear.

"Happy hour! So, while I'm sitting up here worried sick, you're enjoying cocktails, and not even thinking about my misery?" she shrieked.

"Carla, tomorrow. Besides, Kevin is calling, and if I don't answer, he's gonna have a cow! In the morning," I repeated.

My eyes glanced upward to the rearview mirror, and I tried to focus on my driving. I really wasn't in the mood to talk to her or Kevin.

Pushy neighbors, overzealous PTA moms, bratty kids, and controlling husbands made me want to run to Eddie V's and camp out from Thursday to Thursday. Did they allow that?

Oftentimes, I hated to leave happy hour. For the four of us, it may have started with happy hour, but it had morphed into a night of much-needed partying.

I rolled my eyes as Carla babbled away in my ear. When I agreed to go in with her and the business, I had no idea the headaches that would be involved.

Lord knew the extra money would come in handy, but Carla had a way of making me wish I would've thought of the business alone. I was slightly desperate because Kevin was more than a little frugal. He behaved like our finances were so tight that any extra expense might send us straight to the poorhouse. So having my own secret stash helped avoid potential conflict in the house.

I finally got Carla off the phone when I switched over and took my husband's call.

"Hello?" I answered.

"When are you coming home?" he whined the minute I answered. I hated when he did that.

It really irritated me that I had to leave the party early. But since I planned to hang out next week, I let him get his way this week.

"I'm on my way now," I said.

"Oh, how far away are you?"

The sound of relief in his voice really rubbed me the wrong way. I wanted to say, "Isn't it bad enough that I'm on my way home when everyone else is still partying it up?" I resisted that urge. At times, Kevin tried to be a control freak.

"I'll be there shortly."

It had been nearly an hour since I had left Eddie V's, and as usual, we'd had a damn good time.

I hated to leave. The girls took the party over to Saint Genevieve, but if I didn't get home by a certain time on a weeknight, Kevin would send a search party out. It wasn't that he had plans for us, or needed me home to do anything in particular. It seemed like he wanted to restrict anything that might bring me too much joy.

"Okay, well, I'll see you when you get home," he said. When he yawned, I wanted to reach through the phone and strangle him. I ended our call, and took the Fry Road exit off the freeway. My mind swirled with thoughts of all the fun the girls would probably have without me.

The next call really should've been ignored, but I answered anyway.

"Yeah, Roger."

"Dang, that's how you greet me now? Darby, if you really in your heart of hearts don't think what you're doing is wrong, then why have you isolated yourself from the family? Why do your kids and Kevin have to suffer?"

I wanted to tell him that Kevin wasn't suffering in the least. But the last thing I needed to do was encourage a conversation. My mind was still stuck on happy hour, and all that I'd miss.

"Roger, what do you want from me? What do you want me to do? I can't erase all of the vile, evil things your mother said to me. She made her feelings known. Why would I want my kids around someone who thinks so poorly of me?"

"She was hurt. We're all hurt. Haven't you ever said things you regretted later?"

I had to give my brother credit. Ever since Chandler went on trial but got off with no jail time, Roger had been the only person who worked hard to try and mend the broken bridge. I would never admit it to him, but sometimes I wondered how my plans for Chandler Buckingham had gone off track. In the beginning, I really wanted revenge, but that quest somehow took a turn. I think when I learned that he was also hurt by what he had done, it made me look at him differently. Somehow, we became emotionally attached to each other.

"Darby, just because a person isn't physically behind bars, it doesn't mean that they are not in prison," Chandler once told me. Before then, I had never looked at it like that. He told me how he was unable to sleep at night for months after the accident. Knowing that he had suffered too, made me view him in a different light. He seemed to understand me. Where the playground moms judged me, Chandler never did. Where Kevin behaved like I was as much a part of the house as the furniture, Chandler made me feel desired as a woman.

We mostly communicated through Facebook and text messages, but there was something else that made me feel like staying connected to him. I couldn't explain it, but being close to Chandler made me feel like I was somehow holding on to my sister.

"Darby, tell me this," my brother said.

"What?"

"What is it about Chandler Buckingham that makes you so willing to drop your entire family for this friendship? Damn, Darby. He killed your sister—*our* sister. How come you're not mad at him? How come you don't hate him? Anytime I think about him, bastard-loser-murderer is the only thing that comes to mind!"

I didn't say a word.

"Darby!"

My brother screamed my name, but I had no desire to answer. In fact, I ended the call and turned my cell phone off. I didn't try to stop the tears that fell down my cheeks. Everything was a mess. My entire life was an utter and complete mess. What had drawn me to Chandler? How did I convince myself that he understood me when those who knew me best couldn't? I turned into a deserted parking lot.

"I shoulda stayed my ass at the bar!" I screamed.

Being with Ivee and the other girls was a recipe for a good time, and our once-a-week gathering was never enough for me.

19

IVEE

I could've taken my bare hands and wrapped them around Carson's neck. I simply could not believe that this thing with him, all because he couldn't get a refund, was being drawn out this way.

"So, tell me again, at what point did you find yourself disappointed with Mrs. Henderson's work performance?"

My eyes focused in on the low-down weasel. He knew damn well there was nothing substandard about the work I had done for him. I understood that Geneva thought this was the best way to handle conflict between staff and clients, but it made me angry.

Carson turned to Geneva. "How long has this firm been handling my family's business?"

Her cheeks reddened, and she smiled. I wanted to be far away from the madness, but I had no choice. I had to stay and take part in the mediation that Geneva thought was necessary to maintain the relationship with Carson and to keep his business.

"It's been a long while," Geneva finally answered. "But I gotta tell you, Ivee here, she's one of the very best." She scrunched her face as if that emphasized her words.

Carson had the gall to shake his head in disagreement. I wanted to lunge across the table at him.

"Do I get to speak?" I finally asked. It was so hard to remove the sarcasm from my voice. When I had met with Geneva, I thought she was going to handle this in a fair way. Yet, the longer I sat in on the meeting, the more I felt like I was the enemy.

"Yes, just a second, Ivee. We're here to focus on the client's needs."

That was totally Geneva. She turned her focus back to Carson. "So, as I was saying, what can we do to fix this situation?"

Carson looked at me, and it took everything in me not to look away. I forced a smile, and I could see the hint of approval that passed across Geneva's face.

The meeting with Carson and Geneva was grueling. In the end, he agreed to honor the remainder of his contract if he was moved to one of my colleagues.

It was hard for me to understand why Geneva felt I needed to be in the meeting, but she was the boss, and I had to do what she thought was best. I understood the entire idea that the customer was always correct, but I didn't think they deserved *carte blanche* to make demands, and bully their way out of contracts if they didn't like the way things were going.

After the meeting, I walked back to my office. I wanted to lock myself away from everyone for the rest of the day. But I had calls to return and other reports to monitor. I also realized that I hadn't heard the last of Carson Liam, and I fully expected Geneva to hold him and his contract against me.

When my phone rang, I was glad for the distraction.

"Hey, Felicia, what's going on?" I answered.

"Hey, lady, checking on you. Wanna see if we're still on for happy hour tonight?"

"I'm sitting right here at work counting down the minutes. Are we still going?"

"Well, I've already talked to Peta and Darby, and they're cool with it. We wanna take the party over to Mr. Peeples tonight," Felicia said.

She didn't have to work to convince me. After the madness at work, she'd be lucky if I waited for happy hour. I was tempted to take my flask into the bathroom, and get a jump-start on the festivities.

"What time are we meeting, 'cause I can't wait 'til six-thirty this week?" I asked.

"Oooh, one of those days, huh? I hear it all in your voice."

"It's all over my face, too."

"Well, girl, I've got one for you tonight for sure," Felicia said. "I may tell them to simply open your mouth and pour the liquor straight in with no chaser."

20

PETA

"You have got to be kidding me!"

I leaned back in my chair and tried to absorb the information.

"Please, let me get a pen," I said. My voice was very shaky, and I tried not to sound too emotional.

I struggled to keep up and not break down.

"Do we know how this happened?"

"No, ma'am," the officer said.

"Okay, well, it's just that we've used that lot for nearly four years now, and we've never had anything like this happen before."

"I understand, ma'am. The damage to the trucks is pretty significant, and I'm afraid you might have lost inventory if it's kept inside the vehicles."

"Damn! Yes, my inventory is kept inside the vehicles. Do I need to go somewhere and see what's missing?" I asked.

"No, not unless you want to. We have the drivers there and they're providing us with quite a bit of information. If we need you to fill in the blanks, we'll be in touch."

"Oh, okay, but I need a police report for the insurance company, right?"

"Yes, and you can come by and pick that up, or I can make arrangements to send it to you electronically."

I felt like I was going to be sick. Someone had vandalized two of our trucks. I needed to talk to Beverly and Cecily. I couldn't believe that someone had destroyed what I had worked so hard to create. This was going to put me in a bind. Of course insurance would cover the loss, but that process would take so long, and I needed to start repairs and restocking.

"Kendal!"

After I screamed for my daughter, and she didn't come running, I realized she was probably upstairs with earphones on. I needed to go and see about the trucks. Before I left, I logged on to check my bank accounts. I frowned a bit when I still didn't see the automatic deposit from Kyle for child support.

There were only a few things that were as certain as clockwork, and his checks were one of them. It wasn't until the other day that I realized the money had not hit my account. When I went back to the previous month, Kyle's payment was posted by the twenty-eighth of each month.

"I wonder what the hell is going on." Since I didn't have time to investigate it at that moment, I decided to figure it out later.

I rushed upstairs and walked into my daughter's room. She jumped and snatched off the headphones.

"Hey, Mom, what's up?"

"You didn't hear me, but I called you. We need to run somewhere real quick. I just got a call. Two of the trucks were vandalized, and I need to go see about them."

"Oh, wow, Mom!" My daughter frowned and jumped up from her bed. "Do they know who did it?"

"I doubt it, sweetie. We weren't safe at that lot, but I had no place else that could fit all four trucks."

My daughter slipped on her tennis shoes and followed me out of the room. The business was my other baby. I felt violated and robbed.

"Thank God no one was hurt," Kendal said.

I was grateful for that, too. The trucks, then inventory, could all be replaced. My mind raced with crazy thoughts about who would've burglarized my business. It was one thing to break in and steal the merchandise, but did they have to vandalize the trucks, too?

We rushed to the car and headed over to the lot. It was located off Highway 6 and Addicks-Clodine Road in Southwest Houston near the Westpark Tollway. By the time I arrived, the officers and my drivers were about to leave.

"Oh, there she is right now," I heard Beverly say as I approached.

"I'm Peta Nixon." I stretched my hand to the officer.

"Oh, yes, Mrs. Nixon."

"Ah, Miss." My eyes scanned his broad shoulders.

"Okay, Miss Nixon. Let's go over so you can see the damage to your property."

I followed the officer in complete silence. I needed to see something quickly. In my mind, the damages were worse than anything I could imagine.

When we arrived at the row in the back where my RVs were parked, I nearly fell over.

"OH MY GOD!"

For a moment, I couldn't move. My limbs felt as if they were frozen in place. At first sight, the custom paint and wrap job was littered with obscene words that were spray painted over the large glossy pictures on the side of the RV. In addition to that, all of the custom tires were flat and several were slashed.

"This is awful!"

I was afraid to look inside. From what I had seen on the outside of the vehicles, I already knew the interior damage would take my breath away.

My brain couldn't fathom who would do a thing like that to me and my business. The neighborhood wasn't the very best, but again, it wasn't like we were able to park anywhere. In the four years we'd been parking there, we never had any issues or problems.

"The property manager was just here, but he walked back to the office with one of the detectives," Cecily said.

"Are the two of you okay?" I asked.

"Yeah, Miss Peta. Ain't nothing wrong with us. They called us out here when they found our contact information inside. Shoot, we wasn't here when this all went down," Cecily said.

"This means we're off the job 'til you get these fixed?" Beverly asked. She motioned toward the trucks with her pursed lips. "I gots bills to pay," she muttered.

I understood her concern, but I couldn't deal with that. I needed to assess the damages and the loss before I could determine when we'd be back on the road.

My eyes caught another glimpse of the damaged RVs, and my heart began to crumble. As Beverly went on about the state of the economy and her missed income, I moved toward my vehicles. Several windows were shattered. Why anyone would want to bust out the windows was beyond me. They'd still have to be replaced. The doors looked like they were dented in several places and no longer fit the frames.

"You don't want to go in there." Cecily touched my arm. "It's a mess. These are your babies, and I don't know why anyone did what they did. Let us get someone out here to clean things up first."

I appreciated what she said and what she was trying to do. "I wanna see," I said.

"The upholstery is ripped to shreds and paint was splashed all over everything. If I didn't know any better, I'd say that this was a personal attack. I'm no detective, but I'd start checking on possible enemies."

Cecily had my attention with that comment. I had no enemies that I could think of. In this city, I didn't even have competition. My Boutiques on Wheels were unique, and the only mobile fashion stores, so I didn't know what to think.

"My mom doesn't have any enemies," Kendal said. "Do you, Mom?"

That's when I remembered she was there with me. I had fully intended to go in and survey the damages for myself until I realized she had tagged along.

"No, honey, I don't. You know what? On second thought, as long as you and Beverly are fine, I'll let the police and insurance handle the rest of it."

"That's probably the best thing to do. Seriously, it's a mess in there. Besides, we're both going to take inventory and give you a detailed list of everything that's missing and or damaged," Cecily said.

How could I thank her for her work? I stood numb. She reached over and rubbed my back.

"Miss Peta, we'll take care of this. Take your daughter on home," said Cecily.

Of course dollar signs burned into my brain. Even before anyone confirmed it, I realized this would cost me a mint. I took one final glance toward the vehicles and turned to leave.

"Are we getting paid to help with the clean up?" I heard Beverly ask.

I couldn't deal with that question at that moment. I'd have to come up off some serious cash before the insurance company cut a single check. That reminded me that I needed to call and see what was going on with Kyle's check that still hadn't come in.

21

DARBY

I ignored yet another call from Roger. I was sick of him, sick of my mother, and the rest of my entire damn family. I stayed away from them since I didn't need the constant reminder.

When I'd walk into my mom's house, it was as if I had walked through a time capsule. The place looked like a shrine. There were pictures of us all in there, but the number of Darlene's pictures were ridiculous. My mother had gone way over and above. It was the main reason I colored my hair. I hadn't forgotten Darlene. I simply understood that I needed to move on. My plan to avenge her death would've worked like a charm, and I wasn't completely convinced that it wouldn't still work. Or at least that's what I continued to tell myself.

My meeting with Kevin Jr.'s teacher was at two forty-five. After meeting with Principal Johnson, his solution was yet another meeting with the teacher. I had already done a conference call with Carla and several of her coworkers, and thought I was about to go and soak in the tub when the doorbell rang.

"Who is it?" I asked.

I stopped when there was no answer. I wasn't in the mood for any drama. It was obvious my bath would have to wait.

I dragged myself to the front door, and wanted to kick myself when I pulled the door open. I thought it was Carla, but I was wrong.

"What are you guys—" I shook my head.

My overbearing mother barged her way into my house, and my brother was right behind her. I stood at the door and tried to contain my fury.

Roger was so wrong for this.

"You have got to stop this right now!" my mother yelled. I thought she was in the kitchen, but to my surprise she was at the mantel in the family room. She moved from one picture to the next. There weren't nearly as many as she had, but enough to see the progression of my young family.

The sight of my mother made me feel bad. It was wrong to keep the kids from her, and my entire family, but I couldn't trust that they wouldn't bad mouth me in front of my kids, and I couldn't have that.

"Your sister would've been a great mother," my mother said. She still hadn't turned to face me. "But she didn't get that chance. Her life was taken away in her prime." She sobbed.

I threw daggers at my brother with my eyes.

He shrugged like this was beyond his control, but that, it wasn't. He didn't have to bring my mother to my house. He knew what she was going to do.

When my mother finally turned to me, she looked at me with disgust or hatred in her eyes. It was hard for me to tell the difference. She couldn't even look at me for long. She turned back to the pictures.

"Darby, are you still betraying your family? Are you still bringing shame to us all?" she asked. Her back was still to me as she studied the pictures.

Oh, the theatrics. I would never outright disrespect my mother, but we would never see eye-to-eye on so many things. Nearly three years ago, I simply decided to put distance between us.

"I'm not betraying anyone."

"Does your husband know? How do you sleep at night?" She finally faced me again. Her lips trembled as she spoke. "This is not the way to deal with your grief!"

I wanted to ask if she was really the right person to give advice on how to handle grief, but I decided that would be too disrespectful. I hoped to never learn the pain of losing a child. My mother had been through too much.

"Tell her you're not doing it anymore," Roger pleaded. "God! I don't get it! What do you even think you're gonna get out of this?" He shook his head and rushed to our mother's side.

My cell phone rang, and I didn't hesitate to answer the phone. I needed the break.

"Hello?"

"Darby, are you busy?" Carla sounded like she was out of breath. As usual, her timing was off, but I completely needed the break.

"Ummm, kind of Carla. Why? What's up?"

"I've got lots of cash over here, and I don't feel comfortable. I wanted to know if you could make a pick up. My next client comes in about an hour."

"So, why can't you drop it off?" I asked.

"I was hoping you felt like getting out for a few."

"Well, I can't come now. So, if you can't bring it, you're gonna have to hang on to it until later," I told her.

I heard her grumble through the phone, and the rest of what she said was hard to understand. The call ended abruptly.

I turned my attention back to my mother. She broke my heart. The moment my focus was on something else, she zoned back in on the pictures on my mantel. It was as if she needed to study them all. She didn't say another word to me.

Suddenly, she turned, looked at Roger, then said, "I've seen my grandkids; let's go."

Their timing was actually perfect. I had told Carla to bring the cash, but I decided the walk would do me some good after all.

If I stayed around in the house alone, I'd start thinking about the sad and faraway look in my mother's eyes. Then I'd start to ask myself whether I really had done something wrong.

An hour after I left Carla's house, I counted the money again, and put it away in my secret hiding spot. Once that was done, I tried to busy myself with little chores around the house. Every so often, I'd glance up at the computer monitor. When I did, I'd find something else to do.

My house was clean, the beans in the crock pot were nearly done, and there was nothing else for me to do until I left to meet with my son's teacher. I was nearly about to relax when the phone rang. It was Kevin.

"Hey, honey, what's up?"

"Just checking up on you," he said.

Checking up on me? His choice of words seemed a bit odd, but I let it go.

"Okay, did you need something?"

"You have that meeting at the school, so I wanted to let you know I'll be home a little late. Bruce needs me to come by after work to look at some new equipment he just bought," Kevin said.

I wondered why Kevin felt the need to share that with me, but I wasn't invested enough to ask. He made more small talk, and then told me he had to go.

Later, when my phone chirped, I wasn't sure who it was. I was emotionally spent, and didn't have the energy to go another round. I fully expected it to be my brother or Carla, but it wasn't. I looked at the phone again, and tried to contain my excitement. My eyes weren't playing tricks on me.

Sup?

When I saw the three letters, I felt the butterflies come alive in the pit of my belly. I didn't even bother to answer the text message. I rushed to the computer, and logged on to Facebook.

What took u so long? he typed.

The question made me feel special.

23

IVEE

I wasn't about to spend all of my time thinking about the mess at work and the drama that would eventually come from it. I hated when work stayed on my mind so strong that I couldn't focus on having a good time or enjoying myself with my girls.

"What's the matter?" Peta asked.

It was hard, but I tried to catch myself before the others detected that my mind was someplace else. Happy hour was designed for dishing the dirt and hot gossip. Work wasn't supposed be on the brain or on the menu.

"We're going upstairs tonight or what?" Felicia asked.

"For sure." I tried to shake it off.

"You sure you good?" Peta asked.

My thoughts simply confirmed for me that I hadn't had enough to drink. Most days, I felt invincible at happy hour, but the fact that my stupid client tried to dog me out, and my boss didn't defend me, kind of put a damper on things.

"I'd be a whole lot better if we could get another round," I said.

All eyes wandered around the room. We searched for our waitress so we could put the order in, but she was nowhere to be found.

"We going upstairs?" I pointed upward.

It was so packed and loud in Eddie V's, I could hardly hear myself think. I was good and fucked up, and I was certain everyone else was, too.

"Yeah, let's go dance," Felicia said. She began to snap her fingers. "Who all is going upstairs?" I tried to ask again.

Our table was crowded and almost everyone was distracted.

Upstairs at Saint Genvieve, the party was really nice. We finally found seats on the balcony after another group got up right as we walked in.

"Who wants another shot?" When no one raised their hands, I gawked at them.

"Seriously? Y'all gon' make me get fucked up even more by myself?"

"We're already fucked up!" Felicia yelled.

"Peta, are you already on water?" I screamed.

"Shit, I was on water while we were still downstairs. Ivee, we can't keep up with your lush behind. You could probably drink a sailor under the damn table," she said.

"Thank you for that compliment." I drained my glass.

Everyone cracked up with laughter again. When the waiter came to our section on the patio, I waved him closer.

"I want you to bring a round of Patrón," I whispered when he leaned in to me.

He pulled his head up and looked like he tried to get a head count. Since everyone was talking and paid no attention to me, they couldn't talk me out of the last round of the night.

The evening was perfect. The DJ was on point, and all the pretty people must've gotten a free pass to hang out. I loved the vibe and atmosphere, and I especially loved the fact that my girls seemed to be having a real good time.

It didn't matter if it was the headaches at work or Zion and his many issues, drinks on Thursday night made it all better. Or maybe the drinks simply made me feel so good, I was only under the impression that it was better. Either way, when the waiter came back, none of it mattered anymore.

I noticed a few eye rolls, but when all was said and done, they'd drink since the premium liquor had been bought and paid for.

"Okay, y'all; c'mon! It's the last shot of the night," I announced.

Everyone was slow to claim their shot glasses, but I didn't let that deter me. The waiter placed a cup of lime wedges in the center of the square coffee table that sat between the two sofas we occupied.

"C'mon!" I grabbed one of the tiny glasses and stood. I waited for everyone else to pick up their shot glasses, and then we began. When I saw the shot glasses hoisted in the air, I started our mantra.

It wasn't as loud and boisterous as it usually was, but in unison, we all shouted.

"Up to it! Down to it! We do it because we're used to it! Fuck those that don't do it! Now let's get fucked up!"

We took our drinks to the head at pretty much the same time, and then dropped the glasses when we were done. As usual, the liquid burned as it blazed down my throat. I winced, swallowed hard, and blinked my watering eyes.

"Now, y'all know that was niiiice," I said.

24

PETA

Two weeks later, I watched my daughter leave for the school bus stop and pitied myself. Quite a bit had happened to me, and I couldn't understand why when it rained, a tsunami had to follow. It was the first time since I could remember that I didn't want to go to happy hour. I was simply not in the mood.

Bills from the trucks' vandalism were taller than a mountain. I decided to have the ladies double up on the two remaining trucks that were not damaged, but that quickly became a nightmare. They couldn't get along.

As I sat and thought about all that had happened, it dawned on me that I'd never called about Kyle's child support check.

The simple thought of his name flooded my mind with memories of the last time we were together. The vision was imprinted on my brain. As usual, it was completely unexpected, but it happened. I tried to block the thoughts, but it didn't work that way. Kyle and I were together more now than during our marriage. The last encounter was last Thursday night, and he had caught me again when I was vulnerable.

"You leaving already?" I asked as I met him at my driveway.

"Y'all gonna get enough of running the streets every week," he said.

"Really? Why's that?" I asked.

I felt good, and that meant trouble wasn't far behind. It didn't matter that I had recently had Gordon. Kyle was at the right place at the right time.

"Where's your purse?" Kyle asked.

Suddenly, I looked around and realized I didn't have my purse. It was gone!

"Oh, shit! I 'ont know," I slurred.

"Maybe it's in the car," Kyle suggested.

He followed me back to the driveway, reached around me from behind, and opened the door. His scent drove me wild. I wasn't sure if it was his cologne mixed with this fresh night air, but it did something for me. When Kyle climbed into the back seat, for whatever reason, I slipped behind the wheel.

"This shit is crazy, Peta. You go get shit-faced with your girls, and for the life of me, most times, I don't even know how you make it home."

One minute we were searching the vehicle, the next, I was in the back seat on my back, and Kyle was between my legs. Everything in me screamed to stop him. There were so many issues I had with him and the things he had done to make my life miserable.

But when my lips moved, it was in response to his tongue's push for entry. I sucked his lips, his tongue, and it felt really good—so much so that I didn't want him to stop. My brain felt like it was on autopilot, and the only message that seemed to register was, *Do it, girl! Do it, and enjoy it!*

"Jesus, Peta, why you do this to me?" he moaned.

His voice sounded so intense, it was as if he needed me.

We tore at each other's clothes. The small space somehow intensified the action, and I couldn't help but react to everything he did.

"Damn, Kyle. Damn you," I cried.

It didn't take long. He tore at my shirt, pulled a breast out of my bra and found my stiffened nipple. When he suckled, it felt like the right thing. Everything felt so good, my blood was on fire. My heart felt like it was on speed, and I was so excited.

I clawed at his head and shoulders, and did whatever I could to keep him where he was.

When he came up for air, I sucked at his mouth. He had undone his belt and zipper. He pulled back momentarily, placed the edge of the black-and-gold wrapper between his teeth and ripped it open.

"Hurry, Kyle; hurry."

I was hungry and on fire.

Once he shielded himself, I grabbed and welcomed him like no man had ventured there in months. Kyle did it all the right way. He knew exactly where to find my spot and what to do once he was there.

"Oh, God, Kyle. Oh, God!"

When he pulled back, I wanted to beg him not to stop. I looked deep into his eyes, and suddenly I felt something strange. I frowned.

"What's wrong?" he asked.

His eyes turned wild, he panted lightly, and I could feel his wild heartbeat.

It was almost as if I'd somehow caught a glimpse of us as we made out like horny teenagers on steroids. I stopped and drew back a little.

"What in the hell are we doing?" I asked.

"Shit, we gettin' it in," Kyle breathed.

I felt ashamed. I was drunk, scared, and my world had suddenly spun completely out of control.

"I need to stop this. We can't be carrying on like this. Damn, Kyle, you're remarried. We need to stop. And all that showing up on Thursday nights—when you know good and well that I'm vulnerable?"

As I talked, I tried to pull my clothes together. All the crap from my purse had spilled out on the floor of the back seat. It was dark, but I tried to feel around for as much as I could.

"So, that's it? We just gon' leave it like this?" he asked. He sucked his teeth, and I could see the veins throbbing at the side of his temple, but I didn't care.

"Kyle, you need to go. Go!"

He fumbled with his pants and tried to get himself together. I felt sick to my stomach. Gordon may have worked my nerves and been a pain, but he wasn't my ex who was married to some other chick.

"You coulda at least let me get my nut," Kyle murmured as he eased out of my car.

I really felt like shit then. Long after Kyle had left, I sat in the back seat of my car and cried. Every damn thing in my life had fallen apart.

The incredible pounding sensation that ricocheted through my head jarred me awake. I jumped up and looked around with wide eyes as I tried to catch my bearings.

"What the…"

That's when I realized I was still in the back seat of my car. The sky was trapped between night and daylight when I stumbled out of the back seat and made my way to the front door.

I was mad at myself for what had happened the night before, but was glad I had gotten up before the sun. How embarrassing would it have been to have my daughter or my neighbors find me asleep in the back seat of the damn car.

The thought made me angry at Kyle all over again. How in the hell did he leave me sleeping in the damn car? Anything could've happened to me!

After I rushed into the house, I took a long, hot shower and got myself cleaned up. By the time I pulled on my thick, terrycloth robe and walked out of my bathroom, I heard Kendal as she moved around downstairs.

"Mom!"

Her loud scream reminded me that I was still hung over. I made my way downstairs and smiled at my daughter.

"Hey, what are you doing up so early?" she asked.

"Hard to sleep with all that's going on," I lied.

"Oh, Mom. I'm so mad about what happened with the trucks, but don't be all sad about it, okay?"

I nodded.

From the mouths of babes, I thought. I had more than enough on my plate to be sad about, and the last thing I needed to do was fall into a dead-end trap with her father.

When the phone rang, it brought my thoughts back from the recent past. The detective updated me about the case, and we hung up. The phone rang again quickly, but when I saw Pamela's number, I hit the *Ignore* button. I wasn't in the mood for any more of her probing questions.

"Oh, Kyle's checks," I reminded myself.

I found the number and called the state attorney general's office. Kyle paid for his child, but before we came to our friendly, mutual agreement, we had fought like nobody's business, so at the time, I needed to get his payment on paper. When the judge finally signed off on the agreement, I felt more comfortable.

"Yes, my name is Peta Nixon, and I'm calling to find out why my ex-husband's child support checks have not been deposited into my account for the second month in a row."

The caseworker seemed very nice. I gave her his social security number and she placed me on hold. When she came back to the phone, what she said next took my breath away.

"Oh, yes, Mrs. Nixon. Did you forget? It took a little while for the change to take effect."

"What change? What are you talking about?"

"The letter you sent absolving your ex-husband of any and all future child support payments," she explained.

"The what?" I cried.

25

DARBY

"I don't get it. How'd you get all these women to agree to do this?"

Carla looked at me like she didn't understand my question. Ours was such a nice neighborhood, it was hard for me to fathom that she'd been able to operate that kind of business and stay under the radar for so long.

Don't get me wrong, I was glad she did. Carla and her soccer moms slash part-time hookers had definitely upgraded my life.

Outside of that mishap when those she-thugs kicked down my front door, no one would've known what the constant mid-morning, mid-afternoon traffic was all about. Carla had replaced the door without as much as a flinch, and paid extra for the same-day service. And, the replacement was far nicer than its predecessor. I had to tell my husband I won it in a contest so we got it for free, and it was all good when he heard that.

"Girl, it may be the oldest profession, but it's still a bona-fide money-maker," Carla said.

"I don't get it. How do y'all do it?"

"Do what? And, hey, what's missing here?" she asked.

For a minute, she had me going. I actually looked around as if I might figure out what was missing.

"Where's the wine? A martini or something," she squealed. "I can't think of a time I've been over here and you didn't have something to sip on," she said. "Oh, no! Don't tell me you're on the wagon."

"Girl, stop! You make it sound like I'm some closet alchy," I joked. Thoughts of the playground moms entered my mind momentarily.

"No, I just know what you like, and I happen to like what you like, too, so, what's up? Why's it all dry in here?"

Once I pulled a couple of wineglasses and poured drinks for us, Carla and I talked about plans to expand. So far, four of our neighbors worked with Carla. I managed the money and made sure that the supplies were well stocked. If my husband paid attention to anything, he'd realize that we had a stash of condoms, spermicidal jelly, and a slew of sex toys hidden in the garage.

The arrangement had been working well. When the phone rang, I prayed it wouldn't be my husband or the kids' school. I felt like they were getting to know me on a personal level that made me most uncomfortable. Unfortunately for me, it was my brother. I didn't answer, but the call threw me back to one of the darkest days of my life.

Kevin and I were dating then, and he had stayed at my apartment. I had a roommate, Jean Bishop, and she was cool with him being there. My first college roommate and I could never agree on when it was cool to have company.

"Is the alarm set?" Kevin had asked.

"Yeah, boo. I told you. I set it."

"I can't be late for the bus," he said before he stabbed the pillow with his fist, and adjusted his head on it. Back then, Kevin was part of a special engineering camp that required him to spend two weekends a month at seminars.

At first, it was hard for me to sleep. We had stayed in and watched a movie, and although we usually stayed up late on weekends, we didn't when he had the seminars.

I lay next to Kevin with my eyes wide open. I couldn't fall asleep. I couldn't watch TV because it would disturb him, so I lay there with thoughts of our future together bouncing around in my mind.

One minute I was wide awake, the next I heard my name being called.

"Darby! Darby!"

At first I thought it was a part of my dream. It felt like I was on a boat that wouldn't stay still.

"Darby! Darby!"

My vision was blurred as I bolted upright in bed. Kevin sat next to me, but he looked lost and confused.

"What's the matter?"

Jean's hand shook as she held the phone toward me. "It's your brother, Roger. It's about Darlene," she said. I glanced around the room. The green numbers on the digital clock flickered 3:48 a.m.

"Who…what?" I couldn't think straight. My head hurt and everyone looked sad.

"Darby, Roger needs you on the phone," Jean repeated. But when she spoke, her words were forced.

I didn't want the phone. I didn't want the bad news. My grandmother always said only bad news came after midnight. When Kevin came close and put his arm around me, I sensed something terrible had happened.

I grabbed the phone. "Hello," I said.

"Darby, it's Darlene. She's gone. Your sister. She's dead. We need you to come home," Roger said. He cried, too.

"No! I just talked to her. She was at a club. She was partying with—"

Kevin pulled me closer. Jean took the phone and talked to my brother. I was numb. I was sick and scared to be left alone. My twin couldn't be gone. I didn't close my eyes for seventy-two hours straight.

Home was never the same again. A doctor gave me pills to calm me and to help me sleep, but that didn't stop the nightmares. The wake, the funeral, the burial; it was all one massive blur. Darlene was the pride of my family—a senior at Texas Southern University who had already been accepted into the Thurgood Marshall School of Law.

At the time, I was at Xavier University in New Orleans. When I found out that Darlene was killed by a drunk driver who had been arrested three different times for DWI, I was sick. I couldn't fathom how a repeat offender was still drinking and driving, and because of Chandler, my sister was gone. Something clicked in my head.

Prior to that, I never drank. I took a year off from school after my sister died. I couldn't bring myself to leave my family. We were, and had always been, very close. In the year that I was home, alcohol suddenly became my only comfort. Kevin and I drifted apart, and he moved on. Three years later, I was sober and couldn't stand the smell of alcohol.

The new job I'd gotten had come right on time. That's where I met Felicia and Ivee, and they were a blast. I had also reconnected with Kevin, and it seemed like my life was finally back on track. At that time, *Sex and the City* was all the rage. I credited that show with my newfound relationship with alcohol. Every time we went out, we had Cosmos like our favorite girls on the show. We patterned our friendship after theirs. Peta was Samantha, Ivee was Carrie, I was Charlotte, and Felicia was Miranda. We bonded over drinks and stories about our lives.

"You're not gonna call him back?" Carla's question pulled me back to the present.

"I'm not in the mood to talk to him right now. Let's finish this business so you can get back to work," I said.

I poured more wine, and Carla and I went over details of the money we expected to make for the month.

Once we finished, Carla leaned back in her chair. She drained her wineglass, then looked at me. Her face was all scrunched up.

"Can I ask you something?"

"Yeah, sure," I said.

"What would Kevin do if he found out that you're a madam?" She giggled.

Her question made me think for a second. I never thought of myself as a madam. Carla and the other ladies had a list of clients that they slept with once a week, and I handled the business part of it. I collected payments through credit cards that went into an account that required both Carla's and my signature.

Our system was pretty sweet since we didn't have to advertise, and we only dealt with a select number of exclusive clients. Outside of that mishap when Carla tried to deviate from what had been working, there hadn't been a single incident.

Carla had picked up a man in a bar and added him to her list. When his wife found out, she told her prison guard sister, and well, the rest was what resulted in my door being kicked in.

The truth was, if Kevin knew I was doing anything illegal, he'd probably call the police himself. If he realized that I now had my own personal stash that had grown substantially, he'd blow a gasket, and then file for divorce. The thought of me with my own money would be a threat to him and the control he tried to maintain.

I leaned in closer to Carla and said, "Isn't it great that we won't ever have to find out?"

26

IVEE

Usually on Thursdays, I took it nice and slow, and I drank lots and lots of water because there was no telling how my night would end. But it would more than likely involve lots and lots of alcohol. So, hydration was a must. However, once I realized I was being watched by Geneva, I wanted to get in a little more work than normal.

"Felicia, remember those possible clients you were telling me about?"

We were holed up inside Escalante's Mexican Restaurant in River Oaks, and Felicia had just sat down.

"Yeah, I got one of 'em joining us for lunch in a little bit. Why you ask?"

I picked up my martini and took a healthy sip. "Girl, Geneva's been on my back after a client complained."

"Oooh, that's not good," Felicia said. "You order yet?"

"No, I just got a drink while I waited for you."

She glanced around the busy restaurant.

"Our waiter should be back in a sec," I told her.

"Okay, cool. That drink looks so good," she said.

"It tastes even better. You should have one."

Felicia shook her head. "Girl, I'm not like you. When I leave here, I gotta go back to the office. You get to go home and crash if you want until happy hour."

"Girl, it's customary to have a cocktail with lunch."

Felicia eyed me suspiciously.

"No, I'm serious. Back in the day when the workforce was filled with men, that's how they used to get down. Some of the largest deals were brokered over drinks. People think decisions are made in the boardroom; chile, please. The movers and shakers do it right over there." I pointed to my left where the bar was packed with men and women dressed in suits and other professional clothes.

"Call it what you want, but I ain't taking my butt back to the office smelling like liquor. Next thing you know, folks start whispering and the higher-ups get wind of it. No thank you! I don't need that kind of headache."

I picked up my glass by the stem and sipped. I savored the taste of the alcohol and allowed it to slowly move down my throat.

When the waiter came, Felicia looked at him. "We're waiting on another person. Will you bring another place setting?"

We ordered, and I watched as the guy as he walked away. "Oh, I'm sorry," I called after him. He turned around and returned to the table. "Can I get another one of these?"

"Sure thing," he said.

"Okay, so, let me tell you about Wayne before he gets here. He and his business partner put on events," Felicia said.

I frowned.

She stopped talking and looked at me.

"What? What's the matter?"

"Girl, I need some serious clients. I ain't got time to be playing with no middle-aged man who's still hung up on his hip-hop wanna-be-a-rapper dream."

"Damn, Ivee, I thought you said you wanted a new client."

"Yeah, but if I realized that's who you were talking about, I woulda told you not to waste my time or his. I'm talking some serious money potential here. Girl, it makes my stomach turn when I see a grown-ass man walking around with his starched jeans sagging, wearing a T-shirt, with a baseball cap on his head, and Jordans on his feet. I'm like, when will our brothas learn? Who's gonna take you seriously if that's your uniform?"

"You can't be serious, Ivee," Felicia said.

"What? Don't tell me you don't agree," I said.

I stopped talking when the waiter came back with my second drink.

"Your food will be out in a second," he said.

I sipped the drink and finished my tirade. "Girl, I'm so doggone serious. One of my coworkers invited us to her house for this party she was having. Her place is laid, I mean top notch all the way. It was a very nice, upscale, mixed crowd; then this thug-looking man walked in. When she introduced him as her daddy, girl, I nearly spit my drink out!"

Felicia laughed so hard, she nearly sprayed her water. "Please stop, Ivee. You are wrong!"

"I'm wrong? His ass was wrong! Nucca, you pushing sixty and walking around with some starched jeans, a jersey, gold chains, and his little Afro was blacker than his daughter's hair! Men think that mess is cute, but ain't nothing cute about that!" I sipped my drink. "I felt embarrassed for her."

"Well, now that I know how you feel, what'd you call them?" Felicia asked.

"A middle-aged man who still hung up on his hip-hop wanna-be-a-rapper dream," I repeated.

Suddenly, Felicia's gaze moved up, her eyes wide and her mouth agape. That meant my words had fallen on ears that weren't meant to hear them.

I turned my head to see a mass of a man with mocha-colored skin, and dark-brown eyes. He smiled mischievously as if he had stumbled upon a great secret.

"Damn, y'all kinda hard on a brotha, huh?" his deep voice boomed.

"Hey, Wayne, this is my girl Ivee I told you about," Felicia said. "Ivee, this is Wayne Ledger."

The waiter came with our food at that moment. He looked at Wayne, who took the seat to my right, and said, "Sir, can I start you off with something to drink?"

"I'm having exactly what they had," he said. He moved his hand in a sweeping motion across the table. "It's a whole bunch of fun happenin' at this table. Forget the fact that it's at the expense of men." He turned to me. "What did you call those worthless, wanna-be-rapper bums again?"

Warm embarrassment washed over me. "You only caught the tail end of what I was trying to say." I tried to defend myself.

"Oh no, no, no, no!" Wayne shook his head. "Don't try and clean it up now for me. I can take it, baby. I'm a real man. I may wear jeans, but shit, if that's your truth, who am I to question it?"

"See, you walked up at the wrong time," I said. "Tell him, Felicia," I begged.

"Nah, don't try to drag her into it. I only heard *you* talking. Felicia here was probably uncomfortable with everything you were say-ing," he joked.

Wayne was friendly enough, and if he hadn't mentioned it, I wouldn't have noticed he'd worn jeans. He had on a sports jacket and a button-down shirt, so he was all right by me.

"My firm handles specialty events. We do about five million annually," he said.

The thing about Wayne was, he didn't brag. He came to lunch with the idea of meeting a business prospect, and once the joking was over, he jumped right in. Every so often, Felicia would glance up at me as if to say, "I told you so."

The only reason I didn't kick her under the table was that by round four, I wasn't sure which leg was hers. I may not have said it then, but she had been absolutely correct.

By the time lunch was over, Wayne and I had exchanged business cards and made promises to set up a meeting the following week. I'd see Felicia later at happy hour, and I couldn't wait to thank her properly for the hook up with Wayne.

Images of the multiple packages I'd be able to sell him danced around in my head, and I couldn't wait to bring my new find to Geneva.

I was so excited and happy, thoughts of how much alcohol I had consumed never even crossed my mind.

27

PETA

"Was that your daddy?" I asked Kendal when I walked into her room to drop off clothes I had folded.

She had just hung up the phone.

"No, Ma, he called me earlier, but I missed it. Why? What's wrong?"

I was tempted. I couldn't think of a time I'd ever come so close to dogging Kyle out. That dirty bastard had avoided my calls for more than a week. I wanted to kill him, and he had to have known that ignoring me wasn't gonna make me go away.

Between issues with the trucks, my dwindling savings account that had kept me afloat, and the way I chased Kyle, I didn't know if I was coming or going.

The insurance company gave me the runaround just as much as Kyle. If they didn't lose some paperwork, they changed claims adjusters who never seemed to be quite caught up on my damn case.

It was two trucks!

"Well, tell me again how it works," one of the adjusters had said. "I mean, so it's a mobile boutique? We don't have any of those up here in Dallas," she twanged.

I rolled my eyes. What difference did it make that Dallas didn't have any mobile boutiques? Neither did any other damn city in America. I had started to get really frustrated. I felt like everyone was out to get me. I needed them to pay the damn claim. Instead, they kept asking useless questions.

When the phone rang again, I snatched it before it could ring a second time. My heart kicked in my chest each time a call came in. I needed it to be Kyle. I needed him to clear up the mess he had created.

"Hello?" I screamed.

"Peta, I, ummm, I wanted to thank you for the help you sent since the other two trucks have been down, but exactly how long do I have to work with this woman?" Farah wanted to know. "It's already been two days too long for me!"

I exhaled. I wasn't in the mood to have this conversation. My anger over Kyle and the insurance company felt like it had gotten the best of me.

"Farah, I thought you could use the help. Also, since her truck is down, it only made sense that she'd hop on to help you out," I snapped.

"Peta, I'm not talking about Beverly. I'm talking about that new one you sent down. With all those darn questions every time I turn around. She's just worrisome!"

My waxed eyebrows dipped into a frown. Beverly had called and left a message. In it, she said something about food poisoning, but I didn't think she meant she wouldn't be on the truck to help Farah. And if Beverly hadn't been there in the past couple of days, then exactly who had been there?

"So, Farah, you're not talking about Beverly?"

"Peta, haven't you heard a word I said? Beverly got herself sick eating those quail tacos. I was there when she left you that message saying she'd be gone for a few days," Farah said.

I was baffled. "So, if it wasn't Beverly, then who has been on that truck?"

"Well, didn't you send her? She's a pretty little thing, but upstairs, the lights are completely out!" Farah laughed.

She wasn't funny, and she wasn't much help. I needed to get to the bottom of what happened or what was happening.

"What's her name?" I asked.

"Oooh, wee," Farah said. "What is that child's name? It's on the very tip of my tongue."

"Do you expect her back in the morning?" I asked.

"That's what I'm calling you to say. I don't want her back. I'd be better off all by myself."

Farah's truck was out at the BP Campuses in Katy. That was less than a twenty-minute drive from my house.

"Okay, Farah, I'll call you, and let you know the plan. I'm sorry she's caused you problems, but I should have a solution for you real soon."

Could this mystery person be connected to the vandalism on the trucks? I considered calling the detective, but reminded myself that Beverly could've had one of her cousins or a friend fill in for her.

I called Kyle's phone again and got voicemail. If my smart phone weren't so expensive, I would've thrown it against the damn wall. It had become really hard to keep my mind straight.

Once Kendal settled in for the night, I crashed on the couch in front of the TV. I was tired of all that had gone wrong. I went to the kitchen and stumbled upon the massive bottle of Skyy Vodka that the bastard had brought to woo me.

"He had me pegged the moment he knocked on the door," I said.

There was probably enough for a couple of drinks left in the bottle. We'd had more than our share and, boy, had it cost me!

This time, when the phone rang, I didn't even budge. I used my finger to stir my drink and made my way back to the sofa.

It was Gordon.

"Hey, Gee, what's up?"

"You know you ain't right, man," Gordon said.

I already knew what he was talking about. I closed my eyes, and suddenly, I wished I had ignored the call.

"Gee, I got too much going on right now," I began.

"Gon' with that BS, man! How you gonna not even call a brotha after what I did for you? What we did for each other?"

I wanted to tell Gee to *man up!* My entire world had damn near crumbled, and he was upset because I had neglected to call after the last pity-bang?

"It's like you expect me to be here waiting for you to call and bless me with some pussy!"

I had to clamp my lips shut to avoid the harsh words I really wanted to say. If Gordon was with someone, I'd totally understand. In fact, I wouldn't even care. What bothered me most about him was the way he constantly bitched.

Something in me told me to let him get it all off his chest. I half-listened as he complained and allowed him to get it out. He wasn't gonna see me soon, so it didn't really matter.

Gordon finally let me off the phone when I agreed to reach out by the end of the week. I polished off the last of my drink, made sure the house was secured, and headed upstairs.

I wanted a hot shower and a good night's sleep. There was only one person who asked too many damn questions. It drove everyone, including me, bat shit crazy!

The next day, early Thursday morning, I nearly beat Farah to the location at the BP Campus off of I-10. I wanted to be one of the first faces she saw when she parked.

"Miss Peta!" She all but jumped into my arms. "You didn't have to come out here all by yourself! I woulda been fine. Between you and me, I just didn't want that dingbat back." She winked.

Once Farah parked, I walked around and opened the door to get into the RV. This truck was done in rich gold and a bold turquoise. There were two plush love seats with large comfy pillows and several vanity chairs that swirled. We had installed a row of floor-to-knee mirrors between the two sofas so that our customers could see their shoe selections, whether they sat or stood.

"It smells really nice in here," I said.

"Well, I try," Farah responded. I watched as she moved around and prepared the RV for the business rush. "In about thirty minutes, this place will be packed," she warned.

She pulled out the pitcher and began to mix the champagne and orange juice.

Fifteen minutes later, the mimosas were ready, and I waited comfortably for the *so-called* assistant to show up.

The doorbell rang and our first customers of the morning poured in.

"Oh, I love it in here," a slender blonde told the two women she had in tow.

It didn't take long for them to start sipping and selecting various items.

"I'm baaaaaack, and I brought kolaches." Pamela Evans grinned as she opened the door and walked in.

At the sight of me, she froze. Her smile turned into a scowl, the color drained from her cheeks, and she dropped the bag she held.

28

DARBY

I sat, mouth agape, and hang-jawed to be exact. I barely blinked as my eyes focused on the text message. I had dreamed of that very moment for a long time.

"Let's hook up," I muttered as I read it aloud. My hand trembled a bit as I held the phone.

My emotions were all over the place. Alarm settled in. The possibilities also made my stomach dance in quick and tiny flutters. I pulled in a deep breath. I needed to do the right thing, but over time we had become close. What was wrong with a face-to-face meeting between friends?

Should I reply?

My mother's accusations barked in my mind. There was no way I could deny the fact that I still communicated with Chandler Buckingham. I enjoyed the secret friendship that had resulted from my plan to make him pay. He was my dirty, little secret. He had intrigued me from the day we first saw him. Memories of that day flooded back like eager water up against a tight dam.

"Is this him?" I'd asked Roger.

We were huddled in a corner and studied the small, black and white photo Roger had cut out of the newspaper. We weren't supposed to be there. If he had been anyone else, his name and picture would've been plastered all over the TV and newspapers, but money made the difference in this case.

"Yeah, that's him. He's been arrested like five or six times," Roger said.

"For drunk driving?"

"I dunno," Roger said as I stared at the picture.

Chandler was the poster boy for gorgeousness. His olive-colored skin looked as if it had been kissed by the right amount of sunshine. His hair was a light-brown mixture of curls and waves. His hazel eyes had a golden hue that made them pop against his face, and if he didn't have a movie star smile, I had never seen one before.

"What? You think you know him or something?" Roger asked.

I shook my head and refocused. Chandler's recklessness had killed my sister. His near-perfect face hid horror, and held my pain. There was nothing rough about his appearance. He was a complete metrosexual male, and he couldn't deny it if he tried.

"Jesus! Here he comes." Roger nudged me.

We stood in the hall where we hoped we'd catch a glimpse of him as he left the district attorney's office. The head of the mayor's victim's advocate office had given us the heads-up that Chandler's attorney had worked out a quiet deal that would allow him to avoid jail altogether.

My family was devastated by the news. We wanted our day in court. We wanted to see him go to jail, but instead, he was sentenced to several programs, and told something about restricted supervision. I couldn't repeat what happened in court because everything happened so fast. He had a fast-talking, slick, and polished attorney who looked very expensive.

We weren't even given the chance to make a victim's impact statement or anything. Before the hearing ended, I had rushed out of the courtroom. I couldn't take it anymore. The entire scene gave me a clear picture of how different the rules and laws were for the wealthy.

What I didn't expect was to nearly bump right into Chandler as I walked out of the ladies' room a short time later.

"Oh, ma'am. I'm sorry. Are you okay? I wasn't paying attention," he said.

He sounded good.

For the first time, I thought about the fact that the pictures my brother had did him absolutely no justice.

"Uh, I'm good. I'm fine," I managed.

His beauty made me feel intoxicated. When our eyes connected, I had to remember to blink and struggled to avoid an awe-filled stare. He smelled good, but he looked even better. From his designer suit to his manicured fingernails, Chandler did not fit the stereotype of a habitual, reckless drunk driver.

That day remained tattooed on my brain. I guess that was the moment my obsession began. Months after that first encounter, I found him and his family's business. I made trips to the area a part of my regular routine. That was how it all started. At first, I told myself the plan was brilliant. I would get close to him, and take out my very own revenge since the justice system had let us down.

But years later, I had forgotten all about my initial goal. When the phone vibrated again, it brought me back to my dilemma.

Yeah. Let's.

I typed the message; then I erased it. I put the phone down and glanced at the clock. When was happy hour? I grabbed a wineglass and poured myself a drink. After several large gulps of chardonnay, I picked up the phone and retyped the message.

Cool. I'll let U know where and when.

I downed the rest of the wine and refilled my glass. I collapsed onto the chaise, and crooked my elbow over my eyes as if to block out the images that danced through my head. What would an actual face-to-face be like with him? This wouldn't be a chance encounter in the hallway or even stares from a distance across the bar.

The decision had been made. I'd celebrate at happy hour and get ready for the meeting that would change my life. Whether that change would be good or bad was yet to be seen.

29

IVEE

My legs felt a bit shaky as I strolled over to the valet's podium in the parking lot, but I ignored it. I was more concerned about what, if anything, someone might've seen if they watched as I walked.

I turned the ticket over to the attendant, and waited for my car. The warm, fresh air felt and smelled good. I sucked in as much as my lungs could hold, then exhaled. When I felt my lids get heavy, I shook that off quickly. I glanced over my shoulder and saw a group of people headed my way.

"Looks like I got here right on time," I muttered.

My eyes searched the darkened parking lot, and I wondered what was taking the guy so long. My head felt like it was swimming a little, but it was nothing a drive home with the windows down and music blaring wouldn't cure.

"Oooh, excuse me." I pulled my hand up to my lips and hid a frown.

Was that a hiccup? I glanced around discretely to see if anyone had heard me. If they had, they never acted like it. So I kept my vigil on the headlights, and hoped the next car would be mine. My eyes did a strange squint, opened, and then squinted again. I wanted to die where I stood. I couldn't be sleepy.

"What the hell is taking so long? Did someone take my ride for a spin or what?"

I wanted to move away from the podium and look around the corner, but my unsteady legs wouldn't permit it. Right when I decided it was time to look for a supervisor, my caramel-colored Cayenne eased forward, and I was relieved.

The valet driver held the door open for me. I slid a twenty into his hand and eased into my soft, leather bucket seat. I pressed a button and music flooded the space in my SUV. The minute I pulled out of the parking lot, I pressed another button and lowered all of the windows.

The thick, salty, warm air felt good against my skin. I sang along to one of my favorite songs and pressed the pedal as I raced on to the Southwest Freeway going south. I thought about my girls and back to our evening.

When the hook from my song came in for the second time, a flash in my rearview mirror caused my heart to drop to the bottom of my belly. The words caught in my throat as my eyes widened in horror. At first, the flashing, blue lights seemed to be in the distance, but the way they raced behind me made me nervous.

"Shit, I'm being pulled over? What the hell for?"

As I steered my car over to the side of the road, it hit me like a massive bulldozer. I'd had quite a few glasses of vodka. My mind quickly raced to add it all up. *One while we waited, another when everyone got there, then someone bought another round with the crab cakes, and then, ummm, did those guys buy a few rounds too? How many? Had I lost count?* Those thoughts ran through my mind as I brought the car to a complete stop.

I swallowed dry and hard. My gut tightened into a knot, and I drew a complete blank. What should I do? Should I try to explain or be quiet? This could not be happening to me. I glanced up to my rearview mirror and regretted it instantly.

Suddenly, a bright, blinding, white light drowned the inside of my vehicle with warmth as I reached down to the glove compartment for my proof of insurance and registration. Instantly, I felt irritated and then scared. Out of nowhere, perspiration blanketed my forehead. *Did I put the new insurance card in there? Ugh!*

Shit! What if I'm asked to get out of my car? Oh, God! If I have to blow into one of those breathalyzers, I'll die. Wait. I know my rights, don't I?

What was taking him so damn long? I had given up on finding the proper paperwork, convinced myself I could call my lawyer from my cell and rethought it all as I waited on the officer. My stomach felt like it had been twisted in a vise.

What in the hell?

Finally, the officer walked up to my driver's side and looked down at me. To my stunned surprise, he greeted me with a bright and wide smile. He seemed friendly, and I relaxed instantly.

"Good evening," he said.

I released a huge sigh of relief. Thank God he wasn't one of those stuck-up assholes. I felt my body instantly calm down, and my heart returned to its regular pace. The way he grinned with that gum-bearing smile down at me, I felt confident that all I had to do was be straight with him, and I could probably get by with a warning. Of course, I told myself I needed to be humble and remorseful. I closed my eyes, inhaled deeply, and prepared myself for the performance of my life.

I tried to ignore that fact that I was probably a spectacle as drivers zoomed by.

"Errr…good evening?" It jumbled out as a question before I could stop myself.

Two hours later, I sat in a jail cell and wondered how the hell had I read the officer so wrong. *How could I have misinterpreted his smile?*

The glare of the overhead fluorescent light seared down on my brain, and I realized the nightmare of the arrest had finally come true. But this time, it was me. It wasn't some faceless guy on the news. It was me!

What the hell? Will my job find out? Is there a morality clause in my contract? I cannot lose my job! Should I call my lawyer? Is he even a criminal attorney? What in the hell? How did this happen to me?

I closed my eyes. It was cold, and goose bumps rose on my skin. The steel bench I sat on was hard and most uncomfortable, but I was lucky to have a seat. Some of the other women were cowered down in a corner on the floor. A few others stood and kept watch down the hall.

Could I actually go to jail? I couldn't imagine a real jail sentence. What would my coworkers say? What would my girls say? What would my family say?

Trying not to be so visibly unnerved, I clamped my eyes shut. This absolutely had to be a dream, or more like a nightmare!

30

PETA

Whan I left happy hour, I felt good. All the normal crap that had been front and center on my mind didn't seem to matter anymore.

I didn't go to the club after happy hour since I had other plans. I was sick and tired of being the victim, and I felt it was time I did something about it. My first step involved some investigating of my own. Between Kyle and Pamela, I felt physically and emotionally abused, and it was time I began to fight back.

The girls all had their own ideas about what I should've done when Pamela walked in and saw me.

"You should've stomped her backstabbing behind," Ivee said.

"You couldn't have had her arrested?" Felicia wanted to know.

"For what? For stalking me, and showing up to help out my employee?" I shrugged. I had no idea why Pamela had clutched on to me, and why she felt she needed to sneak behind my back to work on the truck.

"What the hell, Pamela?" I had asked.

"I can explain!" she stammered. She reached down to pick up the bag she had dropped.

"Explain? What's there to explain? I should call the cops on you!"

When several customers stopped looking at the merchandise and turned their focus to us, I realized that I needed to tone it down a notch. That skank better be glad we had a crowd, or I could've snatched that weave from her scalp and beat the crap out of her.

"Maybe y'all should have a little talk outside while I help get these clients out of here and back to work," Farah said.

I cleared my throat and thanked God someone still had some professionalism left. I squeezed by Pamela, and grabbed her by the arm as I walked out of the RV.

"I don't know what your problem is, but you are trespassing. How dare you lie your way into my place of business?"

Pamela threw her hands up in surrender. She moved back a few steps.

"Wait, whoa! Hold on. You've got it all wrong. I was here the other day when your other lady got sick. She was like throwing up all over the place, and she called you. When I heard her say she couldn't come in, I offered to help out. I didn't mean nothing by it. I mean, I was trying to be helpful."

I heard what she said, and there was a small part of it that made sense. When Beverly called, I was in the midst of the storm. My mind was stuck on the stunt Kyle had pulled. Beverly could've told me she was driving off into the sunset with one of the boutiques, and her words would not have registered. But there was something about Pamela that I couldn't bring myself to trust.

"I'm supposed to believe that you were simply trying to help?" I cocked my head to the side.

"You were so kind to help me out with the meetings and answering all of my questions. I happened to be in the area, and when I saw the truck, I got excited. At first, I thought my timing was perfect. I even tried to call you. I left a message with your daughter. I guess she didn't tell you that I called," Pamela said.

Kendal had told me about her call, but I had other issues on my mind.

"Peta, I admire you and what you do. I really was trying to help. If I would've known you'd be this upset about me trying to help you out, I would've stayed away," she said. Pamela flicked her fingers and shrugged.

She didn't turn around, but took steps backwards and left me standing there. When a few clients walked off the RV with bags in hand, I told myself to suck it up. I went back in, and worked with Farah until it was time to go and meet the girls at happy hour.

As I eased off the freeway, I turned the radio down. I never had a reason to go by Kyle's house since he came over so much. But after all of my unsuccessful attempts to reach him by phone, I decided tonight was the night.

It also helped that I was riding high on liquid courage. I had convinced myself that I was prepared for whatever might happen.

I could imagine the shock his wife would be in, but what the hell? If he didn't fix what he had done to me, I'd personally tell her about our little romps.

When I turned onto his street, I told myself there was no need to turn off my headlights. It wasn't like they'd be outside.

"You brought this on yourself, you dirty bastard," I said as I pulled in front of his house. But I was the one who was stunned speechless when I brought my car to a complete stop.

I sat in amazed shock as my eyes registered on the massive For Sale sign that hung out front. It was like a hard slap to the face that stung. I hopped out of my car barely before I put it in park, and marched up to the sign. It was real! The bastard had put his house on the market?

I glanced around to see whether anyone was outside. I needed answers, and since Kyle wouldn't take my calls, I had very few options. I rushed to the windows and the front door.

Kyle's house was completely empty! How had I missed all of

that? My first thought was to call my daughter. For sure, he'd be in touch with her if no one else.

Before I called, I told myself the conversation would have to wait until the next day since it was already late.

The drive home was long and lonely with lots of unanswered questions. I didn't understand why I was being tested. I couldn't imagine what else could be going on.

Thoughts of the trucks being vandalized, Kyle tricking me out of child support, and his house up for sale really threw me for a loop. I couldn't wait to get home, and have a drink. I needed something to help me try to figure the entire mess out.

31

DARBY

"I don't want no stupid waffles!" Taylor screamed.

If he was gonna have a fit, he'd have to have it alone. I was not in the mood. I walked to the refrigerator and removed the gallon of juice. I wanted sleep, and I didn't mean the kind of light sleep on the couch either. I wanted to crawl back upstairs and get up under the comforter. I'd get my sleep mask, close the blinds, and sleep until my body was tired of sleep. That was the plan as soon as I cleared the house.

"Boy, you need to hurry up and eat this food." I moved over to the table and poured orange juice into my son's cup, and then into a glass near my husband's plate. What was he doing?

Kevin Jr. ate so fast, I started to tell him to slow down before he choked. But even the sound of my own voice made my head hurt.

"Kevin!" I screamed. "Your breakfast is getting cold! What are you doing?"

I rubbed my temple and prayed for my husband to hurry down. I didn't know what was worse—the fact that I had to get up early to fix breakfast after a night at happy hour, or the fact that my husband hadn't come down to eat yet. My biggest goal on Friday mornings was to get everyone out of the door as quickly as possible. The longer they lingered, the greater the chances something would go wrong. I didn't want anyone to stay at home. I had neither the time nor the energy to look after anybody.

Finally, Kevin rushed in. He snatched one of the waffles from the plate, took three large bites, then rushed over to the stainless steel refrigerator and began to fiddle with his tie. He scrutinized his reflection a couple of times.

I rolled my eyes and prayed he'd hurry.

"C'mon, boys. We need to go," he barked at the kids.

"Oh, babe, I'm almost out of my body wash and deodorant," he said to me.

My eyebrows curled downward. Surely, he didn't expect me to make a mental note of the toiletries he needed. But if I had told him that, it would've only slowed them down, so I didn't say a word.

"I'm serious, Darby. I told you last week, and today I had to mix water in my bottle. It's as good as gone," he said.

I nodded and strained not to sigh out loud. I needed to remember to restock his stuff. The last thing I needed was him to fall back into his mix-with-water-to-make-it-stretch habit.

He walked back to the table, snatched two strips of bacon from his plate, and looked at our sons.

"C'mon, fellas. It's time to roll," he said.

The boys scrambled from their chairs, grabbed their insulated lunch bags, and followed Kevin out of the door.

"Bye, Mom," Kevin Jr. said. He was being kind of standoffish, and I still hadn't figured out the issue with his behavioral problems.

"Love you, Mommy," Taylor said.

"I'll call you in a bit," Kevin added. I wanted to tell him don't bother. I'd be asleep for sure, but I figured he didn't need that information.

Once they were gone, the house returned to its day-after-happy-hour state, and I was happy again. I glanced at the table and the counters. I decided all of the dirty dishes could wait until later.

I fixed myself a Bloody Mary to help with the wicked hangover and rinsed that glass. I turned the lights off and dragged myself back up to bed.

When the phone rang, at first, I thought it was in my dream. But no matter how much I tossed and turned, the ringing continued. I wondered if the noise could be all in my head, but then it stopped.

I adjusted myself and tried to return to the rest I had been enjoying, when the phone rang again.

That time, I knew for sure it was neither a dream nor the effects of the alcohol. I eased up onto my elbow, pulled up the sleep mask and snatched the phone from the nightstand.

"Hello?"

"Oh, God, Darby, I need you to come over!" she screamed.

"Carla, I can't deal with this right now. My head is killing me, and I'm tired."

"Yeah, but, Darby, I'm in a real bind here. My client brought along a friend."

"And what the hell are you telling me for?"

"Darby, after what went down with that woman, I don't feel right," she whined.

"I'm tired and don't know what to tell you!"

"Darby, this is a good-paying client. We don't want to lose him. Please, can you come over?"

"Carla, I am not about to screw some stranger because you double booked!" I screamed into the phone.

"Did you hear a word I said? I told you the client brought him. I didn't double book. Look, either we're gonna be adults about this, or you're gonna sit over there and act like some virginal child."

"Carla, I understand that I'm a part of this business, but I'm a part of the brains behind the operation. I'm not the hired help. I'm not here to fill in at your convenience."

"So, you're telling me we're about to let this money go?"

"If keeping it means I gotta come over there and screw somebody, yes. Yes, Carla, we are gonna have to let that money go."

I had come to enjoy the money from the business, and when I made sure the ladies got their share, the gravity of what we were doing didn't really weigh down on me. Carla didn't get it.

"I thought we were in this together. I mean, damn, I really thought if you needed to, you'd be willing to step up to the plate," she said.

"Carla, you are asking me to screw some man? Yes, I will step up to the plate and make sure the finances are where they need to be, but I'm not about to have sex with strangers for money."

"So, lemme get this straight. It's okay for me and the other ladies to lie on our backs, and rake in the money, but you're too good to get down like that?"

It happened in an instant. My head felt good and clear, and then instantly, a sharp pain ricocheted from my temple to the backs of my eyes. The hangover had returned.

"Carla, I'm not trying to tell you or any other grown woman what to do, but all I'm saying is I won't be sleeping with anybody for money." I tried to speak calmly. The angrier I got, the more my head seemed to hurt.

"You trying to tell me you expect me to handle both of these clients alone?"

"Carla, I'm about to hang up. Let me tell you why. At no point when we've talked about me partnering with you did I agree to screw anybody. I told you I could be a silent partner and help with the finances. I'm married."

"Whoop-tee-do!" Carla screamed. "Several of the ladies are married! You think you're too good to screw for money? And you think you're better than the rest of us because you give it up for free?" she said with a sharp laugh.

I waited for a moment to respond. I was furious.

"You know what, don't even worry about it," Carla said. I felt relieved until the next words dropped from her mouth.

"And don't worry about our books either; I'm sure we'll be able to figure it all out."

First, I heard my heartbeat in my ears, then the dial tone.

"Oh no, the hell she didn't!"

Had that bitch just fired me?

I got up to go get my iPad. I hated when the kids played with it, and still reeling after Carla fired me, I was not prepared for what I found on the iPad after I picked it up from underneath Kevin Jr.'s bed.

"Jesus!" I fell back onto the floor. "What in the hell?" My eyebrows knitted in concentration as I flipped through the stunning images.

Not only had I been fired, but I'd also been sucker punched. I was about to be sick.

32

IVEE

It had all come back, and the memory hit me like a massive boulder.

Once at the station, I was asked to submit to a blood test. Of course they had already read me my Miranda Rights. I was handcuffed and placed under arrest, but in the back of my mind, I kept thinking that maybe they'd let me go. Maybe no one had to know about this.

"Henderson!"

The voice that barked my name killed that thought. I jumped from the bench and rushed to the small opening. The second I moved, my seat was gone, but what could I do? Three women stood close to the area, like they were being paid to hold those spots. It was still cold and crowded.

"You can make your call now," an officer said.

In a different setting, he would've been trying to buy me a drink. Instead, I stood back as he unlocked a door to let me out so I could use the phone. That's when another thought hit me. I stood transfixed for a moment. My husband was probably going berserk! It had been nearly twenty-four hours since I'd seen him. OMG! This thing had gotten so out of control. I stood behind another woman who looked like she wasn't even a little fazed by being in jail and making a collect call.

When it was my turn to use the phone, I wanted to cry. What in the hell would I say? Should I call Zion? Maybe I should call Darby or Peta? Darby would be home. It was Friday morning. But my husband was probably already livid beyond words.

I took a deep breath and pulled the phone's receiver from its cradle. As I waited for an answer, I went over in my head the many ways I could explain that this was all a big misunderstanding.

As the automated voice warned the caller that this was a call from the Harris County Jail from an inmate in custody, I lost it.

"Ivee, what the hell?" Zion screamed.

"I'm so sorry! I wasn't drunk; at least I didn't think I was. I felt fine," I sobbed.

"Okay, okay, listen. Pull yourself together. Have you seen a judge yet?"

"No, but I overheard someone say they're real crowded and things were moving slower than normal."

"Okay." My husband sighed hard. "I was worried sick. I've called Darby, Peta, and Felicia. No one knew where you were."

"I got arrested leaving the restaurant. I couldn't call until now," I explained.

"Don't worry about it, babe. I'm glad you're safe, and you're not hurt or anything like that. What about your job? You need me to call them?"

"Oh, God! No. It's Friday, so unless they've called, it's not unusual for me to work from home."

"Where are you?"

"Downtown, I think. Or wherever the Harris County Jail is."

"Okay, babe, hold tight. I'm on my way," he said.

"Call the lawyer first," I told him.

"Yeah, that's probably the smartest thing to do. Okay, well, you hold tight, and I'll see you soon," he said.

Hours after that call, I listened as, a thin-haired, red-faced woman was holding court. She must've been an attorney or worked in the legal field. She seemed to know her stuff.

"So, before you see a judge, you'll be seen by Pretrial Services for an interview," the jailhouse lawyer said.

"I need to see a judge so I can get the hell up outta here," a woman seated in the corner said. "I ain't got no time for no pretrial nothing!"

"You want to meet with them, honey," the speaker said in her direction. "You see, they determine your flight risk, and that's what determines what bond the judge will set for you."

Speaker lawyer-lady looked at a woman to her left. "You—is this your first time?"

The meek woman nodded.

"Hmmm, okay, so, for you, a bondsman is probably the best and fastest way to go. Pretrial can take a lot longer."

"Henderson, you've bonded out!" a deep voice yelled.

It took a moment for the words to settle in my brain. It wasn't until people glanced around in confusion that I realized it was me. I was the one who had bonded out. I scrambled to my feet and rushed to leave.

The stench of the holding cell really registered in my sinuses as I walked out of jail. The scent of stale paint mixed with the stench, but I didn't mind since I was finally on my way out.

"Oh, Zion!" I leaped into my husband's arms and hugged him so tight it felt like I was attached to him.

"It's gonna be okay," another voice said.

Before he'd spoken, I never even realized he was there. Ted Dennison and my husband were business associates. We used him in emergencies, and he would refer us in the right direction at a later time. Until now, we never had the need for a criminal attorney.

"Ted. I'm sorry about this," I said. My eyes shifted downward.

It didn't take long for me to become very self-conscious. I had been in the same clothes for more than twenty-four hours. My breath was probably a mixture of stale liquor, morning funk, and nothing else nice. I eased away from the two men and fell back a little while Ted spoke on my behalf.

"Okay, we've gotta move fast here to protect her right to drive. I will request a hearing within fifteen days. Let me handle the administrative side of this. You can sit tight and prepare for your arraignment."

I opened the large envelope and sifted through my property as Ted and Zion talked. Once I confirmed that everything was there, I turned to the men and smiled.

"It's all there?" Ted asked.

Afraid to speak, I nodded.

"Well, that's everything then. Zion has already gotten your car out of impound," he said. "Unless you guys have any more questions, I'd say it's time to get outta here," Ted said.

"Thanks, man. I'm gonna get her home, and we can talk later," Zion said.

Unsure of what to expect when we got in the car, I kept my mouth shut. How do you explain getting arrested and charged with a DWI? I assumed my husband was pissed, but in case he wasn't, I didn't want to give him the idea that he should be.

We had been on the road for a little more than twenty minutes when Zion finally spoke up. "What in the hell happened, Ivee?"

The sound of his palm as it slammed against the steering wheel made me jump. My heart flipped backwards. I wasn't sure if it was a rhetorical question. It was obvious what had happened. I was arrested for driving drunk. He'd had to bail me out of jail. There wasn't much else to the story.

"How many times have I asked you to call when you've had too much? I don't get it," he said.

Zion spoke like he didn't need any input from me. He was pissed, and I was scared that if I said anything more, it would only make things worse.

I swallowed nervously.

Other people got DWIs. People who drank too much, had drinking problems that they wouldn't acknowledge, and those who didn't know when to say when, got caught up like that. This was foreign to me.

"You don't have anything to say for yourself?" he finally asked.

That was when I turned and looked at him. "What do you want me to say? You had to come and bail me out of jail. It's not like I intentionally set out to drive while I was drunk!"

I felt smaller than an ant beneath the weight of his words. My mind began to wonder if it would've been better to stay in jail and let the judge throw the book at me.

33

PETA

I didn't know how much longer I'd be able to take it. The tears threatened to push through, but I needed to hold it together. There was no one to catch me if I fell. The realization that my business was vulnerable was real to me, and I felt like there was nothing I could do. I couldn't imagine I'd still be stuck, but the insurance company was no closer to cutting a check, and I thought I was gonna die for certain. I didn't understand why they didn't realize that my business was about to go under as I waited on the bureaucracy of their "red tape."

I slammed my phone down after yet another unproductive phone call with the claims adjuster. I felt like I wanted to cry. The other trucks were doing okay, and that helped to keep me afloat, but the lack of money from the others hurt. And I felt like I couldn't recover regardless of how hard I tried.

After I heard about what had happened to Ivee, I figured I needed to put things into perspective. I couldn't believe she had been arrested and had gone to jail. She wasn't there for a long time, but it made me think. If I ever went to jail, I'd be in a real bad place since it was just me and me alone. Kyle couldn't even return a damn phone call!

After I talked with Kendal and learned that Kyle had been sneaking to the house to talk to her, I was more than pissed. I didn't want to drag my daughter into the middle of our mess, but I felt like he had set me up, and had gone out of his way to avoid facing me.

"Mom! You home?" my daughter yelled as she walked through the front door.

"I'm in the kitchen!"

She walked in, and I tried to calm myself. I had so many questions, but I didn't want to startle her. I also didn't want her to know how mad I was at Kyle.

"Sweetpea, you didn't you tell me your daddy moved," I said casually.

She lit up like a light bulb. "Oh, Mom! You should see his new house! It's like a mansion!" Her eyes grew wide in excitement. She smiled like she was genuinely happy for him and his new home.

"Really? You hungry?" I asked.

I turned and finished my work on the salad.

"There's a swimming pool, a hot tub, and oooh, Mom, it's so cool," Kendal gushed. "The stairs are the truth!"

There was no way I could face my daughter. I didn't want her to see how upset I had become. I couldn't believe Kyle had suckered me the way he did. She went on about her room at his house as I worked.

"When was the last time you saw him?"

"Oh, Mom, he said he's gonna call you back," she said. She didn't answer the question, but what she told me said quite a bit.

It made me turn around. A combination of fear and anger hit my heart like an electric jolt. But I had to be careful. I closed my eyes and took a deep breath.

"He said *what?*" I asked as I turned back to face her.

"Oh, yeah, Dad told me you tried to call him. He said he was real busy, but he's gonna call you back," she said.

The ease with which Kendal delivered his lie had broken my heart. That told me he knew exactly what was going on. It was probably best that I didn't see him. The anger I felt was like nothing I had ever experienced before. Kyle knew I'd suffer without his money. I wondered why he didn't realize that meant his daughter would suffer, too.

Over the years, I had worked so hard to get the boutiques up and running. I had made sacrifices. For months, I went without visits to the hair and nail shops. I only bought the essentials for Kendal. Kyle's money kept us afloat for a while when every dime I had was tied up in getting the trucks off the ground. I still wasn't at a point where I could establish a rainy-day fund.

"Have the police figured anything out yet?" my daughter asked.

I wanted to go back to her dad and his new house. I wanted to find out when he met with her. I also wanted to hear more about the call that he claimed he was going to return, but I couldn't press the issue. Kendal would pick up on a problem before I could cover it up.

"No, still nothing," I said. "You want your dressing on the salad or you gonna put it on yourself?"

"I can do it alone, Mom," she said, and reached for the bottle.

My daughter's tone reminded me that I had fallen into my mommy mode. Kendal hated when I treated her like a kid, and I didn't mean to, but I felt helpless myself.

When my cell phone rang, my pulse began to race. I was hopeful until I saw the caller ID.

The moment my eyes focused on Felicia's number, I went back to the thoughts that had dominated my mind lately. I needed to figure out a way to get to Kyle.

34

DARBY

The following week felt like it had dragged along slowly for several reasons. Imagine trying to explain away naked pictures of yourself to your young son. Kevin Jr. had seen the pictures I had sent to Chandler. I felt like a real filthy slut as I sat and waited to talk with him before his grandmother came over.

"Son, I want to discuss something with you," I said.

He had been playing one of his car games on the floor in the family room. He barely looked up at me. I deserved it, but I also needed to fix the situation regardless of how uncomfortable it made me.

I swallowed hard and exhaled.

Things had improved at school, but knowing my son had seen raunchy and obscene pictures of me made *me* want to act out.

I walked over and removed the two cars he was playing with.

"Mom!" he cried, and finally looked up at me.

"I need to talk to you," I said, searching for the right words. "I wanted to talk to you about the pictures you saw on the iPad," I said softly.

"I didn't look at all of those, Mom," he said. My child's eyes grew wide and began to water; his lip began to quiver. I felt so small. Suddenly, I wasn't so sure the talk was a good idea.

When massive teardrops began to roll down his cheeks, I wanted to cry myself.

"Son, it's okay; it's okay."

"Are you and Daddy getting a divorce?" he asked between sobs.

My eyebrows curled downward.

"A divorce?"

My heart raced. Did he know something I didn't?

"Yeah, when me and Lucas saw the pictures, he said you and Daddy was getting divorced."

There wasn't enough saliva left to swallow the boulder-sized lump in my throat. I needed a drink now more than ever before. Not only had my son seen the pictures, but his friend had, too. That explained some things.

"Honey, no one is getting a divorce. I'm sorry you saw those pictures, but that's why Mommy tells you and your brother not to play with the iPad. Those were intended for Daddy's eyes only. I had a skin irritation and needed to take pictures to show the doctor."

My son's little face twisted into a frown. It looked like he wanted to believe my explanation.

"Did you have to get a shot?" he finally asked.

I nodded slowly, and instantly his focus was off the most embarrassing moment of my life.

"Whoa! Shots hurt!" he said.

I made a mental note to unsync my iPhone and iPad. I also made sure my text messages and pictures were all removed from both.

No wonder the poor boy had been acting out. I was looking forward to washing away the sick images of him and his friend twisting and turning the iPad to make sense of my raunchy X-rated pictures with some mommy juice.

When my mother-in-law came in, I was relieved. I grabbed my purse and ran out of there before she could ask any questions.

"Happy hour is supposed to be happy!" I muttered, nearly to myself, later at the bar. I rolled my eyes, and wanted to curse when I took the last sip of my first drink.

For hours, I had been looking forward to getting drunk. The picture discussion with my son and the stupid situation with Carla had worn me out. I should've told her she had every right to tell the client she wasn't down for a threesome. I couldn't believe she thought I'd agree to hooking.

The last of my drink only made me want more. I couldn't imagine a more somber gathering than the one I felt stuck in with Felicia. She was about as interesting as a faucet that dripped slowly.

"Where is everybody?" she asked and looked around at the other people at the bar. She waved with a few fingers, smiled, and then turned back to me. Those other people seemed to be having a great time. I felt like *they* understood the concept of happy hour!

"You heard about what happened to Ivee, right?" I asked.

Felicia leaned in. "Can you imagine? She was in jail!" Felicia's eyes widened when she said the word jail.

"I tried to call her a few times, but she didn't answer."

"I knooow. She's not talking to anybody. Imagine how I feel? I was with her at lunch. I tried to hook her up with a new client, and you know how Ivee is. She must've gone way overboard."

"Felicia, please! What time did you guys go to lunch?"

She shrugged as if she understood the point I tried to make.

"That was last Thursday mid-afternoon, and then of course we met up here for happy hour, so I don't see how you can blame yourself for her getting arrested. She was arrested after happy hour, not after lunch."

It really bugged me when people tried to make other people's problems somehow relate to them.

Felicia got up from her chair and rushed to my side of the table.

She picked up her glass and put it back down again. Felicia looked like her mind was on overload. That wasn't the kind of company I needed at a bar. I wondered whether people realized that our usually loud, fun, and boisterous table had fallen off drastically.

"Darby, the truth is, what happened to Ivee could've happened to any one of us. Think how many times we've thrown back tons of drinks, and then gotten behind the wheel."

"Okay, Felicia. I'm really not happy right now, and this is supposed to be *happy* hour—you know, with an emphasis on *happy*. This conversation right here, it's messing with my buzz, and if something is messing with my buzz, I ain't so *happy!*"

Felicia threw her hands up and shrugged as she frowned.

"Now, move on back to your side. I don't need you bringing any more misery close to me. Lord knows I've got my own pile of mess to deal with."

"I'm just trying to—"

"Yeah, yeah yeah. I know what you're trying to do, and all I'm saying is, I'm not in the mood!"

When the waitress walked by, I reached out and tapped her. "Can I get another one, please?"

"Sure." She smiled. "Hey, where's everyone else tonight?" she asked as she reached for the empty glass in front of me.

"Who knows?" I eyed the glass on her tray.

She got the message and moved on. Felicia was not the kind of company I needed, and I knew it. I needed someone to tell me that what I had decided to do wasn't the best move. But Felicia only wanted to have a pity party.

"First, Peta and her trucks! Who the hell would want to do something like that to her? Then, Ivee going to jail," Felicia deadpanned.

I picked up my phone and sent a text message. The night was

still very young. The last thing I wanted to do was sit around and drown other people's sorrows in my martini.

I tried not to stare at the phone, but it was hard.

By the time the waitress had returned with my new drink, and Felicia had delved into her theory about the happy hour curse, I was ready to slit my own wrists.

I couldn't think of a time when we didn't have a great time together. Over the years, we had brought everything to the table on Thursday nights. It didn't matter whether the issues were, big or minor.

The idea that my friends were struggling and felt like the best thing to do was stay away, made me sad, but I didn't want to linger on it.

"…so, all I could think about is, what if Zion is tripping out on her after this whole arrest thing. You know how he gets."

I stared at Felicia. She insisted on trying to bring me down.

When my phone vibrated, I nearly didn't want to check it. I couldn't handle another disappointment after I had stomached all of Felicia's suspicion about all that was wrong with everyone's life.

Out with friends. 'Sup w U?

Looking for trouble. I texted back.

Ppl say trouble is my middle name.

I'm at Eddie V's.

I can be at hotel Derek in under an hr.

My heart nearly stopped.

Sure, what started out as my master plan for revenge had grown into something more. It had turned into us chatting online, through text messages, then blossomed into something that I could've never guessed. We'd been flirting for a long time, but I never stopped to think about where it would go. I never expected it, or us to end up in a hotel room. But the liquor made me feel adventurous, and nothing appealed to me about Felicia.

"Oh my God! What is it now? Who is it?" Felicia asked, her face twisted up as she waited anxiously for bad news.

I looked up from my phone and knew exactly what I had to do.

"Oh, this?" I raised the phone. "It's nothing, um, Kevin, going on about the kids," I lied. My eyes began to search the busy restaurant. I needed to find the waitress and end the depressing evening with Felicia.

"Oh no, what's going on?" Felicia asked. Her voice was as worried as ever.

"I need to go. Something is wrong with his mom, and he's freaking out. You know how they can be," I said.

If I had to wait for the bill, I'd never make it in under an hour. I looked at the table and did the math in my head. I placed two crisp twenty-dollar bills on the table, and eased out of my chair.

"You're about to leave, like right now?" Felicia frowned.

"Yeah, Kevin is worried sick, and I don't want him doing something stupid to our son," I said.

Felicia's frown deepened. Her busy eyes followed my every move. "But I thought you said it was your mother-in-law," she said and looked at me like she was confused.

"Oh, yeah, that's what I meant," I said. I shook my head a little. "Okay, honey, I'll check in with you later tomorrow."

I did two air kisses on the side of each cheek and moved away from the bar.

"But what about Ivee and Peta?" she yelled after me.

"Oh, they'll be fine." I dashed toward the door.

On the drive over, I tried to play devil's advocate.

Why does he want to meet now?

We already had plans. Why not stick to the plan?

What if he is trying to set me up?

What will I do when we are finally alone together?

Why am I about to go and meet this man?

I had no common-sense answers to any of the questions I asked myself, but that didn't stop me. At the corner of Sage and Westheimer Roads, my phone vibrated again. Chandler's text message was simple.

Rm 7654.

When I pulled in front of the hotel, I considered whether I should park myself, or use the valet service. I made my decision since they didn't have self-parking and rushed into the hotel's lobby. The sleek, wooden panel against the wall and the shiny, gray cement floors gave the lobby a slick and modern appearance. My eyes fixed on the numbers inside the elevator car. As it took off and rose, it felt like my heart dropped to my toes.

I stood outside of Room 7654 and pulled in a deep breath. I glanced down the hall in both directions, then dug into my purse and pulled out my flask. I unscrewed the top, took a couple of swigs and tried to calm my nerves. Once I put the flask back, I raised my closed hand to knock, but decided against it. I turned and took a few steps away from the door.

Being there was wrong. Being with him was wrong. It…us…we had gone too far. I felt a sudden urge to get away as fast as I could.

"Change of heart?" a deep voice behind me boomed. The low and sensual sound made my insides quiver. I stopped.

When I turned back, the smile he bore had to have been the sexiest I could've ever imagined. My insides went soft.

He held a small glass of liquor, and sexiness all but oozed from his entire body.

My legs threatened to give out on me. My throat felt scratchy, and I could hardly swallow.

"You came all this way, and you were going to leave and not even knock?" he asked. He sounded hurt.

Chandler stared at me so intensely that I struggled, but swallowed hard and dry. I scrutinized him, sized him up, and looked for any inkling of a possible character flaw.

When I found none, like a brainless zombie, I followed him into the room. The bed looked lush and inviting from where I stood. Instantly, my mind thought of how comfortable the high-thread count sheets and fluffy pillows would be.

35

IVEE

"Is everything okay?" Jessica asked.

"Oh, yeah," I lied. There was no way I'd admit to her, or anyone in the office, that I had been arrested. Since I had gotten out of jail, the nightmares had been wicked and frequent.

"Yes, I won't be in the office for a few days," I explained over the phone. "I'm still working, and you should definitely call me if Geneva calls a meeting,"

"Okay, well, you mean this is not a vacation or something like that?"

"No, just me working from home. That's it. That's all."

Once I finished that call, I tried not to look at the clock. I picked up the proposal that I was working on for Wayne, and decided I'd call and set up a meeting with him. I tried to keep myself busy so I wouldn't be focused on what Ted was doing to make sure I could keep my license.

We only had fifteen days to avoid the possible suspension.

I had the pleasure of sitting and not watching the clock or the phone as I waited for the results of the Administrative License Hearing. I was grateful my lawyer could attend that in my place. I didn't want to go near a jail cell ever again.

Also, Zion thought it would be better if I didn't drive until we got word about the hearing. This thing made him near neurotic, and it was all I could do to not go off on him at times.

My last call with Ted left me hopeful.

"What's the worst-case scenario for me?" I asked.

"I think you're gonna be okay. Trust me on this. Since you have an otherwise clean record, and this is your first alcohol or drug-related offense, you will not be required to serve any jail time. I'm gonna push for probation here," he said.

The way he dismissed jail made me happy. As long as I didn't have to think about going back to that hellhole, I could handle pretty much anything else.

"Probation? Are you sure about that?" I asked. "Or I guess the better question is has a person ever gone to jail after their very first DWI arrest?"

"Well, of course," he said.

I sighed. That was what I was afraid of. If it was possible, I felt like there was a good chance it might happen to me. The entire experience had left me completely petrified and nervous.

"But hear me out here, Ivee. As long as the DWI didn't result in serious bodily injury or a death, the judge can give you anything from six months to two years probation." He continued when I didn't respond. "Believe it or not, Ivee, no one wants to throw a harmless, nonviolent woman in jail. That serves no one any good. Now let me get in here and get back to you later, after the hearing," he said.

That conversation had taken place more than six hours earlier, and I had been going bananas ever since.

Later that evening, I fixed dinner and waited anxiously for Zion and Ted. Ted didn't call me like I expected him to do. Instead, he had called Zion.

When the phone rang later in the day, I fully expected it to be Ted, but it was my husband.

"Hey, listen, Ivee, Ted's stuck in court on a different case, but I told him he should come on over to the house for dinner tonight. That way, he can give us the skinny on the best move here," he said.

I was confused. I thought the best move was going to be the probation Ted had assured me I qualified to get. I was more upset that he hadn't bothered to call me back, but called my husband instead. I had spent the bulk of my day stressed and worried over it, and he had left me to suffer.

"So, he called you instead of me?"

"Well, I'm paying the damn bill," Zion snapped.

When I didn't say anything, I heard him breathe hard in my ear. The last thing I needed was an argument.

"Okay, you can tell, I'm still a little bent out of shape over this whole thing, but, Ivee, I'm not trying to argue with you. I was actually calling to tell you that Ted was able to save your license, but there's a catch. You're only supposed to drive to and from work or for work-related events. He also mentioned another option that he wants to talk with us about, which is why I suggested he come over for dinner," Zion said.

"I wasn't planning on cooking."

I had mixed emotions about what he'd said. I felt put out because he snapped at me, and tried to throw it in my face that he was picking up the tab for Ted. On the other hand, I was relieved that I'd get to keep my driver's license.

"I'll order some takeout," I offered.

"Baby, that's cool. I don't think Ted cares whether you cook or not. I figured it would be easier for Ted to talk to us together, in person," he said.

I was ready for our conversation to be over. I wondered how long I'd have to endure Zion's outbursts over my mistake.

"Okay, well, let me go. I need to figure out what we're eating. As soon as I place the order, I'll call and let you know."

"Ivee," Zion called out to me.

"Yeah?"

"You can't ever screw up like this again," he said.

He actually tried to sound sweet. It had been more reassuring to talk to Ted than my own damn husband. I wanted to tell him that I didn't set out to drink, drive, and get arrested, but that breakdown would've been lost on him.

"I'll talk to you soon," I said.

If he wanted to say anything else, he didn't get the chance. I ended the call.

"Why would Ted call him and not me?" I told myself not to focus on the negative. The important thing was there was another possibility for me. That was really good news because whatever it was, it had come after court.

I felt trapped. I'd spent the bulk of my day waiting, only to have to return to the waiting game again.

36

PETA

Three minutes! That was the amount of time that had passed since I looked up and thought I saw the back of Kyle's car turn the corner down the street from my house. I didn't know whether I should try to chase him, or come up with another idea of how to make him come to me.

"If I spent my time chasing down every glimpse I see of him, I wouldn't get anything done!"

Lately, I'd been on the verge of losing my mind. At the grocery store, every other man looked like Kyle from behind. Then in traffic, his car either whizzed by me in the opposite direction, or it was several cars up ahead. I barely recognized my life anymore. Things had started tightening up around the house, and I had run out of ways to hide it from Kendal.

"Mom, why are we eating spaghetti again? Isn't it like the third time this week?" she asked.

"Dang, Mom, we're out of juice."

"Mom, can I use your body wash? We're out of soap."

Two weeks had passed since the last time I had spoken with the insurance company, and each day I prayed I'd find a check in the mailbox, but I never did.

Inside, I tried to ignore the bottle that seemed to call my name louder and louder since my world had flipped. Beverly had returned to work, and things had slowly gotten back on track, but it wasn't the sense of security I enjoyed when all four trucks were out and working. Still, life was getting back to what was about to be my new normal.

Since I didn't feel up to a battle with the insurance company or the stonewall from the detective, I decided a drink wouldn't hurt.

I grabbed a glass and was about to grab a bottle when the doorbell rang. My spirits rose momentarily as visions of an insurance check by special delivery danced through my mind.

"Coming!"

As I skipped to the door, I didn't even bother to ask who was there. I would've bet anything that good news was on the other side. That was exactly what I needed.

When I pulled the door open, and Ivee stood there with bags in her hands and at her feet, I wasn't sure what to say.

"Darby is parking the car. We don't know what the hell is going on, but we're not about to let you go through it alone."

"Oh sweet Jesus! What are you talking about?"

"Peta, with two of those trucks down, I can only imagine how hard it must be for you. Then Felicia mentioned something about Kyle no longer paying child support, and well...we knew you'd never ask for anything."

"So, we brought a few things we thought you and Kendal could use," Darby said as she walked up to the doorway.

Ivee motioned to the bags that were at her feet. Both of her hands were full. "Here, grab this bag," she said.

"You guys." I sobbed.

"Can you move? This stuff is heavy!" Ivee said.

I stepped aside to allow them in, and grabbed the bags Ivee had stepped over. Tears rolled down my cheeks as I struggled to carry all of the bags of groceries inside.

As I was about to close the door, Felicia screamed, "Hey, hold on! Hold on! I need some help out here."

Darby met me back at the door to grab the bags from me. "I've got these. Go help her."

My pantry, refrigerator, and cabinets were full. By the time the ladies finished unloading and unpacking the groceries, I was so overwhelmed. They had come in right on time.

"You guys did not have to do all of this."

"Girl, please. Crack open some wine or something," Darby said.

I looked around a bit. "Ummm, I have some leftover vodka."

It felt horrible that all I could offer besides the vodka was water. Outside of the things they'd bought, I was down to nearly nothing. I didn't want to think what would've happened if they hadn't stepped in when they did. Felicia jumped up. "Oh, I forgot the box I was trying to get in before you closed the door."

"You left the drinks in the car?" Ivee asked.

"I couldn't carry everything!" Felicia grabbed her keys. "Darby, come help me?"

When the two of them walked out, I looked at Ivee and shook my head. "This was nothing but you, huh?"

"No, girl. It was all of us. And don't be acting all silly and stuff. We ain't doing nothing you wouldn't do for all of us if the tables were turned."

Once everything was put away, and I poured us all drinks, we sat and got ready to catch up.

"What are you gonna do about Kyle?" Darby asked.

"I can't find him. I finally went by his house a week or so ago only to discover that he had moved! I told the AG's office that I didn't intend to sign the letter, but no one seems sympathetic to what I'm saying. It's my signature, so saying I was coaxed into signing apparently sounds so ridiculous that no one believes me."

"Wait, you never did say what happened. How'd he get you to sign?" Felecia asked.

"That bastard! He got me drunk. I'm almost ashamed to admit it, but he brought an extra large bottle of Skyy Vodka over and we got drunk. By the time he started talking about needing my signature on something, I could barely see straight," I admitted.

"Oh, that was dirty," Ivee said.

"And he gets away with it just like that?" Darby asked.

"He had a letter with my signature saying it was no longer necessary for him to pay. They were doing their job and cut me off. For all they knew, we had worked something out together and it was what I had requested."

"They didn't need to verify anything with you first?"

I shrugged. "I guess that's not how they work down there. Now, I'm gonna have to hire a lawyer and take him back to court." I shook my head. "And that, like every damn thing else, costs money."

"The state has money to prosecute my ass, but bastards like Kyle can get away with falsifying documents, so he could basically rob you and his own flesh and blood!" Ivee said.

"I know things are tight, but last week, Felicia and I looked around and we were the only two at happy hour," Darby said.

Ivee and I looked at her.

"We've always been close, and we're all going through it right now, but if we start pulling away from each other, then who knows what will happen."

Her voice cracked a bit. Now, all eyes were on her.

"What, you mean like folks might start getting arrested for DWI or something?" Ivee suggested.

"Yeah, that, or maybe someone might meet up with a dangerous, but sexy murderer at a hotel room and do unspeakable, but pleasurable things," Darby said dreamily.

When she suddenly stopped talking as if she'd caught herself and realized she'd said too much, all of our faces were stunned frozen.

Darby threw her hands up as if to say, "What the hell," and then dropped another bombshell.

"Oh, and if that isn't enough, the playground moms held a telephone intervention about my bringing my mommy juice to the park. Then I had to explain to my seven-year-old why his mommy took pictures in her birthday suit and they ended up on the family iPad."

Ivee spat out her drink.

Felecia nearly gagged, but all eyes were stuck on Darby.

"Yup, let that be a lesson. Unsync your stuff before you go texting someone other than your husband!"

"Aren't you scared he's going to tell his father?"

"I bribed him with the promise of a new bike," Darby confessed.

We all cracked up at that. These ladies let it all hang loose.

37

DARBY

"Thanks for dinner, babe. It was good," Kevin said. He stooped down to kiss my forehead as he passed.

"Thanks for dinner, babe," Kevin Jr. mocked, then pursed his little lips. He was slowly but surely coming back after we had that little talk about the birthday suit pictures, and of course the new bike.

"Yeah, it was good, babe," his brother teased. They made smooching noises and cracked themselves up with laughter.

"Oh, cut it out you, clowns," I teased.

"Okay, fellas. Finish up at the table, and then it's time for showers and bed!"

When Kevin took the boys off to shower, I got up and started to clean the kitchen. Once I prepared the water, I grabbed a glass and poured some wine. I swallowed it in two gulps, poured another glass, and then started to wash the dishes.

Once alone, my mind traveled back to heaven right here on earth. No one had ever kissed the soles of my feet. Chandler had done that and then some. He had done remarkable things—things my husband had never done. Kevin was immensely cheap, responsible, straight-laced, and had been goal-oriented from day one.

Chandler was a reckless free spirit. He was a trust-fund baby who lived a privileged life, and he never made excuses for his sense of entitlement. The very things I hated about him were what I loved most. He handled my body as if we'd been together many times before. We didn't talk too much, but he gave me everything I needed. Most of which I never even knew I wanted.

"Hey, where are the towels?" Kevin rushed out of the bathroom and asked.

"In the linen closet to your right," I said.

"Oh, my bad!"

He turned back toward the bathroom and opened the closet door. When he ducked back into the bathroom, I took another sip of my wine.

Regardless of how much I tried to shake the memories from my head, they wouldn't leave. Chandler had me hanging off the sofa in the hotel room, then on the corner of the massive four-poster, king-sized bed. We screwed like rabbits, and everything he did made me feel like I was on the edge of ecstasy.

"We got any lotion?" Kevin peeked out from the hallway and asked a little while later.

"Under the sink in the yellow bin," I said.

"Gotcha!"

I drank more wine, then a little more, and started to wash the pots.

I couldn't drink enough wine to erase the memory of the very best night of sex I had ever experienced. My emotions had been at war ever since. It was hard to look at myself in the mirror, but I felt so good, I was damn near ashamed.

Before the showers were over, I was asked about toothpaste, house shoes, and pajamas. When they finally finished, my sons ran out of the bathroom and filled the room with scents from their Cars and Spiderman body wash fragrances.

Only then, did I force thoughts of Chandler's sweat-drenched body slamming into me from behind out of my mind. It was all I could do to wait for our next rendezvous.

38

IVEE

As I eased into the back seat of the car, I thought about the fear I felt over going to work. My time outside of the office had spoiled me. I barely wanted to go back in, but the moment those thoughts tried to get the best of me, I reminded myself of one fact—things could've been a whole lot worse for me if anyone at the office had gotten wind of my recent trip to the slammer. When I thought about that, it really put things into perspective and made me realize how fortunate I was.

Inside my office, I familiarized myself with some of my files and projects. Nearly everything looked good except that one thorn in my side.

"Nothing I can do about that now," I said.

I clicked out of the network files and pulled up my agenda for the day. It didn't take long for the buzzer on my desk to go off.

"There's someone named Wayne Ledger here to see you," Jessica said.

Her tone of voice told me she wanted to know who he was and why he was here. Typically, only clients who were already on the roster came into the office. When I was wooing a new client, I usually did that over a very expensive lunch or dinner and drinks. A lot of my life revolved around alcohol, and I didn't realize it until I was forced to go without.

"Yes, send him in, please," I said.

I straightened small knick-knacks on my desk and adjusted my picture frames as I waited for Wayne. He strolled into my office in a pair of jeans and a white T-shirt. All that was missing was the baseball cap turned backwards.

The smirk across his face told me he thought he was being funny. I held in my laughter and gave him a knowing look.

"I know what you're thinking," he said. "But I came straight here from someplace else."

"Uh-huh," I said.

"No, seriously, before you start to look down that pretty nose of yours at me, hear me out," he said.

His cell phone rang, and he looked at it. The friendly smile vanished from his face. "I'm so sorry. I really need to take this. Is that cool? I need about twenty minutes," he said.

I nodded. "You're fine. Go ahead."

He stepped out of my office, and I stepped back in time. My mind focused on all of the information Ted had thrown my way.

"There are some uncomfortable things we're going to have to do," he explained.

My eyebrows went up. Since I had been arrested on the side of a road, my car was towed and impounded, and my short stint in jail had already been uncomfortable for me. To me, that had been more than enough discomfort.

"Ivee can handle it," Zion said with all confidence. He stabbed his fork into the lasagna.

"A provision of your restricted license calls for you to install an ignition interlock device. You'll be on probation for two years, and of course there are the associated court costs and fees," he said.

"What is an ignition lock, or whatever you called it?" I asked.

My heart immediately began to race. I thought we had paid him to go to court, talk to the judge, and bring me back probation, maybe with a stint of community service. I didn't want any kind of locking device on my damn car.

"Listen. It was either that or no license. The ignition interlock device simply requires you to pass a breathalyzer test before you're able to operate your vehicle," he explained.

He shrugged and behaved as if that was not a big deal. I swallowed hard and told myself not to say a word.

"In addition to that, sometimes while you're driving, it'll randomly ask you to test your breath," he added.

My eyebrow danced upward. "You mean while I'm driving? That can't be safe. And I thought we were going to plead not guilty," I said.

"Ivee, this is a part of what's required in order to keep your license, once you pay the necessary fees," he said.

"Fees? What fees? Isn't that what we're paying you for?"

Ted chuckled. He picked up his crystal water glass and took two healthy gulps.

"Ivee, you need to hear him out. You got yourself into this mess, and now he's trying to tell you what it's gonna take to get out," Zion tossed in.

My head had begun to hurt. Zion had made it clear that he was more than pissed over the DWI arrest, but more and more he acted like this was more than he could handle.

"Ivee, my legal fees, which are being incredibly discounted, are only the tip of the iceberg in terms of what you will have to pay."

"I don't understand," I said.

But before Ted could say another word, Zion put down his fork and spoke.

"Hell, it's already added up when you look at the towing and impound fees, then lawyer costs—even at a discount. There are still court and device fees and bail…" Zion exhaled, hard and long. He seemed exasperated.

I had grown sick and tired of him and the way he had to remind me of how much I had fucked up. Yeah, I got busted and had to fight a DWI, but I didn't need his constant commentary or his re-minders about how much everything had cost and was going to cost.

The rest of our time over dinner was spent with Ted's detailed description of what it would cost to install the device and the monthly rental fees. Also, there would be possible costs associated with the mandatory DWI treatment program along with the increase we were sure to have to pay for our auto insurance.

I was pulled from my reverie when Wayne suddenly stepped back into my office, and not a moment too soon. Thoughts of my problems didn't do anything but bring me down. I welcomed the distraction.

"Was that an entire twenty minutes?" I joked.

He cut his eyes at me and took a seat in front of my desk. I had already drawn up the proposal for him to review. If I was able to lock him down, that would go a long way to help improve my standing with Geneva and at the firm.

The mess with Carson was still underway, and it pissed me off every time I thought about it. A part of me wanted Geneva to return Carson's money and tell him to hit the road. No single client was worth all of that. Still, the last thing I needed was the mess with him to blow up in my face, and word of the arrest to leak. I'd been extra careful to remain on my toes and made sure my face had been visible around the office as much as possible.

39

PETA

I didn't want to think about what my life would've been like had my girls not stepped in and rescued me. Bills were stacked as high as the ceiling, and I had made no progress whatsoever with the insurance company.

As I sat at the table and waited for my daughter to come in, I had gone over my speech several times. I didn't want to drag her into the mess with Kyle and me, but it was time for me to see if she could help.

Over the last couple of weeks, Kyle had picked her up from school, and it became clear that he knew he'd run into me at the house sooner or later if he didn't change his routine.

Once I heard her at the door, I checked dinner to make sure we had time to talk.

"M-o-o-o-m," she called from the front door. "Oooh, it smells good in here. What are you fixing?" Kendal asked.

"Your favorite." I smiled.

"You made crab cakes?" she asked.

I frowned. "Since when did crab cakes become your favorite?"

"Mom, Dad turned me on to seafood awhile back. We've been going to some really good seafood restaurants lately, and I realized what I've been missing all my life."

That burned me up. Here I was barely able to keep food on the table and Kyle was spending money like it had gone out of style. It hurt me so much to have to keep quiet about something like that. It would hurt my daughter.

"Well, I didn't make any seafood. I made a pasta casserole that you used to love," I said. "You know, before you got a taste of the good life with all that seafood."

Her eyes lit up. "Mom! You know that's my old favorite, too. Yummy!"

"Good."

"I'm gonna go upstairs and change before dinner." She moved toward the stairs.

"Wait!" I patted the area next to me. "Before you go up, there's something I need to talk to you about."

Concern spread across her face. She fumbled with the chair, pulled it out, and eased down onto the seat.

"Oh, God, Mom. What's wrong?"

"Hey, it's nothing that serious, but I need to know what's going on with your daddy. He's been trying to avoid me, and I really need to talk to him."

Kendal's entire demeanor changed. She tilted her head slightly and said, "Oh, Mom, he's not avoiding you. Here, I'll call him right now."

I watched as my daughter pulled out her cell phone, pressed a number, and pulled the phone up to her ear. A few seconds later, she smiled.

"Hey, Daddy, are you busy?"

She looked at me. It wasn't a disrespectful glance, but it said, "See, he picked right up. What's the problem?"

"Yes, Daddy, uh-huh."

I sat and listened to the one-sided conversation.

"Mom needs to talk to you," Kendal said. "Okay. Here she is." She passed me the phone.

I was almost scared to take it. Kendal got up from the table, and all but skipped out of the kitchen.

"I'm gonna go change, Mom," she said over her shoulder.

"Hello?" I said into the phone.

For a moment, there was quiet and I was concerned.

"Hey, what's up?" Kyle said.

He greeted me as if life was cheery. His voice held no care or concern in the world. I had been struggling and suffering for what felt like months, and he was cool as a cucumber. I swallowed back my bitterness and tried to remain focused.

"Kyle, why haven't you paid any child support?" I asked. "How do you think your daughter's been eating?"

"What? What are you talking about?" He sounded put out by what I said. It wasn't anger. It was as if I was a mere interruption in his day. His voice held irritation that he didn't even try to hide.

"Kyle, you have really put me in a bind. You know what happened with the trucks. My savings are just about gone, and a couple of weeks ago, my friends had to bring food for your daughter and me," I said.

"Peta, I'm sorry about your business. But as a business owner, you know the sacrifices and risks involved. Besides, I don't support your business. The money I gave you was to support our daughter. You need to get that other dude to handle your bills or whatever it is you're struggling with." His casual, easy-going solution stung. "That's why men trip over child support. That money is supposed to go to take care of our daughter—not make up your shortcoming or put your business in the black."

"Kyle, you have not paid child support; that's all I'm talking about.

If my head's not on straight, then I can't give our daughter one hundred percent."

"Listen. You signed those papers. I tried to talk to you about it. Yeah, I asked you to free me up, so I could finish up and close on the new house, and you were cool with it," he said.

"Are you kidding me? You know damn well I had no idea I was signing a letter to prevent you from paying child support."

"Oh, so now you didn't know, huh?" He laughed.

I burned with fury.

"You a trip, Peta. What's wrong? Your man trippin' on you? Things didn't work out with y'all, so now you trying to backpedal on what you promised me?"

"Kyle, you're not supporting your daughter! What does that have to do with me and any man? She is your financial responsibility," I said.

"No, she's *our* financial responsibility, and even though you allowed me to stop making monthly payments, I support my daughter. I'm present in her life. She spends time with me at my home. Our relationship is healthy. You're mad because I'm no longer footing the bill for your weekly drink fest with your girls. I'm not paying for your designer shoes, clothes, and your hair weaves!"

"Kyle, we need to talk about this some more. I had no idea I was signing that bogus letter, and you know it. You intentionally got me drunk and tricked me into signing it."

"Listen. My wife is calling me, so I need to wrap this up. I hope everything works out for you," he said. "Oh, and don't be talking about me getting you drunk, and bogus anything. If it's that easy, then maybe you have yourself a drinking problem."

Drinking problem, my ass; it was clear what Kyle had done. I felt like he was being cold toward me because of the way I abruptly ended the action in the back seat of the car. It wasn't that I didn't want the sex, but I wanted the madness to stop. Kyle knew what he was doing by showing up at the house on Thursday night. To him, being present, and adding vodka, was a guarantee for easy ass. I was fed up.

I sighed. "Well, I guess I'm gonna have to do what I have to do to survive. I realize you need to run, but when you get some time, we need to talk about my new living arrangements. Since my man is moving in, you're really gonna need to give me advance notice to pick Kendal up and visit with her."

"Your what? Oh, ain't no man moving into a house with my daughter under the same roof," he barked.

"Look, I need to run, too, Kyle. I can't maintain this household alone without your financial support. Either we're moving him in here, or he's gonna move us into his place, but you'd better go since your wife is calling. We'll have to catch up some other time."

Before Kyle could protest or say another word, I ended the call.

I should've been fighting fire with fire a long time ago. Thoughts of my conversation with Kyle pissed me off so much, my body shook after the call. What really lit a fire under me was the commercial that came on the small TV mounted beneath my kitchen cabinets.

"Oh, no she didn't!"

My mouth dropped to the floor, and I could hardly believe my eyes or my ears.

40

DARBY

C handler and I were at a standoff after what was quickly becoming our regular weekly meeting. The conversation was not going well and I hated to end our time this way.

"I didn't ask for this. Do you think I planned this? How could you even think I'd choose this? Where we are right now? I mean, look at how we're doing this. I'm not stupid. It makes no sense, but I can't bring myself to stop. It's like you're…like you're a drug or something, and I can't get enough."

I regretted the words as soon as they spewed from my lips. But what was done was done. It wasn't like it was a big secret or anything. He knew the power he held over me. He knew it, and I knew it.

I sniffled now as I heard the words rolling around in my head. I shouldn't have said any of that. I should've walked out, made a dramatic exit, but I had to do it. I had to pour my heart out. And look where it had gotten me—nowhere. Now I was driving home alone with tears and love songs blaring through my speakers. I felt like a fool, but back there at the hotel, my mouth had definitely written a check my heart wasn't prepared to cash.

I thought back to the rendezvous that left me wallowing in misery instead of pleasure like it should have. This was dysfunction at its worst, and I knew it. I wasn't a simple woman. I was well-educated with common sense, but I also knew what I couldn't deny. The heart wants what the heart wants, and mine wanted Chandler Buckingham.

"Why are you trippin'?" his deep husky voice had asked.

I looked deep into his eyes. He couldn't be serious. He couldn't be. But he was. He was, and that made it hurt even more.

"I'm not trippin'. I wanna know what's going on between us. Really, what's happening here?" I gestured with my arms to emphasize my words.

Chandler looked at me in that way that always made me weak. I inhaled a rugged breath and tried to understand why he had such power over me. Honestly, everything about him was too much for me to handle. It was those dark, hazel eyes, and the way they held me and threatened to pierce right through the armor I hid behind. His lips always looked incredibly inviting, but still flinched ever so slightly. He was sexy. Those strong hands were included in every single thing I loved about him—right down to that little scar above his left eye. It gave his face character.

I knew what he was thinking. As a matter of fact, I knew him better than he knew himself. I knew his thoughts before he could even formulate them into words. His handsome face always gave him away.

Our story was tragic, forbidden, and now there was a serious disconnect. Something had to give.

"You come here only able to spare a few hours, get what you want, then you expect me to be grateful for what little I got," he said.

We'd had this discussion before, and he was right, but what could I do? What could I say? Was I wrong to long for the passion we'd shared? More and more, it made me feel like Kevin and I were going through the motions.

"What we have is real. I recognize what I feel. This isn't a game for me," I said.

The silence was so thick it felt like I could slice it with a dull butter knife. It hung in the air until I felt like I had to say something else, to bring sound back into the room.

"There are no guarantees. You can say it's all about missed opportunities, but the truth is, something brought us close in this way," I said. "I wish we…"

"You wish we could what, Darby?"

"I wish we could make the best of it. I don't want to fight with you." I moved closer to him, but he pulled away. It was subtle. He turned his cheek ever so slightly, but still I noticed it—felt it—and he may as well have slapped me clear across the face. That's how much it hurt.

"Don't do this. Don't mess up what we have here," I urged.

That really made him pull away. He turned and walked to the other side of the room. From there, he stood and looked at me. He wore nothing but his briefs. His skin was still covered with a thin layer of sweat. My sweat, our sweat. I couldn't fathom why it had to end like this.

"What do we have, Darby?"

The tone of his voice was so cold and disconnected, it shook me to my core. Moments before, that same voice was whispering hot and heavy explicit words in my ears.

"Is this what you like?" *It* had asked, in sensual whispers.

"Right there? Is that your spot?" *It* teased.

"Tell me it's mine." *It* insisted.

Now, he stood across the room, looked at me like he needed me to make a choice. A choice he knew deep inside I couldn't make.

"Seriously." He chuckled. "Tell me. What do we really have here?"

"Don't do this," I begged.

"Don't do what?" Now his tone had changed. He was angry. He frowned as he spoke.

I inched a bit closer, but I didn't want to crowd him. I wanted him to remember what we had shared. How could he love me like that, then minutes later look at me with such disdain in his eyes? Yes, there was definitely a serious disconnect.

I couldn't help myself. Despite the tension in the room, my eyes quickly glanced down at my watch.

"That's the kind of shit I'm talking about!" he snapped.

I already knew what he was talking about, but what could I do? This wasn't supposed to happen. I was supposed to rush, get dressed, and hit the road. Who knew he'd choose this moment to have a complete melt down?

"You should go," he finally said. He sounded frustrated and through.

I didn't want to leave him like this. I needed to comfort him, to tell him whatever might get him back on board. There was no way I could walk out and leave him like that, despite the fact that I needed to go.

"We need to talk," I said.

He closed his eyes and shook his head. It was as if he thought our situation was hopeless, and that was the very last thing I needed. What happened to the loving and understanding we had shared?

"Go on home. Go home to your husband before he calls again and you expect me to be quiet."

As luck would have it, the moment I exhaled, my cell phone rang. Without saying another word, I looked at Chandler, shook my head, pressed the talk button, and walked out of the hotel room.

"I'm on my way," I answered.

41

IVEE

As I sat at my desk, on the phone, a sobering thought flooded my mind. I was very close to the point where I could say I hated my life. It seemed like every day there was a new stipulation related to the damn DWI charge.

"I don't understand why I have to do all of this, and I have an attorney. And let's not forget, it's not like I've admitted guilt. I haven't even had my day in court or anything like that."

"Ivee, I tried to explain this process to you. This is all part of the fighting process."

"How is me going to a drug rehab part of the fight? I don't understand. That's like saying I'm guilty!" I yelled.

I heard Ted exhale on the other end, but I didn't care. He was my lawyer. He was the one being paid to make the mess go away, and instead, all he had done was come back with one stipulation after another—none of which had been good for me. What in the hell would've happened if I had gone at it alone?

"It's not drug rehab. It's DWI education classes. There is a huge difference. You simply need to take some alcohol education courses. They're not that expensive, and in all honesty, it's three, four-hour sessions. You can knock that out in one week."

My eyes burned. I didn't want to go to drunk-driving classes, and I damn sure didn't want to have to pay for the misery of going.

"First, I'm treated like a criminal, handcuffed, and sent to jail. Then, even with a lawyer, I've gotta pay all these damn fines, plus I have to blow into a freakin' device just to start my car, and now I have to go to some meeting like I have a drinking problem. This is all too damn much, and I'm not doing it!"

"And you don't have to. You don't have to do anything you don't want to do. But if you want to be able to drive at your own free will, you will need to complete the ignition interlock program. And, if you want to qualify for probation instead of jail, you will have to show the judge proof that you've successfully completed the alcohol education courses. Then once you get probation, it's still not over. You will get community service, in addition to whatever fine the judge slaps you with."

I allowed his words to sink in. The lengthy summary made it all hard for me to swallow.

"So many other people have more of a drinking problem than me. I made one mistake. My girlfriend—she carries a flask in her purse," I said.

Ted chuckled. "Yeah, that's probably a person with a problem, but the difference between you and that person is, she didn't get arrested and charged with DWI. You did. I'm trying to work with you here, Ivee, but if you don't think my services are up to par, I will gladly refer you to another attorney. I've handled enough of these cases to tell you this—gone are the days when you get caught with a DWI and get a slap on the wrist."

"I'm not looking for a slap on the wrist. All I'm saying is there's all of these stipulations, and I haven't even been convicted yet," I stressed.

"And you don't want to be either. I'm working on a diversion program, but, Ivee, even with that, you will still have to come out of pocket, and the judge can still decide to do whatever he wants. That is the reason we are taking all of these precautions. It's our hope that when we go before the judge and he sees what we've already put in place, there will be no doubt in his mind that you've learned your lesson, and that you would be a perfect candidate for probation."

There was silence.

I sighed hard. Based on what Ted had told me, it didn't appear that I really had a choice. I always thought if I had an attorney, my chances of beating this whole thing would be easier. This all felt like stuff I couldn't have gotten on my own or with a public defender. I couldn't come right out and say that to Ted, but in my heart of hearts, I didn't feel like we were getting our money's worth.

"Probation is a privilege—not a luxury," he said.

"Okay, Ted, I understand, but there's something that's really bothering me. With all due respect, what would this experience be like for me if I didn't have a lawyer?"

"It wouldn't be good, Ivee. It's like I told you before, if you have any problem with the work I'm doing on your behalf, and you don't think the services I provide are worth the discounted fee I'm charging, I'll gladly refer you to another lawyer. The call is yours."

I felt like crap after we ended the call. I wasn't sure what I expected him to do. I was confused. I really thought this whole thing would play out differently. I thought with him as my front man, my life would barely be impacted. But as it stood, I rarely drove because of the embarrassment of the ignition lock, and I had all but turned into a hermit.

When my cell phone rang, I didn't even want to answer it. I felt completely helpless. That single mistake had turned my entire life upside down. I thought about my friends and how much we enjoyed our time at happy hour. I rarely returned their calls, and they were probably wondering whether I had fallen off the face of the earth. Even after we talked at Peta's house about not isolating ourselves, I simply didn't feel like being bothered.

My eyes focused on Felicia's name on my caller ID screen. Voice-mail clicked in and the phone stopped ringing. *Why had this happened to me?* Before my mind could answer the question, the phone began to ring again. I rolled my eyes. It was Felicia again. Why couldn't she take no for an answer? I wasn't in the mood to talk to anyone.

The ringing stopped, and I decided to gather my things so I could wait for my ride.

As I picked up the folders from my desk, the cell phone rang yet again. And it was Felicia again.

"Hello?" I answered.

"Dang, Ivee, what's going on with you these days? It's so hard to catch you on the phone," she complained.

Felicia spoke so fast it was as if she needed to get all of her thoughts out for fear she wouldn't be able to reach me again.

"Lots going on. That's all," I said.

"Uh, who doesn't have lots going on? You're not the only person going through stuff, you know. When was the last time you talked to anyone? We haven't had a good session for quite some time. It's like happy hour is so dead these days."

The sudden change in her voice gave me pause.

"Oh, I'm sorry, Ivee. I didn't mean to bring up happy hour."

"Felicia, you can talk about alcohol. You can even talk about happy hour. I still drink. You act like I'm some delicate alcoholic. I made a simple mistake! How many times have we all stumbled out of the bar and gotten behind the wheel? We've taken that gamble multiple times. I'm no more of a drunk than Peta, Darby, or even you! The police happened to catch me, and now my life is a living hell," I said.

When I looked up and saw Geneva who stood in my doorway, I nearly dropped the phone.

"Oh, damn!" I murmured.

42

PETA

The thick, dark curtains were drawn to keep the room gloomy to match my mood. I ignored one call after another, including Gordon's. If I didn't have a daughter who looked up to me, I would've stayed in bed for days at a time. Everything in my world had gone in the wrong direction, and I didn't see a way out.

After the twentieth call in a row, I finally gave in and answered.

"It's about time," Darby greeted me. "What's wrong with you?"

"Too much. She's running commercials! I've seen them for the past two weeks, and I'm sick over this!" I barked into the phone.

"Calm down."

For a while longer, Darby filled me in on details about her rendezvous. As she spoke, my mind was on all that was wrong in my own life. If it wasn't Kyle skirting his responsibilities, it was Gordon bitching about me not calling.

"...so just roll with it, that's what I'm doing," said Darby.

We were supposed to be talking about the strange and awkward affair she was caught up in, but the scream I belted out when Pamela's commercial came on again, brought that conversation to a halt.

"Pamela? Is that the same woman who kept calling you and asking all the doggone questions?"

"Yes, that's her! I swore she was up to something, but for the life of me, I didn't think she was trying to get next to me so she could become my competition. I'm so tired, Darby. I'm so tired. Every damn thing is falling apart. Kyle keeps trying to make me believe I wanted him to stop supporting his child, and this dirty trick stole my business idea right from under me! I don't know how much more I can handle," I cried.

"Wait, Peta, don't talk like that. Here, I'm coming over."

"Oh, God! No, please don't. I'm in no condition to entertain company. My place is a mess. I'm low on food, and I wouldn't make the best company right now."

"You've got a lot on your plate, and I'm worried about you. You don't get to become a recluse. It's not gonna happen on my watch. Get up and wash your behind. I'll be there in thirty minutes!"

The next thing I knew, the call had ended. I should've kept my mouth shut. I didn't need to vent. I should've kept the thoughts to myself.

It felt more like five minutes instead of thirty had passed when the doorbell rang.

I sighed and pulled myself to the front door.

"Hey, honey," Darby greeted me. Before I could respond, she grabbed my hand. "C'mon."

I frowned. "Where are we going?"

"The spa. They were able to squeeze us in. We don't have a lot of time. We need to go." Darby pulled her purse up on her shoulder.

"The spa? I haven't been to a spa in so long, I wouldn't know what to—"

"Enough of the talking. I've already paid, so we have to go. I don't have money to waste."

"Oh, Darby. You shouldn't have spent that kind of money. What's gonna happen when Kevin finds out?"

Darby's face clouded over. She pursed her lips and twisted her mouth then spoke.

"He don't know nothing about this money, and this ain't none of his business," she said with a sassy tone.

"Well, I guess when you put it like that." The truth was, I didn't feel like going anywhere. I wanted to stay home, monitor my TV for Pamela's flashy, new commercials, and have my own little pity party.

Darby wasn't having it. She all but dragged me out of the house, put me in the passenger seat of her car, and even tried to buckle my seatbelt.

"Ummm, I can handle that," I said.

"I can't believe Pamela did that to you." Darby frowned as she drove.

"You can add her to the list of people who act like I'm nothing more than a doormat. You still carry that flask?"

"You know I do." Darby smiled. "My bag is on the floor behind your seat."

I reached back and grabbed Darby's Michael Kors bag. I dug in and pulled out the flashy flask. After several swigs from the little bottle, I started to feel better.

"Oh, I'm sorry. We were supposed to be talking about you and Chandler, and you had to come over and rescue me."

"That Chandler situation is a big ol' funky hot mess!" Darby exited the freeway and prepared to turn right. "I don't know how we've developed such strong feelings for each other over such a short period of time."

"How often do you guys see each other?"

"At least three times a week," she admitted. "Sometimes more."

"Wow!"

"I know. I know, but I go through the motions at home with Kevin and the kids, and the minute I get some free time, I'm rushing off to meet him somewhere," Darby said. "And it seems like we're meeting even more even after he tried to dump me!"

"Do you think he really cares about you?"

"It doesn't matter whether he does or not. When I'm with him, I feel like I'm the most important woman in the world. He's everything Kevin is not, and I don't know how to pull away from him."

"Damn, Darby, what are you gonna do?"

"I don't know. I really don't."

We arrived at the spa with only a few minutes to spare. We changed into our thick, white terry robes, and slipped right into relaxation. I had nearly drained Darby's flask by the time we arrived, but we were greeted with wine, so I felt better than I had in a very long time.

Darby paid for massages, facials, and footbaths. For a long while, we enjoyed the quiet and serenity of the place. I was so glad she had forced me to go. During my quiet time, I thought about everything that had happened to me. I thought about the trucks, Kyle and the letter, and Pamela, who had infiltrated my business to duplicate it and start her own.

We didn't get to stay at the spa for the entire day, since Darby had to get home to cook for her family, but the few hours we spent there were priceless.

"You are the very best," I told her.

"Sometimes, with all the craziness going on in our lives, we need to take some time out for ourselves."

"What are you gonna do, Darby? Your emotional attachment to Chandler is so bizarre to me."

"Girl, imagine how it is to me! Years ago, when I started communicating with him, it really was so I could get close to him and get revenge."

"What was the plan?" I asked.

Darby paused, as if she was trying to think of how to answer the question. She shook her head and a smirk made its way to her face.

"You're not gonna believe me if I tell you."

I pulled back a little. Now, I desperately wanted to know.

"Try me," I said.

"I was gonna plant some drugs at his place."

"Girl! Stop!" That's not what I expected her to say.

She laughed a little to herself. I watched as her expression changed like she had gone to a faraway place.

"Yes. That's what I was gonna do, and you couldn't tell me it wasn't a good plan. I was gonna get close, and then move in for the kill," she said.

"Drugs and all, huh? But, okay, what happened to that plan?"

"First of all, I watched him for a very long time, before I made my move. Then, it took a lot longer to get close to him than I expected. Finally, once I got close to him, I realized he wasn't this horrible person I'd made him out to be. By then, we had to established trust, and once that happened, things took a turn."

"I don't know what to say," I admitted.

The idea that Darby was falling in love with the man who had killed her sister was completely outside the realm of possibility to me. I didn't know what to say.

"And what's worse, the man is too damn good in bed. It's all I can think about. I compare him to Kevin in everything he does. It's wrong. It's dysfunctional, but it feels so good, and I don't even know how to begin to try and get out."

As I listened to Darby pour her heart out, I felt like such a fraud.

I had nothing to offer. I listened to her story, but my mind was fixed on what I needed to do to get back at Kyle and Pamela.

"And Kevin is clueless?" I asked.

"You know he's so damn self-absorbed, as long as I fix his food and wait on him and the boys, I could move Chandler in and he wouldn't be the wiser."

We laughed.

"You gotta go back home, or can you come over?" she asked me.

I had a free night since Kyle was picking Kendal up from school, but I needed a different kind of company, and I had to find a delicate way to tell her.

"The spa was good, but now I need a different kind of release, and I've gotta put in some work to get Gordon over," I said skittishly.

Darby laughed.

"Girl, go get yours in, 'cause I definitely get mine in. We'll spend some time together tomorrow once I get everyone out the door, okay?"

"That'll work," I said as Darby pulled up at my house. Before I got out of the car, she reached into the console in her car and pulled out an envelope.

"Don't make anything out of this. I've had this side hustle that's done better than I expected."

I looked at the thick envelope as she extended it in my direction.

"What is this?"

"It's a gift to you and Kendal," Darby said.

I peeked inside the envelope and saw bills that I hadn't seen in a very long time. I paused for a moment and tried to tame my trembling hands.

"Oh, Darby, I can't," I said.

"Like hell you can't! This is not a loan. This is a gift. Don't take it for you. Take it for Kendal," she said.

When she looked at her watch, I realized that I needed to go. Darby had to get home.

"I don't know what to say," I said as I accepted the envelope.

I hugged her and got out of the car.

43

DARBY

Wednesdays were kind of tricky in the Jaxon household. Sometimes, we met with some of Kevin's coworkers and their families for dinner, and other times, we had takeout. It was my easy day of the week. But this week, they were going to a restaurant I didn't care for, and I let it be known that I would not be going. Kevin was okay with that. He had some business he needed to discuss with his coworkers, so I would've been setting myself up for a major snooze fest if I had gone.

"You want us to bring you something back?" Kevin asked.

He and the boys were about to walk out of the door.

"No, I'm good. If I get hungry, I'll pull something from the freezer," I said.

In truth, I wanted him out the door. I had already received two text messages that I hadn't been able to respond to, and the agony was nearly killing me. Chandler didn't usually text during family hours. We communicated during the day, when he knew I was alone, or very late at night.

"Okay, later then," Kevin said as he eased out the door behind the boys. "Oh, and we need to discuss that new bike you bought for Jr."

I rolled my eyes. That was a conversation we'd never have if I could help it. That new bike had been paid off, and worth every penny.

Once alone, I fixed a drink. Then, I waited a good ten minutes before I picked up my cell phone. Out of courtesy, I sent Chandler a text first to see if he was available.

When I asked the question, I expected him to reply with a text message. Instead, my phone rang.

"What are you doing?" His voice always did something to me. I couldn't explain it, but it made me weak and wanting.

"I'm having a drink now, and am about to warm up some food. Why do you ask?"

"I'm close to you," he said.

The certainty, with which he said it, triggered something in me that made me giddy. The butterflies sprang to life in the pit of my belly. This was completely unexpected, but it was a pleasant surprise. Chandler didn't know exactly where I lived, but he knew I was in Katy.

"How close is close?" I finished off the drink.

"I'm at the Omni, off of I-10," he said.

Lately, we'd been meeting up more frequently. Carla mentioned to me that she knew something was up because she'd come by the house to talk to me several times, and I was gone. I hadn't come clean to her about Chandler. The closest I'd come was to the girls and when I was at Peta's house, but her misery was far more serious than mine.

I had gone off the deep end, but it felt so incredible, I couldn't pull back.

"The Omni." I didn't ask. I simply repeated what he'd said.

"Yes, Room 9872," he said. "The view from here is magnificent. I'd like to fuck you up against the window. I know how much you enjoy me from behind," he said.

He stated that as if it was a fact. I didn't understand the hold he had over me, and I never spent too much time trying to figure it out. I considered another drink, but decided not to since I'd be driving.

Chandler's voice was the kind wet dreams were made of. His body was beyond exceptional, and although there was no future for us, I couldn't get enough of him or what he gave me.

"That *is* really close to me," I said.

"You should go into the office in your house, lock the door, and sneak out. I can send a car for you," he offered.

"No need. I'm free tonight, but I can't stay all night," I warned.

"I understand. So, when should I expect you?"

"I'll be there in twenty. Let me freshen up," I said.

"No, come like you are. You can freshen up here," he said.

"Okay," I lied.

Once I hung up, I stripped, rushed into the bathroom and wet a face towel with warm water. I lathered soap and cleaned myself up the best I could. I slipped into an off-the-shoulder, hip-hugging dress, and stepped into high-heeled sandals.

Before I left, I walked into the pantry and removed the vodka from my hiding place. I took two quick shots and replaced the bottle.

The Omni Hotel wasn't far from my house, and as I drove, I thought of how long I'd be able to stay. When I got to I-10, it made sense that I'd stay until eleven o'clock. Kevin and the boys would be back, but they'd be in bed. That would give me four solid hours.

When I pulled up in front of the hotel, I told myself that midnight wouldn't be bad, especially since I decided I could say I went out with one of the girls who had a fight with her man or something. Midnight it would be.

As I rode the elevator up, the fight idea began to sound better and better.

The moment I stepped into the nice room, Chandler's tongue

was down my throat. I nearly melted, right there in his arms, up against the door. The hint of liquor on his tongue was like an aphrodisiac to me. I wanted more.

He slid his hands up my thighs and pulled back.

"Wow, no panties. I like the way your mind works, Darby." A wicked grin spread across his handsome face.

We peeled each other's clothes off at the door. I waited for him to put the condom on, then I straddled him as he sat with his back against the door. I rode him methodically and felt every single inch of him.

"You feel so damn good," Chandler huffed. "I enjoy the naked shots you text, but there's nothing better than having you here in the flesh."

I bit at his ear, clawed at his neck, and lowered my head to take his nipple into my mouth.

"Oh, Chandler," I cried.

Moments later, I exploded and felt suspended in an indiscernible bliss.

Afterward, we shared a drink. It was aged scotch, and it smelled expensive before it settled onto my taste buds. It was silky smooth. Chandler poured us a refill the moment he fed me the last drops from the glass.

I felt myself as I began to slip away. It felt good, and just when my head was swimming in mellow waves, Chandler manhandled me. He pinned my naked body against the large, smoked glass, floor-to-ceiling window like he had promised.

Twinkling lights glistened out as far as my eyes could see, and it looked like we floated high above a blanket of stars. He had been correct. I did enjoy him when he took me from behind. We enjoyed each other for hours.

My head felt like a bulldozer had done major damage. I grabbed it, eased up in bed, struggled to catch my bearings as I wondered why I was looking at a pink and orange light outside. Suddenly it registered. My heart slammed against my ribcage when I realized that I had a front row seat to daybreak, courtesy of the magnificent view from the Omni Hotel room.

I had spent the entire night with Chandler.

"OH MY GOD!"

44

IVEE

Geneva didn't have to eavesdrop to hear what I had fought so hard to hide. I had all but spelled it out over the damn phone to Felicia. There was a reason I had avoided all of their calls before. It had taken one simple phone call to undermine weeks of careful thought and plotting.

Is there something you want to share with me? Those were Geneva's words and they rang in my head over and over again.

As I sat in the back seat of the chauffeured car, my mind was stuck on instant replay. Geneva's words haunted me. What else could she have been referring to? I was beyond paranoid since I couldn't be sure how much she had overheard.

She had never been one to play her full hand. For all I knew, she was probably already planning my demise. This was probably the final thing she needed to nail my coffin closed for good. Back in the day, something like a DWI arrest would've been a small bleep on her radar.

Geneva was crass and hardcore. She worked hard, and played even harder, so I could only imagine she might have had run-ins with alcohol and the law before. But now that the Carson thing was still in a state of disarray, what would've once been a small incident could now be a major collision.

Why had she even asked the question? It wasn't like she waited on the answer.

Before I could answer her question, she'd flicked her wrist, glanced at her watch, and said, "Oh, look at the time. I have a conference call in less than five. I'll be back by tomorrow. That's Thursday. You will be in, right?"

Unable to speak, I simply nodded. Was my mouth agape?

It had all been completely fake, the whole look-at-the-time act. That was not like Geneva. She shot straight from the hip at all times. Geneva didn't care how it went down. She gave it to us raw, and before anyone could adjust, she'd give some more.

"Hello? Hello?"

That was when I realized I hadn't ended the call with Felicia. It had all happened so fast. I was sick to my stomach. Could I lose my job over the DWI arrest? I needed to talk to Ted.

"Felicia, I need to go," I said.

"But, Ivee, I wanted to ask you—"

"Not now. I need to go. I'll catch up with you later."

The minute I ended the call with her, Jessica's voice boomed through the phone on my desk.

"Your ride is here," she sang.

"Oh, okay, I'll be right there."

I was flustered and thrown completely off. Geneva's little maneuver had left me uneasy. That's when the lie I had told Jessica came to mind.

My first day back at the office, I told Jessica that Zion had wrecked my car in an accident and it was being repaired.

"Well, the least he could've done was gotten you a rental, huh?"

"Oh, the whole idea of the accident spooked me so much, I decided I could use the break and be chauffeured around for a while."

That, I thought, would hold me over until I got used to the idea of blowing into a device to check my breath before I could drive.

What if someone at work saw me doing that crap? Then what?

I dialed Ted's office. His secretary told me he had been in court all day. She assured me that she'd deliver my message, but that did nothing to ease my concern.

In my mind, I combed over every little thing I had said to everyone after the arrest. Luckily, I hadn't discussed my personal business with too many people. But what if Geneva started to interview people about what I had told them? The little I had made up would probably be enough to incriminate me.

She probably heard the entire thing about me being arrested, and my talk about a drinking problem, and oh, God! I grabbed my forehead. My mind spun out of control. There was no way in the world that I could lose my job. The fact that I had snagged Wayne and his business as a client would soon mean nothing. All of that hard work would be overshadowed by one simple mistake.

The way Geneva's face twisted when she asked me the question. Then, before I could even formulate an answer, the way she high-tailed it out of there, it all spelled trouble for me. I just knew it.

At home, I waited for Ted to return my call. When I called the office again, they said he still hadn't called in for messages. I didn't want to call back, but I needed him to recognize that he did work for me, and that my calls were very important.

I was a nervous wreck. Geneva had heard enough to put two and two together. The more I wracked my brain over the conversation with Felicia, the more I'd forgotten exactly what I had said.

Zion wasn't home yet, and I had no one else to bounce my destructive thoughts off of. I walked over to the bar and pulled out a bottle.

Suddenly, I stopped.

Did I have a drinking problem? I had always considered myself to be little more than a social drinker. I was like most women. We enjoyed a cocktail here and there, but it wasn't like I'd take a bottle of vodka and turn it up, was it?

I stood and stared at the bottle.

When does it cross the line?

Was my arrest a simple mistake, or was it a sign of something far worse? What if I did have a problem, but I was too close to it to recognize or acknowledge it? Zion and I would usually unwind with drinks in the evening. I always had a cocktail with lunch, and our old, weekly happy hour outings were tales that legends and urban myths were made of.

For years, I had told myself I felt more at ease, better, and less stressed after I had enjoyed a drink, but I only indulged socially.

Could there be such a thing as a social alcoholic?

"For Christ's sake! Hasn't that caused us enough problems?"

Zion's voice took me by surprise. I looked over at him and wondered if it would even be worth it to respond to his little comment.

"Ted called me," he said as he walked all the way into the house. "I know good and well you're not about to drink some more."

His tone was laced with a mixture of shock and disgust.

"I'm sorry. Since when did I become an alcoholic?" I asked sarcastically.

"Since we've been slapped with what's about to be damn near a ten-thousand-dollar bill connected to your DWI arrest," he huffed.

There it was. That was what had become the dig that kept on giving.

"How long, Zion?"

He edged past me and pulled the refrigerator open.

I turned and asked, "Seriously. How much longer?"

Once he closed the door, Zion cocked his head and looked at

me quizzically. He removed the cap from a sports drink, and then took a swig. Afterwards, he fell back against the refrigerator door, and appeared as if he needed to study me before he answered.

I waited.

"What are you talking about, woman?" he finally asked.

"I just wanna know. How long are you gonna continue to spank me for the same mistake?"

45

PETA

"We ain't tryin' to tell you how to run your business or nothin' like that, but I don't know why you would put two trucks at the same location," Beverly said into my ear. I put my drink down. I had learned my lesson after I failed to pay attention to her last warning phone call, but that was not about to happen again. "What are you talking about?"

"Farah and I were talking about the new truck, and we've been so slow all morning. I couldn't take it anymore. Farah over there talking about 'Ms. Peta knows what she's doing,' and maybe you do, but the mess don't make no sense to me. I could've been at home watching *Judge Judy* if I'd known it was gonna be this slow," she complained.

"Beverly, the other truck is in Sugar Land. I don't know what you're talking about."

While I was still on the phone, she began to talk to Farah. I polished off my drink. I had long convinced myself that with all the crap that now dominated my life, happy hour was any time of day I felt the need to get away.

"Farah, is that another mobile boutique parked right over there with a line wrapped damn near around the courtyard?" Beverly asked sarcastically. She returned to our call. "Like I said, I coulda stayed at home for this foolishness!"

"Beverly, there are only two trucks. If Sugar Land is there, I need to call Cecily and figure out what's going on. I did not approve a move, and why would I send it out there anyway? That makes no sense."

"That's what I tried to tell Farah. You know what. I'ma 'bout to go and see what the hell they giving out for free over there, 'cause ain't no way folks gon' be standing in a line like that to spend money," Beverly said. "'Specially when we sittin' over here on empty like this!"

I had a strong feeling about exactly what was going on, and I wouldn't get any answers if I stayed on the phone. I went to the bathroom, brushed my teeth, and rushed to my car.

When I arrived at the campus in Katy, I could see exactly why Beverly was confused. The new mobile boutique was nearly twice the size of mine. The line she complained about had shrunk a bit, and several people had wandered over to our truck. But that new, big fancy truck was not mine.

I poured myself a glass of mimosa in hopes that it would help calm my building temper.

"Hey, Ms. Peta, they're giving away one item with the purchase of two! And with that, they're offering a coupon for fifty percent off on the next visit."

I rolled my eyes. *The very last thing I needed on top of everything else was—*

That's when it slapped me all upside my face.

"She brought it right here to my very own backyard. I had finally had enough!" I swallowed the rest of my drink and got up.

Farah's eyebrows were knitted in concentration as she focused on the activity that buzzed across the courtyard. It was all-quiet in our RV. I was ready to spit fire.

"If that trick is over there in that truck, so help me God, I may be going to jail today," I said. I put the empty glass down and hopped out of the vehicle.

"Oh, Ms. Peta, don't you do nothing stupid now!" Farah yelled after me.

By the time she had gotten out to follow me, I had already made my way across the courtyard and up to the front of the line.

"Excuse me," I said. "Pardon me. Can I squeeze by?"

It didn't take long for me to get to the front of the line, but that's where I had to stop. The RV was packed to the hilt. Sounds of chatter, music, and laughter floated out toward those of us who were unfortunate enough to have to stand in line and wait.

"Is Pamela in there?" I yelled from my perch in line.

A few heads turned in my direction, but no one responded. I was fit to be tied. With all the problems I'd had, I couldn't believe that backstabbing skank had the audacity to show up on my turf. I was full of liquid courage and fed up. That was a dangerous combination but still, I charged forward.

"Excuse me. Heee-llo," I repeated more loudly.

I felt bad for the person in front of me and the one behind me, but this was not about them. It was about the bitch who had pushed me to the limit.

Once I got tired of being ignored, I began to charge my way forward.

"I'm sorry. I need to get in there," I said as I moved.

"You need to wait your turn," another woman said and shoved me back.

Farah stood off to the side and tried to reason with me. "Ms. Peta, can I have a word, please?"

I ignored her and the woman who pushed me, and moved until

I worked my way up to the door. I squeezed onto the steps and could hardly believe my eyes when I caught a glimpse of the inside of the RV.

Pamela had studied my business to the tee. Her custom-designed interior looked like she had spent a mint.

A woman whose cute outfit matched the brown and turquoise setting looked at me as if I was a nuisance.

"Ma'am, you need to wait your turn like everyone else," she snarled.

"You don't understand. Where's Pamela Evans?" I asked.

By then, I was nearly out of breath and must've seemed as crazy as I jumped the line.

"Ma'am, Pamela is not here."

At that point, she had stopped working with her customer to focus her wrath on me. "If you don't leave, we're gonna have to call security. You are disrupting business." She pointed a crooked, bony finger toward a sign that was plastered up against the door.

It read that they had the right to refuse service to anyone. I wanted to rip it from the wall and tell her what she could do with her sign. I also wanted to tell her that had it not been for me, she wouldn't have a job or a meaningless sign to point to in the first damn place.

"Get Pamela on the phone, please," I said.

"Lady, I don't have time for this. Can't you see we are super busy? Leave your name and number, and I'll get a message to Pamela for you."

"I need you to get her out here now!"

"Lady!" The woman whipped around and threw a hand onto her hip. She shifted her weight to one side and gave me a look that could kill. "You are really trying me. I'm busy. I don't have time to call Pamela right now. Now, I've already offered to put you in touch with her. That's the best I can do for you," she said.

"I'm not moving an inch until you get her on the phone!"

Several people in line threw up their hands and stormed away in a huff. When the saleswoman saw them go over to my RV, she fumbled and grabbed a phone.

The chattering around me prevented me from hearing her entire conversation, but it was clear she was not happy.

"I don't know. Keeps yelling for you," she said into the phone.

She turned back and looked at me. The RV was still crowded, so she couldn't move too far away.

"Okay. I'll tell her."

A few seconds later, she ended the call and turned her attention back to me.

"Ms. Evans is at a meeting, but she says she'll call you when she's free. She also told me to tell you that if you continue to disrupt business she will have no other choice but to call security on you," the woman said.

That was when I lost it.

47

DARBY

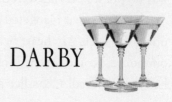

I felt like a wayward teenager who had to try and sneak back into the house after she had missed her curfew again. As I sped along I-10 toward my exit, I prayed that Kevin was not downstairs asleep on the sofa.

For the first time since I woke next to Chandler, I was grateful that he had the wherewithal to come close to me. That meant I'd make it home in record time. Since the only people on the roads at that time of morning were obviously adulterers and shift workers, there was no traffic jam.

I had never wanted a job so badly.

Crazy thoughts flew around in my brain like frantic, trapped birds. *What can I possibly say to explain away the fact that I've been out all night long?*

"Please, don't let him be on the friggin' couch!"

Usually, when I was out with the girls, Kevin would meet me right at the sofa. When I had pried myself away from Chandler, who was still in a drunken fog, I tried to explain I had to go, and I wanted to kick myself. He knew better. Hell, I knew better.

How in the world could I have allowed that to happen? Would it be wrong for me to pray to God for mercy in this situation?

It was five-fifteen in the morning, and I had to hightail it home before my husband realized I had been gone all night. I didn't even attempt to look at my cell phone. I had turned it off the minute I got off the freeway and slipped it under the seat of my car. There was no point in trying to retrieve it now.

A layer of sweat blanketed my forehead, and I felt a trickle run down my back. My heart beat so fast and loud as I pulled up to our house, I could barely think straight. Then it dawned on me—I hadn't showered! Chandler and I drank and fucked all over the room so many times, we probably passed out and fell off to sleep.

"Damn! I can't crawl home in the wee hours of the morning smelling like liquor and stale sex!"

I stopped the car as I reached for the button on the garage opener. It was clear I hadn't thought the situation through. It dawned on me that there was no way I could put my car back into the garage. That's where it was when Kevin and the boys left earlier, or actually, yesterday.

If I opened the garage door, the sound would wake Kevin and the boys, and there would be no question that I had just made it home. I decided to take my chances and park on the street. It didn't matter that I never did that. Desperate measures called for desperate actions.

After I parked the car, I searched for the wet wipes I kept in the middle console. I snatched a couple sheets from the packet and tried to wipe my lover's scent off my body.

That didn't help since the moist towelettes left me smelling fresh. Suddenly, I didn't know what would be worse. It seemed like I couldn't stop messing up. If I couldn't explain away the scent of sex and alcohol that seeped from my pores, how would I explain why I smelled so refreshed at the crack of dawn?

"To hell with it all!"

I eased out of my shoes when I stepped out of the car. The air smelled dewy fresh and felt damp against my skin. Barefoot, I calmly padded my way up to the door. With sunrise on my heels, I quietly unlocked the front door and slipped inside. When I realized that the entire house was still calm and quiet, I released a breath that felt as if I had held it trapped in my lungs all the way home.

I could've cried tears of joy when it became obvious to me that I had literally made it home scot-free.

Quietly, I removed the top from the large basket near the door and dropped my shoes into it. Kevin was upstairs, so I crept into the laundry room and grabbed a sheet. It didn't matter that it was dirty. I eased onto the sofa and pulled the sheet over my body.

Moments after I had closed my eyes, my heart froze when I felt sudden brightness flood the room.

"This shit has got to stop!"

Busted!

Fear gripped my heart like a vise, and I didn't want to open my eyes. I wondered how long he'd stand there as I hoped my pounding heart didn't crack my ribcage. I couldn't continue to live the way I had been going for the past few months. It was time to come clean.

"You don't know how to answer your phone anymore, huh?" he asked.

Visions of my life, as I knew it, flashed before my eyes as the end drew near. I didn't budge. Fear rippled up and down my spine.

"You and your girls need to realize you're not in college anymore, dammit! You come sneaking up in here like I wouldn't know that you've been out damn near all night?"

My eyes snapped open. My entire body was flushed with heat as Kevin's words ran through me. I was totally taken aback. The only question I asked myself was whether I was going to accept the obvious help God had graciously handed me.

I turned my head toward my husband, who stood with a justified scowl across his face. Just when I thought I didn't have the stamina for lying anymore, some words upchucked and spilled from my lips. It was as if my brain and lips took on a life of their own. I had been ready to throw in the towel the minute the bright lights blared on, but suddenly, I heard myself say, "Peta is really having a hard time right now, that's all," I murmured.

I purposely averted my eyes as I spoke.

For a long time, he didn't say anything. And that awkward silence forced me to look at him. Kevin's jaw tensed. He gulped and stared back at me, seemingly unable to speak. He jerked his head sideways, and I braced myself for the worst. He angled his body, edged past the sofa, and strode toward the front door.

Without another word, he threw the deadbolt, flicked off the light, and grumbled under his breath before he grasped the railing and barreled up the steps.

I fell back onto the sofa and tried to calm myself.

48

IVEE

An entire week had passed since I had seen Geneva. I didn't know if she avoided me intentionally, but I didn't go out of my way to search for her either. In my mind, everyone was either against me, or they were busily thinking up ways to try and bring me down.

Zion and I moved around our house like two strangers who needed to get out of each other's way. It really bothered me, but since most of our conversations ended in yelling matches, I decided I'd keep my thoughts, fears, and ideas to myself.

I had to admit, being home on Thursday evenings was already a foreign concept to me, but our awkwardness made it even stranger.

"You need something?" he asked.

We had been in the living room watching the local news on TV when a story about a drunk driver who killed a deputy came on. I was tempted to change the channel, but luckily, Zion hadn't uttered a word about it. In the midst of all my complaints and all my rumblings, I was grateful to God that no one was hurt or killed when I got arrested.

"No, I'm good," I told him.

"Okay. Running to the store. I'll be back." He got up, put on his tennis shoes, grabbed his keys, and walked out of the door.

Once alone, I began to think about how I needed to protect myself at work. Ted had simply asked for a copy of my work contract, but I still hadn't heard back from him.

I had been tempted so many times to feel sorry for myself, but when I thought about what Kyle had done to Peta, or the mess Darby was stuck in, I tried to look at the bright side of my own horrible situation.

It hadn't been easy, but I had started to drive again. I still didn't drive to work, but I did drive to the Metro Park and Ride lot to get on a commuter bus that took dozens of professionals into downtown Houston.

For a change, I decided to do something I had avoided for far too long. I picked up my cell phone, dialed a number and waited.

"Heeeey, stranger!"

"Hey, Felicia, girl, I'm so sorry about the last time we were talking. I looked up and saw Geneva's butt standing there listening to my doggone conversation," I confessed.

"Uh-oh," Felicia said.

"Tell me about it."

"Has she struck yet?"

"No, and you know that's what's killing me the most. The wait for the other shoe to drop ain't no joke when it's one of Geneva's spiked heels. Well, I don't have to tell you. You know exactly what she's like."

"Yeah, she probably ran with that information and immediately went to work to see what destruction, if any, she could cause," Felicia said.

"Girl, I feel like such a head case. Seriously, now I'm always thinking someone is out to get me. This crap with the DWI has left me utterly messed up in the head. And I swear, I can't feel any benefits of having this doggone lawyer!"

"What do you mean, you don't feel the benefits? You're free, aren't you? I mean, you're not in jail, Ivee. Now, don't get me wrong. I can only imagine how hard this is for you, but, honey, let me tell you. That lawyer of yours has saved you unimaginable heartache."

"How do you know that? You ever been arrested for DWI?" I asked.

I really didn't mean for my question to sound as sarcastic as it did, but I hated when Zion, and even Ted, tried to convince me that I was better off because we had an attorney. We may have had Ted, but we still paid a grip in other fees. I still had a provisional license, had to sign up for classes, and much more.

"No, not me personally, but I have a cousin who spent six months in the county jail for it!"

"What? Six months in jail!"

"Ummm, yeah, and that ain't even the half of it. By the time she finished paying all those fees, she still had to drive around with this contraption on her car, and they made her pick up trash at the park," Felicia said.

"Girl, bite your tongue!"

"I'm dead serious."

"Well, shoot, how come she didn't have a lawyer?"

"Get real, Ivee. Do you think everyone can afford to pay for an attorney? She was trying to hide the whole thing from everyone, so she went with the public defender. Not only did her case drag on for months on end, but she said every time she had a court date, which was at least once every month, she'd be assigned to someone new, and that was like starting her case all over again."

I couldn't absorb all of what Felicia said. I didn't want to.

"Well, that's downright crazy. But public defenders are real attorneys, aren't they? And why was her case passed around so much?"

"That's what I'm trying to tell you. Yeah, they're real attorneys, but in many cases, they're just starting out. They don't have the years of experience of a lawyer who specializes in a particular area, and one day they may be working on a DWI case, the next, it could be shoplifting, then it could be rape. They don't have the time or the resources to focus on any one case in particular."

"I'm sorry, but I don't see how a first-time offender, with no prior criminal record, could spend more than a day in jail," I said adamantly.

"Well, you don't have to *see* it, but I'm telling you what happened to my cousin. And if you don't believe me, I can have her give you a call. You better believe you are way better off with representation than without!"

"Yeah, I guess so," I said.

I made a mental note to myself. I wouldn't express my concerns about Ted to anyone else.

"Oh, and also, she can barely get a good-paying job, since that damn arrest. It's still on her record, and if I'm not mistaken, I wanna say it's been something like three or four years now."

"Girl, please!"

I was suddenly mad that I had called Felicia back. The last thing I needed was something else to worry about connected to the arrest. Not only did I not know how it would impact my current job, but I hadn't even given thoughts to how it would impact my future. So, now I'd have an arrest record. Good Lord!

Before long, Zion came back. He had several bags that he brought in and took into the kitchen.

"Hey, babe?" he said.

That sounded odd to me because lately he'd call me by my name, if he called me at all.

"Yeah, what's up?"

"Ted wanted to know how much you know about your company's morality clause."

I whipped my head around in his direction. "The morality clause," I slowly repeated.

"Yeah, you do know one exists, right?"

Dammit! I need a drink!

49

PETA

In the midst of my belligerent tirade, I didn't see Pamela when she walked up. Had it not been for Beverly, she could've cold-cocked me, and I wouldn't have known what hit me. I could've killed that trick with my bare hands.

"Hey, Peta, how are you, honey?" She had the nerve to greet me like we were old friends.

When she approached, something in me clicked, and I swung.

"Oh my God! What the hell!" she screamed. She grabbed the side of her face and stumbled.

All of my rage and frustration barreled out at once, and my fists wouldn't stop. Soon, several women screamed and began to pull at us. We fell.

In one swift move, I felt myself being pulled up from the group that had tumbled to the ground. As I was pulled away, I swung and kicked at Pamela one last time.

"You backstabbing bitch! You used me!" I yelled.

"Get her off of me! Oh God! Get her off me!" Pamela screamed.

When I looked up, it was Beverly who had ushered me away from the melee and not a moment too soon. As she drove off in my car, I heard the faint sounds of sirens in the distance.

"I don't know what got into me," I said. "I'm tired. I'm so sick and tired." I buckled my seatbelt as she sped along the feeder road of I-10.

"I feel ya, Peta. I woulda whupped her ass for you if you had told me what that tramp did to you! She deserved that thumpin', no doubt!"

My nerves were a complete wreck, so I was glad Beverly decided to drive. For sure, I had lost it. I couldn't remember the last time I had gotten into an actual fistfight. I eased back in the seat and wondered how the hell my life had become this train wreck.

"You think she gon' try to press charges against you?" Beverly asked.

"Honestly, I really don't give a damn. She sought me out, blew my phone up, and begged for meetings so she could duplicate my business idea. I almost would've rather she'd been up front about what she was trying to do," I said. "And then, to park her truck in the exact same spot!"

"Yeah, that's ratchetness for real right there. Well, as far as I'm concerned, you did the right thing, and I'd tell anybody who wants to know that all I saw was you defending yourself."

Beverly was trying to be helpful, but I needed to think. I needed to figure out my next move. Pamela's trucks were now spread out across the city, and my business was in trouble.

Even if the insurance company came through with the money for the other two trucks, I didn't think it'd be enough to get me out of the hole. And then Kyle still refused to make this thing right with his child support, and that only made things harder.

"Turn at the next light," I told Beverly. "I really appreciate you helping me out back there. I probably would've killed that woman," I admitted.

"She deserved that ass whupping, for real. That was dirty what she did, and then she had the balls to sneak onto the RV? Oh, just thinking about it makes me want to turn this car around," Beverly said.

I laughed for the first time in a very long while and said, "That wouldn't be a good idea. If I go to jail, I'll need someone to bail me out."

She laughed at that.

As she drove along I-10, I didn't even want to ask her how she'd get back home or back to the RV. I wanted to get inside and get a drink.

"I'm gonna call and have my dude pick me up from here if that's okay with you, or I could walk up to the gas station around the corner," she said.

I swatted away the idea of her walking to the gas station.

"Of course your man can pick you up here. I'm glad you were there. Poor Farah looked like she didn't know what to do," I said.

"Yeah, that lil' old white lady ain't used to seeing no mess like that." Beverly chuckled. "I gotta be honest. I didn't think you had it in you. All I know is one minute ol' girl walked up on you, and the next, she was stumbling backwards and trying to find her legs. Then, you kept swinging." She laughed.

I laughed, too. It must've looked like a real circus. I couldn't believe I actually hit the woman. She deserved it, but once I was removed from the situation and was able to think straight, I hoped she didn't call to have me arrested.

Imagine my shock when we pulled up and Kyle's car was in the driveway. I could barely wait for Beverly to park my car.

"You know, Beverly, why don't you go ahead and take my car. My ex-husband is here, and I need to talk to him about something," I said.

"Peta, you're gonna let me have your car?"

I tilted my head and frowned. "Uh, no, but you can drive it home and pick me up tomorrow on your way to work," I clarified.

Beverly laughed. "I didn't mean let me have the car. I meant I don't want to leave you without your vehicle. If something happened with your daughter, I wouldn't even feel right."

She looked toward the house.

"Go on. Talk to your ol' man. I can sit here and wait for my dude to come. It won't take long. He works close to here. You ain't gotta worry about me. I'm glad I was there to help you out, Rocky!"

I laughed at her comment and got out of the car. I may have been nervous, but I hoped, for Kyle's sake, that I'd left all the fighting back at the BP campus. It was obvious I wasn't scared to throw a blow or two.

When I walked into the house, I didn't see him right away. It was too early for my daughter to be home from school, so I was baffled by why he was there. I was glad he had finally surfaced, but I didn't appreciate the way he welcomed his way into my house after I had been trying for months to catch up with him.

"Kyle!" I yelled.

He rounded the corner and emerged from the kitchen with wide eyes. So, he had been popping in and out of my house when he thought no one was home. I hated him with a passion.

"Hey, I was dropping off some stuff. Kendal said something about y'all being low on food when I talked to her last night," he said.

I stared at him.

"You don't have anything to say for yourself, and what you did to me—to your daughter?"

Kyle stood with the familiar simple expression on his face, and I wanted to slap the taste out of his mouth. He dropped back against the wall and looked as if he was trying to brace himself for what he thought was coming next.

"I tried to talk to you, but you were too busy. I didn't mean for stuff to go down like this," he said.

"What am I supposed to do? For the past several months, your daughter and I have been eating off the kindness of friends. What kind of shit is that?" I moved closer to him.

Kyle inched backward.

"Why you always gotta be so damn extra, Peta?" he asked.

A wave of raw hurt gushed over me. My world had literally been flipped upside down, and this fool thought I was being extra.

"That's what you think I'm doing? You think I'm being *extra?* You have no clue what's been going on with me over the last few months. How could you be so damn condescending?"

He rolled his eyes as if I had gone exactly where he expected. There was nothing I could do to inflict on him the kind of pain I had suffered.

"Look, I brought some food, and I refilled your favorite," he said as he motioned toward a massive bottle of Skyy Vodka.

"You think a couple of meals and a few drinks will do the trick? I need you to undo what you did," I said.

Kyle shook his head at my suggestion.

"No can do. I tried to talk to you. I tried to tell you that I needed that order lifted so we could qualify for our new house. Ain't nothing I could do about that. Besides, you signed the papers, Peta."

"Kyle, you know good and well I had no clue what I was signing. You slipped those papers in front of me after a night of drinking. Any judge would throw it out," I said.

"See, this is why I don't take your calls. You think I wanna hear all this crap? Damn, Peta, handle your business and stop leeching off of me! You thought I was gonna support you forever?"

He shook his head.

My blood boiled until it felt like my skin might melt right off my bones. His indifference to my suffering and callous comments made me sick to my stomach.

"Oh, and by the way, my wife and I talked, and we decided with all you've got on your plate, maybe Kendal should move in with us for a while. You know, just 'til you get back on your feet. Especially since you're talking about shacking with some man."

I heard his words, and then the blood flowed from his mouth. I looked into his wide, panic-stricken eyes and couldn't move. The sound of his head as it thumped against the edge of the granite countertop stayed with me.

I stared at the knife that I'd shoved into his chest, and looked down at his hand that covered a growing crimson spot on his shirt.

"Peta, hh-help me," he managed.

"The way you helped me?" I asked.

He fell to the floor like a rag doll. I stood over him and watched as the life began to drain from his horror filled eyes. The joy I felt, scared me, but only a little.

50

DARBY

The thing about guilt is it kind of had this power to make me want to do right, at least initially. Despite the fact that I had barely laid my head down two hours before, I was up and in the kitchen before Kevin and the boys came downstairs.

I wondered whether Kevin was going to say anything else about the way I had crept into the house. They'd been at the table for a good ten minutes, and he hadn't said a word.

"Eat your food, boy," Kevin finally said to one of the kids.

He looked over at me when I turned around from the sink and said, "Where you been getting all this money to go hang out like you've been doing?"

That question made me think about Carla, and how much I missed the money I made when I used to work with her. I still hadn't talked to her, but after that stunt she tried to pull, I hadn't been in a hurry to reconnect. I needed to do something. Chandler had taken up way too much of my time.

It was one thing when we sexted each other, creeping around through text messages and Facebook, but we had moved up to a full-fledged affair. It was as if the devil rested on one shoulder and an angel on the other. I knew in my heart of hearts that screwing around with the man who was responsible for my sister's death was an asinine thing to do. I never set out to catch feelings for Chandler, but somehow I did.

The angel on my shoulder reminded me of the family I had. Images of my boys smiling and sometimes fighting popped up in my mind, but I was quick to shake those away.

Kevin was a different story all together. For years, I had put up with his cheap and chauvinistic ways. But I had grown accustomed to his behavior.

"I have been helping Carla do some bookkeeping for her business," I said.

The flesh around his eyes quivered, and he frowned.

"You mean Carla, as in our neighbor down the block, Carla?" Kevin asked.

"Yeah, how do you know her?"

Kevin finished off the last of his food. He drank the rest of his juice and pushed his chair back from the table. Once he stood, he dug into his pocket and pulled out his keys. He hit a button and the car chirped.

"I know nearly everybody in this subdivision. Hey, boys, go get in the car. I'm right behind you," he said.

We watched as our sons shuffled out the door and raced each other to get into the car.

"I'm the man of this house. You shouldn't be asking me anything about how I know someone who lives on our street. I may have been underestimating you for far too long," he said.

I was baffled by his statement, but there was also a part of me that didn't really care. If he had been screwing Carla or some of the other women, he had done a good job hiding it.

Kevin pecked me on my forehead and left.

As I cleared the table, a funny thought popped into my mind. The way my husband pinched pennies, I doubt I had to worry about him paying for some ass.

I shouldn't put anything past him because he was still human, and he was still a man, but the way he was, he'd be hard pressed to spend more than twenty-five dollars. And because I handled the books, I fully understood that little bit of change wouldn't get you a simple hello from Carla and the other ladies.

When I finished the kitchen, I decided to take a long bath. My plan was to try and meet with Carla around lunchtime, and that was several hours away.

Upstairs, the scent of vanilla floated out of my Jacuzzi garden tub, and I couldn't wait to get in with a great book. I still had on my robe, so I decided mimosas would make the bath even better.

I went downstairs and pulled a chilled bottle of champagne from the wine cooler. Once I mixed my drink, I poured myself a glass and started back upstairs.

The sound of the doorbell's chime stopped me.

"Shoot, Carla, your timing sucks," I muttered as I padded over to the front door.

When I pulled it open and saw Chandler, a mixture of fear and excitement shot through my veins.

"Aren't you gonna ask me in?" he asked.

I wanted to slap his face, and then slam the door in it. I wanted to ask if he had gone and lost his rabbit mind. But I didn't. I stood frozen with my door wide open, my hand clutching a flute full of mimosa, and my eyes fixated on my lover at my front door. It finally registered. My lover was at my front door! Obviously, he knew exactly where I lived.

"Okay, not quite what I expected, but here, let me invite myself in," he said.

Chandler eased past me and used a hand to push the door closed.

"Ah, what are you doing here?" I managed.

"I wanted to see you. I waited 'til he pulled off with the kids and waited for nearly an hour after that before I got out of my car," he said.

He spoke as if his explanation made complete sense. Did he not know the ethical rules he had shattered when he decided he had to see me at my house?

There was nothing I could do once he was inside. A small part of me had no desire to try to put up a struggle. I watched as Chandler wandered down the hall. He glanced at the pictures that lined the wall, and then he moved into my family room and began to look at the pictures on the mantel. Warning lights flashed brightly in my head.

"It smells good in here," he said. He turned to look at me and added, "Kind of like bacon, eggs, and vanilla?"

That's when I remembered my bath.

"You have to go. Go, and I will come meet you," I said.

"I'm going to stay," he said calmly.

I stared at him in utter disbelief. He hadn't moved an inch.

"You can't. Kevin could come back," I stammered.

"He won't. It's been more than an hour. He's gone for the day," Chandler said. He looked around the room again. "So, were you cooking?"

"Oh, no, I was about to take a bath when the doorbell rang," I said.

His eyebrows inched upward and a twinkle danced in his eyes. When the devilish grin spread across his face, I read what was on his mind. That was another opportunity for me to do the right thing, but I didn't want to.

"You have to go, Chandler." I didn't sound convincing, but I tried.

He waved his arm in a sweeping movement and smiled.

"After you. Where's the bath? Upstairs?" He tilted his head upward.

"Let's not do this, not here," I pleaded.

He inched closer and pulled me into his arms. His scent awakened something in me, and I was in trouble. The hold he had over me was like nothing I'd ever felt before. As if in a trance, I put one foot in front of the other and took shaky steps.

Chandler pointed to the drink in my hand. "Oh, wait. Where's the rest of that?"

I motioned silently in the direction of the refrigerator. I used the back of my hand to wipe the moistness from his kiss. He stepped toward the refrigerator, opened the door, and grabbed the glass pitcher.

"Okay. I'm ready now," he said.

I couldn't move.

"Let's go. I won't do anything you don't want me to," he whispered.

51

PETA

I jumped when I heard the frantic knock at my front door. I looked down at the bloody mess near my feet and felt conflicted. *Has the knocking gone on for an eternity? What if I don't answer? Who was it anyway?*

My heart raced as I tried to figure out the best thing to do. It didn't matter who was at the door, they had to have known I was home—both my car and Kyle's were outside. Beverly was going to leave it after her ride came.

My mouth felt dry and my hands were unsteady. When I heard the door open, I didn't know whether I should walk up front to try to keep whoever it was away or simply stand there.

There wasn't much time to decide.

"Peta, sorry. I had to pee," Beverly said, then suddenly screamed. "Oh, shit! What the hell—" She stumbled back a bit. "What in the hell happened here? Oh, sweet Jesus! Is he—" She started breathing hard. "Oh, God, don't tell me he's—"

I shook my head. I had no idea. I could hardly feel my feet. "I don't know. I don't know," I repeated.

"What the hell?" Beverly rushed toward us and bent down over Kyle's body. I didn't move a muscle.

I watched as she reached down and pressed a couple of fingers near his neck. I couldn't move.

"Where do you keep your dishtowels?" Beverly asked. She was frantic.

It was an odd question, but I pointed toward the drawer. She moved quickly. She opened it, grabbed a can of vegetables from the pantry, wrapped it in the towel and opened the French doors that stood to the left of the kitchen.

I watched as she used the towel to turn the knob. She stepped outside and then broke one of the windowpanes closest to the lock and came back in. Once back inside, Beverly's wild eyes looked around. She put the towel and can in her purse. Then she grabbed the phone from the counter.

"OH MY GOD!" she cried. "We need an ambulance quickly. We walked in to my boss's house and found someone stabbed on the floor," Beverly cried. "Hurry! He's lost lots of blood!"

Beverly hung up the phone and looked at me.

"Hurry, go wash your hands," she said. "Peta, do you hear me talking to you? Go wash your hands!"

I moved over to the sink and washed my hands. They trembled so much I thought they'd fall off.

"I need you to pull it together. We walked in here and found him like this! Stop looking like you saw a ghost."

A few minutes later, I heard sirens. Everything happened so quickly I could hardly keep up. The moment we heard movement at the door, Beverly guided me down over Kyle's body.

"Put his head in your lap," she instructed.

I did everything she told me without any questions or resistance.

"Houston Fire Department Paramedics," a voice announced.

"In here! Over here," Beverly said. Two uniformed men rushed into the room.

"Ma'am," one of them said to me. "Let us take over from here."

I got up and stepped back. I watched as paramedics put a breathing mask on Kyle's face.

The paramedic looked at me and asked how long we had been in there. I stammered through my answer as Beverly glanced in my direction every few minutes.

An officer asked Beverly to repeat her story.

"Yeah, so we pulled up, and when we came in, there he was," she said.

"Ma'am, what happened?"

"I-ah, I tried to move the knife," I stammered.

He wrote that down on his notepad.

"Yeah, that's when I told her not to touch it. I explained to her that he could die if she did," Beverly chimed in.

The officer looked at her and said, "Yeah, that was very smart."

He turned his focus back on me.

"Who lives here?" he asked.

"My daughter and I," I said. "But he came over a lot," I added.

"She's real shaken up over this," Beverly said to the officer. "The paramedics had to tell her to move out of the way because she kept trying to help."

"Yeah, she was cradling his head in her lap," a paramedic confirmed, "and from what I can tell, he suffered blunt trauma to the back of the head."

Another officer walked up. He looked at the detective who spoke to Beverly and me and said, "Looks like forced entry over there." The officer pointed toward the back door where broken glass still lay scattered on the floor.

"Okay," the detective said.

His glare raked over me, then switched to Beverly. "You do know we are going to interview Mr. Nixon, right?"

Beverly put on a tough-girl stance.

"Shoot, he better tell y'all the truth! We heroes! We saved his life, if you ask me," she proudly proclaimed.

The gravity of what I had done fell heavy on my shoulders. Kyle would be dead had Beverly not come in when she did. I stood and watched, but I had no desire to help him.

As far as I was concerned, he had ruined my life, and I didn't feel like he deserved to live. The drinks I'd had may have clouded my judgment a bit, but I was still very pissed.

The detective looked at us for a long while, and I wasn't sure if he wanted to arrest us, or was simply trying to intimidate us with his mean-mug stare. It didn't seem to have any impact on Beverly, but two minutes more, and I would've probably confessed to everything.

"If you don't have any more questions for us, I wanna take her upstairs so she can lie down," Beverly said.

All I could think was, *What in the world would I have done without her?*

"That's it for now," he said. "But don't go anywhere far. We'll be in touch after we've had a chance to talk to Mr. Nixon."

"Okay, good. You do that," Beverly said.

I watched as she walked with him toward the front door.

When she came back alone, she looked at me and frowned.

"What the hell were you thinking?" she asked.

I shook my head. I had no words. I felt defeated. It was obvious to me that my days of freedom were numbered and none of it really mattered anymore.

"What time does your daughter get home?" she asked.

"Oh, God, Kendal," I stammered.

"Here, let's get this mess cleaned up. Where's your bleach? You got any candles?" Beverly asked.

52

DARBY

No jury in the state of Texas would ever convict him! All Kevin would need was one sympathetic man or woman who had ever been done wrong before being seated in that box. That's all it would take for him to walk out of jail a free man. There was absolutely no doubt in my mind.

Chandler and I had polished off the mimosas, and I sent him downstairs to get something stronger. What started out in the bathroom as him simply watching as I eased into the tub had taken a turn, and I was completely lost.

I mulled over it for a few seconds. Then I raised my wet leg out of the water and into the air. I was in bliss when Chandler and I were together.

"You are so sexy," he said.

I turned to see him leaned against the wall as if he'd been watching me. It didn't matter. I basked in the glow of his attention like it was the most natural thing to do.

"So very, very sexy," he said.

It could've been the alcohol talking, or he could've meant every single word. But it didn't change a thing. We were both so completely out of order, that at times, I stunned myself.

By the time we had finished off the third round of drinks, I had lost all inhabitations and common sense. I moved around the tub like a carefree teen in love.

"You should get in with me," I teased. "The water's perfect." I felt good.

Chandler didn't need much coaxing. He had gone from spectator to full-fledged participant in less than sixty seconds. I watched as he undressed. His body was beautiful.

Once in the tub with me, he pulled my body close to his and held me tightly. We kissed long and hard. I ran my fingers through his thick, wavy hair and pulled and tugged at it.

Everything about him felt so incredibly good to me. He had a way of making me feel like I'd die without his touch.

Suddenly, he pulled back and began to manhandle me. Chandler grabbed my hair, turned my body around, and pushed me over the edge of the tub.

"This is what you like, isn't it?" he growled.

I didn't get the chance to answer. When I opened my mouth to speak, the sensation of him filling me all but took my breath away.

"Give it to me," he said.

I tried. I pushed back against his thrusts and gave in when his body told me he wanted me to. Our bodies moved in sync. It had gotten to the point that I didn't even want sex with my husband anymore. All I wanted was Chandler.

"Oh, shit! I'm cumming," he cried.

That announcement brought me so much joy, it hadn't occurred to me that he didn't have on a condom. When I felt him release inside of me, and he collapsed onto my back, I actually felt fortunate.

"Let's move to the bed," he said. "I want to satisfy you completely."

I wanted to tell him that he already had, but instead of putting up any resistance whatsoever, I dipped back into the tub, then got out like he asked. He slid his wet hand up my thigh and rubbed me as I moved.

In the bedroom, atop my marital bed, Chandler dove face first between my thighs.

I loved everything he did to me. We complemented each other in so many ways. I was happy with him. And as we lay in the afterglow of magnificent, unprotected sex, I began to imagine my life with him. On the surface, I understood that it was the ultimate no-no, but that didn't stop me from considering the impossible.

Unable to tell exactly when I had fallen off to sleep, I bolted up and realized what had gone down.

"Chandler, wake up! Wake up!" I shook his body violently. This foolishness had to stop. We had become entirely too careless.

The clock said it was ten minutes after two in the afternoon.

"Damn! I had a lunch meeting I couldn't miss."

Chandler flashed his gorgeous smile. "Oops. Didn't mean to distract you." He laughed groggily.

"C'mon, you. Let's go shower. You need to get out of here."

"Awww, you putting me out already? Thought I had earned the right to hang around," he said.

"As tempting as that offer is, we'd better get cleaned up and get you on your way, so I can fix dinner for later."

"Do you do that every day?"

"What?"

"Fix breakfast, lunch, and dinner?"

"Yup, I sure do. My family wants to eat every single day." I sighed dramatically.

Chandler pulled me into his arms and held me. "Why couldn't we have met long ago?"

I eased back and tilted my head to look up at him.

"Be honest. Would you have been willing to date a black woman back then?"

"Darby, white men don't care about women's skin color. It's you guys who do. Most black women won't date outside their race, but I'm glad you did."

We were not dating. I didn't know what we were doing, but we couldn't date. I began to make my way back to the bathroom. Chandler was hot on my heels.

"Is that what you think we're doing here? I mean, dating? I'm married, Chandler, and I won't leave my husband."

"Oh spare me, Darby. You've told me all of that before, remember? Besides, I didn't ask you to leave him—not yet anyway."

We showered together, had sex one last time, and then got dressed. I walked him to the front door. We embraced, and he held on to me like he wasn't sure whether he should let me go.

"Dinner," I whispered.

"Oh, yes, dinner," he repeated and slid his tongue into my mouth.

We kissed some more. Hotter and heavier than before, and I wasn't sure I wanted him to leave. The clock was ticking, but once again, he had stirred something in me and I felt like I needed him to finish what he had started.

"If you don't let me go now, I'm gonna take you right here on that couch," he said. Chandler took my hand and lowered it to his crotch. I opened my hand and grabbed as much of him as I could.

He felt like steel. And, had the clock not been ticking, I would've had him again. But it was already after four. Kevin and the boys would be home by five-thirty.

"Look at what you do to me." Chandler chuckled. When I moved back and tugged at the door, he had the most massive wood I'd seen protruding from a man's pants.

We laughed as I swung the door open, and suddenly, our laughter stopped and turned to instant shock.

53

IVEE

I looked around the classroom and wanted to gouge my own eyes out. The people who sat in the chairs looked like they belonged behind bars. There were two skinhead-type guys who had tattoos etched into their scalps.

Another guy had a star similar to the Houston Astros Baseball team logo tattooed near his right eye, and all I could wonder was who in their right mind would give him a job.

The women in the class looked just as bad. If they didn't look like masculine she-males, they looked like hookers. And not the high-priced, call girl types either.

"What's your name?" an equally rough-looking woman, who sat at the front of the room, asked.

"Oh, I'm Ivee Henderson."

"Okay, gotcha," she said and marked my name on a list.

I rolled my eyes and walked toward the back of the room. I thought better of it when I realized there was a little gang action going on back there.

The moment I realized I wasn't welcomed in that section, I sat near where I stood. I was not looking forward to being taught anything about alcohol. I knew everything I needed to know. As a matter of fact, I wished I could have a few shots to help me get through my very first class.

Moments after I was seated and tried to think better thoughts, the woman who sat at the front of the room began to speak.

"Hey, everybody, what's up? I'm Diane Watson. If you did *not* get stopped and arrested for DWI, did *not* get arrested for public intoxication, or are *not* court-mandated to take an alcohol, drug awareness program, this ain't the class for you. I'll wait for you to vacate the premises."

She waited and looked around the room. When no one moved, she waited a few more beats before she spoke again.

"Okay, dig that. Now that we all where we supposed to be, why don't we get down to business? All of us in here, we are adults. I don't believe in babysitting no damn body. And they damn sure don't pay me enough to babysit no grown folks. Y'all need to listen real good, so I can tell you how it's gonna go down. And you betta' make sure you listen 'cause I ain't gon' repeat myself. First off, you ain't allowed to be late. Ain't no exceptions to that rule. If you late, you disrupt the rest of us when you come in, and that throws everybody off. I give y'all a five-minute grace period. Not six, not ten. Five minutes, and that's all. If you not up in here when I start, you will be counted absent, and I will report that to your probation officer, your judge, or whoever it was that thought you needed to be here."

She began to pace back and forth in front of the four rows of desks.

"Secondly, ain't nobody allowed to sit in the first two rows in this room. I'll wait for the four of you to get up and move around."

Four people got up and scrambled to seats near the back of the room.

"I don't like feeling all crowded and stuff. Cool. Third, you can't miss any session unless you're in the hospital or dead! Ain't no exceptions to that rule either." She spread her right hand and used the other to count down two fingers. "In the hospital." She pointed to the index finger. "Or dead." She pointed to the middle finger.

When she reached the end of her path, she pivoted, and began again. "The only person allowed to miss a class is yours truly." She pointed at her chest with her thumb. "Now, raise your hand if you don't understand rule number three!"

She stopped and glanced around the room at each of our faces.

"Good. I love when I have me a sharp and attentive group. Also, you can't come up in here high or drunk. If you do, or if I catch a contact, or you even look like you're under the influence of any substance or alcohol, ain't no point in you tryin' to concoct no lie, 'cause I'll call and have you arrested myself. Please do not test me!" she warned.

Her neck snaked while she issued that threat.

"You here 'cause you have a drinking problem. And the problem is more than you just gettin' drunk and fallin' down. I don't care why you drink. I don't care whether you deny your drinkin' problem. The bottom line is, if you didn't have a problem, you wouldn't be here," she said.

I hated her already.

By the time she finished her rules, my desire to cause bodily injury to myself had intensified significantly. I couldn't believe I had to sit through not one, but three, of these retarded, brain-numbing, demeaning sessions.

And, honestly, who was that chick? What made her qualified to teach anybody anything? She looked like a recovering druggie who had lived a very hard life.

I braced myself and prepared for what I was certain would be the most difficult three hours of my life.

Everything she said rubbed me the wrong way. It wasn't simply her ebonics that made me cringe. I understood that my anger was really misdirected, but I didn't care. Compared to the hoodlums in the class, I was a respectable, upstanding citizen, and I didn't appreciate having to be in the same room, much less the same category, as any of them.

What really tripped me out was the fact that some of them had the nerve to be trying to get to know one another. My ears perked as I heard a few of them as they traded notes about which drug classes and which instructors were best.

"Dude, Martinez is the homeboy! I can't tell you how many times he let us sign in and bounce!" one of the gang members boasted.

Hence the reason you're right back here again, I wanted to say, but didn't.

I couldn't understand why the instructor hadn't shut them down. She was so busy laying down the law that the lawbreakers had free reign.

Hours later, unable to wrap my mind around how I'd ever made it through the first session, I nearly bolted for the door the minute the clock struck half past nine.

For the first time since it was installed, I had no problem blowing into the interlock device in my car. I wanted to get home, and I wanted to get there quickly.

Where did that tramp get off telling any of us we had a drinking problem? Who had died and left her in charge of anything? I was fit to be tied by the time I pulled up at home. The truth was, I wish I had someplace else to go. After being in class with that witch, the last place I wanted to be was at home up under Zion and his bad disposition.

I pulled into the driveway and dialed Darby's number. If nothing else, she could come pick me up, and we could go somewhere and have a drink. Just because I drank didn't make me an out-of-control alcoholic, and I didn't appreciate being treated like one either.

When Darby didn't answer, I considered Peta, but figured she'd be home with Kendal, and I wasn't trying to be around any kids.

The realization that my only other option was to go inside made me feel worse than I did in class. Had my life really crumbled to the kind of people who went to work, went home, rested, only to do it all over again?

My front door opened, and the porch light flicked on. All of a sudden, Zion walked out shirtless and barefoot. He approached the car.

"So, how long you planning to hang out in the car?"

"I'm coming in now," I lied.

"Oh good, 'cause I saw you when you pulled up, and I've been waiting for you to come in. Ted called earlier, and I need to fill you in on the latest," he said.

I rolled my eyes as I climbed out of the car. I wasn't sure what bugged me the most—the fact that my attorney always felt the need to update my husband instead of me, or the fact that my husband seemed to get some kind of controlling upper hand when he knew information about my case before I did.

54

PETA

I had to sleep with Kendal. She was too spooked to sleep alone. If only I would've been able to stomach the sad and confused look on her face when she called Kyle and only got his voicemail.

"Honey, come over here. Let me talk to you," I said.

"Okay, Mom, but I'm about to call Dad again. I don't know why he's not answering his phone."

"That's what I wanna talk to you about." I patted an empty space next to me.

"I didn't want you to worry, but your dad is in the hospital."

My child's eyes grew wide and tears quickly spilled over the rims.

"In the hospital?" she asked.

"Yeah, I was trying to wait until I had some information to tell you, but I still don't know anything."

"M-o-o-o-m! We need to go to the hospital. Why are we sitting here doing nothing?"

"We can't, sweetie. I called and they told me he's still in intensive care. That means he can't have any visitors." I needed more time to think, so I had to tell her that she couldn't see him just yet.

Kendal burst into uncontrollable tears. For the first time since it had happened, I felt bad. If Kyle had died, I couldn't imagine what I would've done. I hated him, but my love for her was unshakable.

If I had to do it all over again, I would've thought before I acted on impulse. Kyle and I didn't get along anymore, but he was still my daughter's father. And what he had done was beyond dirty, but I could've handled it differently.

The next morning, I was up before the sun. I had experienced the very worst night of sleep that I could remember. I fixed a large breakfast for my daughter and met her at the bottom of the stairs.

"You're going to school today?" I asked.

"Yeah, Mom, I can't see Dad, and if I stay home, it's only gonna make me sad."

I had done lots of things wrong, but Kendal was by far the best thing I had ever done. I wanted to beg her to stay home—not for her, but for me. What if I was arrested before she made it home from school?

Beverly had called several times last night to check on me, and I assured her I was fine, but inside. I felt like crap.

We ate breakfast quietly, and my daughter looked broken. It hurt me to see her so incredibly sad.

"You sure you're okay to go to school today?"

"Yeah, Mom, but when I get home, if we still haven't heard anything, we should go up there. Okay?"

"Okay, honey."

How could I ever admit to her that I was the reason he was in the hospital in the first place? I had to figure out a way to forgive myself.

After Kendal left, I got up and began to clean up the kitchen. I poured myself a drink and took a break. Emotionally, I was a complete mess.

The only thing I could think to do was go to the hospital and check up on Kyle myself. I thought of a thousand reasons why I should stay away from there, but the desire to make my daughter feel better outweighed each one of them.

I still had tons of time to make up my mind, so I picked up my drink and took a sip. I didn't want to go to the hospital and get arrested, but I hadn't heard back from the detectives so I wasn't too worried about that.

The TV had been on while I cleaned the kitchen, but I didn't become aware of it until one of Pamela's commercials came blaring through it.

"That's who I needed to kill," I said.

I closed my eyes at the thought. I was in a mess! Now I was thinking murderous thoughts. It was unbelievable. When I finished the drink, I decided to change and check in with Beverly and Farah.

If Pamela was back at the site again, I would give myself a free pass to commit murder for sure.

"You doing okay?" Beverly asked when she answered the phone.

"I'm making it. I was calling to see if Pamela's back?"

"No, she didn't show up today. Maybe she developed some common sense and set up shop elsewhere," Beverly said.

"Yeah, let's hope so. I saw one of her commercials and figured I'd call to check in."

"We've had a great morning, so we're doing okay over here," Beverly said. "How are things in Sugar Land?"

"I'm gonna call when I'm off with you. I wanted to make sure Pamela didn't circle back around."

"Nah, she didn't. It's all good out here," Beverly assured me. I was glad to hear that. That was one less thing for me to worry about. "Oh, Peta, before you go, have you heard anything more from the guy who we talked to in your kitchen?"

"No, no, I haven't. Is that a good sign?" I asked.

"Yeah, for now. But when they talk to him, things could change. I'm sure all will be fine as long as you remember what we discussed. Besides, I think it was believable."

"You know, I never said thanks for your help with that," I said.

"Please, boss lady. You thanked me when you gave me another chance on that truck. Speaking of which, any news about when we might hear something?"

"I plan to call them later today, so I'll be sure to check back in with you," I replied.

My mind was made up. I was going to the hospital, and I'd find out what, if anything, Kyle would have to say. It was wild to me that he held the key to my freedom. But that was the hole I had dug for myself.

I rinsed the glass and went upstairs to get dressed. I had a nice little buzz going, and I felt good.

Nearly an hour later, I walked outside and inhaled deeply. I loved springtime in Houston, which would probably be the equivalent to summer in some parts of the country.

Instead of going straight to my car, I decided to check the mail. I hadn't done that in a few days.

The mailbox looked more like I hadn't checked it in weeks instead of days. I stood with the door open and rifled through the stacks of mail.

"Junk, junk, and more junk," I said as I searched for anything of interest. "Bills, bills, and more bills." Something dropped, and I stooped down to pick it up.

"Oh, Jesus!" I quickly grabbed the envelope off the ground and fixed my eyes on it. "Is this a check?"

My adrenaline soared as I ripped the envelope open. After months of the runaround, the insurance company had cut a check. Just like that. I was beyond stunned. But nothing could prepare me for the numbers my eyes fixated on.

"They gave me ninety-five thousand dollars?"

55

DARBY

My head began to pound the moment my eyes connected with theirs. Horror was stretched all across my face. But mine wasn't the only one twisted all out of shape.

His mouth pinched into a scowl and I watched, as all of the color drained from his cheeks.

"I need you to go!" I pointed away from my front door. "Why do you keep doing this?" I screamed at my brother. I couldn't believe Roger had brought her back by again. After the last disaster, I couldn't understand why he insisted on allowing this drama to unfold. My brother and I used to be very close. The things he had done lately made me wonder whether he got some joy out of the craziness that was my mother in my presence.

I inadvertently shoved Chandler behind me, but that did nothing to shield him from the building drama. My mother's performance at the sight of Chandler leaving my house was worthy of nothing less than an Academy Award.

"Oh, dear God Almighty!" she yelped, as she threw a thick arm over her forehead and stumbled backward. A part of me wondered how loud the thump would've been had Roger not rushed to catch her.

"Why me? Why me?" she cried. "Oh dear God, why me, Lord? Why me?"

Chandler looked at the scene that played out before us, and he gave me a look that said how sorry he was. I shook my head.

I was caught in an awful place. I couldn't tell him to go back inside, and I wasn't comfortable that he had to pass the circus to get to his car.

The near-perfect spring afternoon had turned on me quicker than a racecar driver on his victory lap.

"Mama, it's okay. It's gonna be okay." Roger tried to soothe her.

My mother hollered and wailed like she did the day they lowered my sister's coffin into the ground. The only thing missing was flapping arms and legs. Because I knew her, I also knew those antics were not far behind.

"You murderer! You filthy murderer! Every dime of your money has blood on it. Your wealth got you off!"

"Chandler, I'm sorry. Here, let me walk you to your car," I offered. I was totally embarrassed. I didn't know what else to say. But I did know that I needed him gone.

"You traitor! How could you betray your entire family for this filthy, murdering dog? Oh, God! Where did I go wrong? Why am I being punished? Does your husband know what you're doing? Does he know?" she lashed out at me.

"Ma'am, I am so sorry," Chandler said in her direction. I struggled to hold him back and ward her and her over-the-top theatrics off at the same time.

"You sickening, murderous bastard. If you were on fire, I wouldn't spit on your behind. Don't you ever, ever, speak to me!" she yelled. "You killed my child!"

But her best words were saved for me. She whipped her head in my direction. "He will drag you right down to the filthy gutter, and you're gonna lose every damn thing!"

When she began to claw toward her chest, I rolled my eyes. Chandler didn't want to leave, but I desperately needed him to go. People had started to come out of their houses.

The scene my mother created was nothing short of a ripe, ghetto attraction. Who yelled out in the streets and flung themselves all over like a fish out of water? Gawkers pointed and stared in our direction. I felt so ashamed. This wasn't the kind of thing that happened in our quiet, middle-class subdivision.

"Darby, I think she's really hurt," Chandler tried to say.

"Trust me, she's not. The only thing that hurts her is the fact that you are here with me. Please, honey, go. Go, and I'll call you later," I said.

"Mama!" Roger cried.

I was pissed at him. He had to stop bringing her by my house. Enough was enough! The minute I got Chandler on his way, I'd give them both a piece of my mind. The craziness had to stop.

"Please, somebody call nine-one-one!" Roger yelled.

Chandler was nearly on the damn sidewalk. I stopped and sighed. I wanted to tell him to keep it moving, but I knew he wouldn't budge.

"Oh, God, please don't take my mama," Roger wailed.

Chandler sidestepped me and rushed to their side. He kneeled down, pulled out his cell phone and dialed 9-1-1. I thought for sure I might pass out next.

By the time all was said and done, a small crowd that consisted of neighbors and firefighters was spread out all across my yard.

When Kevin drove up with the boys, and Chandler was still there in the thick of things, I begged the Lord to take me right where I stood.

"What the hell is going on? Boys, get in the house," Kevin growled.

My kids scrambled into the house as they looked at all of the activity in our yard.

Kevin looked around at me, and then back at the crowd.

"Okay, folks. Let's break this up. What's going on?" he asked.

Right then, the stretcher was hoisted and loaded into the back of the ambulance. And the timing couldn't have been any worse.

"If our mama dies, I'll never ever forgive you, or him." Roger spat as he climbed into the back of the ambulance.

I closed my eyes and tried to stave off the tears.

"What the hell is this all about?" Kevin asked me.

He looked at Chandler; then he looked at me again.

"What's up, dude, you need help with something?" Chandler eased closer to me, and I was mortified. What was he doing? I needed him to run to his car.

"Darby, what the hell? Who is this joker?" Kevin asked.

"Let's talk later," I said. I wasn't sure which one I had spoken to and it didn't matter.

It was way too late, but Chandler finally caught a clue and started toward his car.

"Yo, man, what business you got with my wife?" Kevin asked.

When he grabbed at Chandler's shoulder, once again, I began to pray. The crowd had started to thin out.

"Ask your wife," Chandler said, and jerked from Kevin.

Kevin looked back at me quizzically; the sneer on his face told me he was ready to kill. I blinked rapidly, swallowed nervously, and tried to pull myself together. Under his narrow-eyed glare, I couldn't stand it. I turned and walked back inside on very shaky legs.

56

IVEE

S ounds of the normal hustle and bustle of any professional business were fully underway when I walked into my office. The noises from people talking, constant chatter, and office machines that hummed filled the air. I was still on my cell phone as I strolled down the hallway and past several offices.

It was official. Wayne had delivered his company and gave me a promising lead on another company to bring to the firm. My hard work had paid off, and I was excited.

I passed by the administrative pods and slowed as I approached my assistant's desk.

"Jessica, please find Geneva for me. I need to talk to her," I said as I passed.

She was on the phone, but pulled it away from her face and covered the mouthpiece with her hand. "Oh, I'm glad you said something. She's looking for you, too."

That stopped me in my tracks. Suddenly, all sounds were mute as my brain absorbed what Jessica had said. The last time I had seen Geneva she had rushed away from my doorway like something was on fire. Nearly three weeks had passed, and I hadn't heard anything from her. Now, all of a sudden, she'd been looking for me.

I took a few steps backward and stopped in front of Jessica's desk.

"What did she want?" I asked. I lowered my voice and scanned the area with my eyes.

Jessica gave me a knowing look, and I read her clearly. I wasn't sure whether I should face the music now, or leave and consult with Ted before I met with Geneva.

The decision was made for me the moment I rounded the corner and walked to my office. Geneva and two men in suits sat waiting for me.

"Good morning, everybody," I said cheerfully.

My voice may have been bright and friendly, but my insides were twisted in tight knots. Geneva always made it her business to trump you with the upper hand.

"Oh, Ivee, you're here." Geneva smiled. The smile was brittle, at best, and as far as the masks Geneva had worn, I'd seen her do better.

She must've thought I was crazy. That smile meant she thought she had me cornered. There was no way she'd need two security guards to meet with me if this was a friendly meeting. It was just like Geneva to grin all up in my face as if it would result in anything other than ridicule for me.

"I was looking for you," I said as I walked around the trio and sat behind my desk.

Ted had told me that it wouldn't come to this, but he didn't know Geneva the way I did. I knew she would strike. I just wasn't sure when it would happen.

"We didn't mean to catch you off-guard like this, but a pressing matter was brought to my attention, and we needed to handle it immediately," Geneva said.

As she spoke, I looked at the men. They looked bored. I had been with Geneva long enough to know how she operated. I may have been nervous, but I'd grown tired of waiting for her to make her move. Quite surely she didn't think I hadn't picked up anything during the years I'd watched her in motion.

"Something was brought to your attention?" I asked.

"Yes. And, well, I'm sure you know, you don't make it in business unless you're one step ahead in the game. So we need to talk about this DWI arrest and conviction, and what it will mean for your career."

"Oh, Geneva, that's a personal matter. I didn't think that was what you came to see me about." I rested my hands on top of the desk.

Geneva tilted her head ever so slightly and she looked at me like she thought I might have lost my mind. She sat erect in her chair and shifted her shoulders.

She cocked an eyebrow. "A personal matter?"

"Yes, as I said before, it's a personal matter, which is quite embarrassing. I'm working with my lawyer to get it dismissed. I should also mention that it was an isolated incident that will not happen again, nor will it in any way affect my job performance. So, we can talk about the new client I just signed, and the other two prospects if you'd like, but I am not about to discuss my personal business."

The stunned expression on her face told me she wasn't prepared for my response.

Geneva needed to watch out. If I didn't know any better, I would've thought I had caught her off guard.

She glanced at the men on both sides of her and turned her focus back to me. Her lower lip curled in distaste as her jaw tightened. My mind had already begun the mental countdown. I was prepared to give Geneva and her bodyguards about ten minutes more of my time.

"Geneva, if you are not here to talk about work, what can I do for you?"

"In light of all that's been going on around here with your client list, this new development speaks to your ethical standing, and I believe it's in the best interest of the firm that you are suspended, pending the outcome of an investigation," she said.

"Geneva, I'm not sure how one unhappy client suddenly becomes my entire client list, but the recent turn of events should have no impact on my work. And just to be sure, I had my attorney take a look at the morality clause in the contract. He has already briefed me on possible steps that we will need to take in the event I'm convicted of a crime. But for now, these charges against me are merely that—charges. I have not pled guilty to anything, have not been convicted by a jury, and am presumed innocent until a conviction says otherwise."

"This is a private firm—" Geneva stated.

"Yes, it is. And according to the contract that we both signed, an arrest or mere charges are not grounds for termination or suspension. But, Geneva, if you don't want me here, then it seems like we should be having a completely different conversation."

"As I was saying before you cut me off," she began, "this is a private firm, and what you and your attorney missed was the fact that we were in the midst of our semi-annual ethics push, where all employees are required to report life events. It states that such events include arrests as significant events. There is an exception for minor traffic violations, but it clearly states that DWI, even arrest only, is specifically listed as a required disclosure."

"So, what are you saying, Geneva?"

"Your failure to disclose puts you in violation of the morality clause. While initially I thought we could clear this up through an investigation and your suspension, this conversation has led me to determine that your services are no longer needed at this firm."

Geneva rose from the chair. The two men stood seconds later.

"So, you can grab your purse, but nothing else. We will mail all of your other personal items to you."

My head felt as though it had spun completely off its axis.

57

PETA

The signs were all there. The gray clouds outside the window as I drove, the mind-numbing traffic I sat in on I-10, and the fact that I couldn't find a single spot in Memorial Herman Hospital's four-level parking garage should've told me to turn around and go back home. After all, I did have a check burning a gaping hole in my purse. But I needed to do what I had set out to do.

I wanted to make sure Kyle would make it and if he was able to speak, I wanted to hear what kind of story he'd tell.

At the Information Desk, a woman raised her index finger to me as she talked on the phone. I waited patiently as she gave the caller directions.

"Okay, ma'am, sorry about that. How may I help you?"

"No problem, ummm, I'm here to see someone," I said.

"Okay, do you know their room number?"

"No, I don't," I said. "His name is Kyle Nixon." She started to type on her keyboard. A few seconds later, she said, "Okay, here we go. Kyle Nixon. He's in room six—oh, wait here." She frowned. As she read from her computer screen, I couldn't help but feel like that was the last of a string of signs that meant I didn't need to be there.

"You know what? Hold on a minute here. I need to make a quick call," she said.

By the time she snatched up the receiver, I turned and walked back out of the door. I didn't need any additional problems.

I didn't want to hang around out of fear that his wife or her family would begin to ask me questions. Besides, my mind couldn't focus on Kyle while that money was in my purse. I was so nervous and excited about the check, I didn't know what I should do first.

"Maybe I should do my own commercials," I muttered as I waited at the traffic light. When the light turned green, I walked across the street to the mall parking lot and climbed into my car. I had far too much to do to be treated like I was trying to break into Fort Knox. Maybe they had Kyle under guarded protection; maybe the receptionist was about to call the police to have them come and arrest me. Either way, I was not about to hang around to find out.

When my cell phone rang, and it was Gordon, I quickly answered.

"Hey, baby," he said. "What's up? Are we gonna get together tonight or what?"

"Yeah, we will, but let me handle some business first, and I'll call you back later. Cool?"

"That's cool."

After I merged on to I-10 and headed back home to Katy, I called Farah.

"Hey, Ms. Peta, how are ya', sweetie?"

"Oh, I'm doing good. I wanted to tell you and Beverly about a meeting. It'll be a dinner meeting tomorrow evening and everything is on me," I said.

"Okay. Where are we meetin'?" she asked.

"We're gonna meet at the California Pizza Kitchen at Memorial City Mall," I said.

"Oh, I love their pizzas," Farah said.

"Good. Let's plan to meet at about four. You ladies should bring the RV."

"Oh, Ms. Peta, you know when we drive these things to the mall, those fashionistas and the gawkers won't let us rest," she said.

Farah was correct. The RVs were a magnet for people who loved to shop. Although I had four of them, it always stunned me to find out how many people had never heard of the business.

As I talked to her and wrapped up that call, a thought popped into my mind.

How come I never considered this before?

I dialed Ivee's number and was surprised that she answered on the second ring.

"Hey, lady," Ivee said. "What's going on with you?"

"Oh, you're probably busy. I actually thought I was gonna get your voicemail," I said.

"No, girl, since I lost my job, I've got all the time in the world. Actually, we should get together soon! What's up with you?"

"You what?" I screamed.

"Yes, Geneva fired my ass." I heard fingers snap. "Just like that, honey! Just like that!"

I couldn't read Ivee's emotions through the call, and I didn't know what I should say about the fact that Geneva had fired her. I really couldn't believe it.

"So, what's up? You down or what? I can call the girls. We can do it like we used to back in the day," she said. "Well, not all the way like we used to since drinking was what got me into this mess in the first damn place!"

"Uh, you know what, Ivee, that's a real good idea. And we don't always have to get together over drinks, you know. We can do anything. It doesn't matter to me."

"Okay, okay, well, let me reach out to Darby and Felicia. I know Felicia'll be down. She's been behaving like I needed to be on suicide watch over being fired. I keep telling her maybe this was the push I needed to branch out on my own. I hate to tell Zion he may have been right all along."

"Ivee, actually that's why I was calling you," I said.

When she stunned me with the news of being fired, I had almost forgotten all about the reason for my call.

"Oh, girl, I'm sorry. Here I am going on and on about my problems. I didn't even give you a chance to get a word in. My bad, but what's up with you?"

"Well, I wanted to hire you to do a media campaign for my mobile boutiques. This would be no different than if you'd still been at the firm with Geneva. To me, the only difference now is that you'll keep all of the money for yourself. I've always respected your expertise, so I'm not looking for any hook-up. I will pay you for your services."

"Awww, Peta! So, you'll be like my very first client!"

That time, there was no way I could be mistaken about the emotions that poured out from her end. Between sobs, she said, "Here I was feeling sorry for myself, and all I needed was one of my girls to remind me that being fired ain't got nothing to do with my God-given talent."

"Ivee, you should've called to tell us what happened," I said.

"Honestly, I was embarrassed. That DWI has been the biggest mistake of my entire life. We are spending way too much money on this, and if you toss in my lost salary, I was deeply depressed. But you know what? All of that is in the past. Working on your project is exactly what I need to get me out of this slump."

I listened as she sniffled a couple of times.

"Good! I'm glad to hear that. Besides, isn't that what we're supposed to do for each other? Y'all brought groceries to my front door when I had no clue where our next meal was coming from. I was broke and waiting on my insurance payoff. Well, now I'm able to do something for you. You need to pull yourself out of that slump, and meet with my staff and me. We're meeting tomorrow to talk about getting the other RVs back on the road again. That would be the perfect time for you to get to know more about us, what we do, so you can draw up a proposal. How does that sound?"

Ivee sighed hard.

"Girl, that sounds like the lifesaver I need."

58

DARBY

As I sat in the room alone, I couldn't help but think about the last twenty-four hours. I had no idea how I had allowed my life to spin so far out of control, but that was exactly what had happened. My first mistake was I had taken Kevin's nonchalant behavior as weakness for far too long. Little did I know, he was smarter than I thought.

Hours after the freak show that unfolded on my front lawn, all I was concerned about was the fact that Kevin hadn't said another word about Chandler. I should've become suspicious right away, but he left to go to the store, then came back home without another word about it. I was relieved.

"I put some air in your back tire," he said when he came back. That was it. One second he was there, and then the next he went and locked himself in his office. With him out of the way, I went on to fix dinner like nothing had changed.

"Kevin Jr., Taylor, dinner's ready!" I yelled from the kitchen nearly three hours later.

When the boys came bursting in, I leaned against the counter. "Where's Dad?"

"Oh, I'll get him," Kevin Jr. offered.

"No, let me!" his younger brother yelled.

The two took off and ran toward the hallway. A few minutes later, my husband followed them into the kitchen.

"Smells good," he said.

Again, he did behave a little standoffish, but nothing that I thought was outside of the norm. My mind stayed on thoughts of how I could escape for a couple of hours.

"Thanks. Sorry it's so late," I said.

"You not eating with us?" he asked as he took his seat.

"Not really hungry. Maybe I'll have a bite later," I said.

"Worried about your mother, huh?" he asked.

Before I could answer his question, my cell phone rang. I picked it up and swiped my finger across the screen to answer.

"What's up, Roger?" I was still so very angry at my brother. I wondered why he couldn't simply leave well enough alone. Maybe it wasn't meant for me to have a close relationship with my mother. I had grown to accept that. I didn't understand why he refused to do the same.

"Ma suffered a mild heart attack," he said.

"Yeah, well, Roger, you shouldn't do things that you know will send her over the edge," I said.

I also repeated my brother's name on purpose so that Kevin would know who was on the phone. Once I made sure he and the boys were occupied with their dinner, I motioned toward the ceiling to let Kevin know I was going upstairs.

He nodded, and I continued in on my brother.

"It makes no sense to me that you keep doing this. Why would you bring her over here unannounced?" I asked as I walked up the stairs.

"Are you serious right now, Darby? I call to tell you that your mother had a heart attack because we caught you with your forbidden fruit of a boyfriend, and that's all you have to say? Wow! You really are a piece of work, aren't you?"

Roger had never talked to me like that before. He made me feel bad, but not so bad that my mind didn't stray to thoughts of Chandler.

"Well, is she okay or not?" I finally asked. But just to say the words left a sour taste in my mouth. It wasn't that I didn't love my mother; I didn't love how we had become.

"Why don't you come and find out for your damn self!"

Suddenly, the call ended. I preferred to say it ended since the obvious would've hurt too much. My younger brother, the peace-maker who had always looked up to me, screamed and cursed at me, and then finally hung up in my face.

I threw on some clothes and grabbed my purse.

"Kevin, can you get the boys tucked in? I need to go see about my mother," I said.

My husband caught me at the front door. I purposely averted my eyes as he stood close to me.

"Is everything okay? You need us to come with you?" he asked.

I shook my head. "No, I'm gonna be late. I don't want to keep the boys out that long. I'll call you after I get there."

Kevin grabbed my arm, and stopped me. I looked down at his hand, then up into his eyes. An odd feeling passed between us momentarily, but I was in a hurry to get out the door.

"Hey, it's gonna be okay," he said.

His words may have been meant to put me at ease, but they made me feel a little out of sorts.

I sighed and closed my eyes with relief.

"Seriously, regardless of what happens, it's gonna be okay," he repeated.

I licked my dry lips, and my nostrils flared a bit. I turned and walked out into the night.

When I got into the car, I could hardly keep my hands steady. It nearly killed me to have to wait to turn the corner before I could call Chandler. I was desperate to get next to him and make sure that everything was going to be okay with us.

Hours later, one o'clock in the morning felt a lot later when I had to creep quietly back into my house. This time, I hadn't made the same mistake of falling asleep with Chandler.

My heart was still racing as I locked the front door behind me and put my purse down on the table in the foyer. I may have smelled like fresh soap, but I felt like hot shit.

I nearly died of cardiac arrest when a small light suddenly flicked on. It was just enough for me to see what Kevin had meticulously lain out across the coffee table and the sofa.

I brought a trembling hand up to my quivering lips as my eyes widened in horror.

"Some bitches never learn," Kevin said calmly.

All of those times he left the house, he had been setting me up all along. I bought his excuses, helping a friend, going to the store, since I was busy doing my own thing. My life literally flashed right before my eyes. Too bad for me. Pictures of me being fucked against a hotel's windows, getting it on in Chandler's car, selfies that included images of me playing with myself, and much more, lay sprawled out right there for me to see. The old baby monitor confused me, but I wasn't about to ask any questions.

"Your own son found nasty, naked pictures that you sent to some other man, and even that shit wasn't enough to stop your dumb ass." Kevin shook his head. "Then you fucked him in our bed! But I was on to your low-down ass well before that," he said.

I was mortified. Tears burned a trail down my cheeks.

"Shit, don't cry now. I can smell dick on your breath from way over here. Where'd you meet him tonight, at the Omni again?"

He gave a little chuckle, but his mouth stayed closed.

"You were good, but not good enough. See, Bruce had to help me figure out how to spy on my own damn wife after I saw text messages from you and that dude. At first, I was like, I take good care of her; she wouldn't dare cheat on me. Boy, guess you fooled me, huh?"

If I weren't scared he might slap me across the room, I would've hung my head in shame.

"The bike move was classic. You thought my boy wouldn't tell me about your naked shots? You're dumber than I thought. And you think I didn't know who ol' boy was yesterday? The only thing worse than a ho is a drunk, tired ho," he said. "You two deserve each other!"

There was a soft knock on the door before it swung open. "You're gonna stay here while I work?" Carla asked.

Her question brought me back from the miserable trip down Memory Lane. When I was alone, I had replayed the night before in my head, like a bad horror flick stuck on repeat.

"Oh, no. I don't know. You know what, I'll call one of my girls to come get me," I said.

"Hey, it's up to you. You can stay here, but I get pretty loud, and I didn't think you'd want to hear me getting it on with my clients. I have two today," she said.

Carla's wouldn't have been my first choice of a temporary place to stay, but I was such an emotional wreck after Kevin confronted me, I needed to go to a place that was within walking distance. Kevin would come to his senses, and we'd talk and work things out. I knew, deep in my gut, that he meant it when he said he'd keep me from the boys.

I grabbed my cell phone and tried to make a call.

"What's up with my damned phone?" I turned it off, then back on again. "Damn, he turned my service off! Oh, wow!"

"It's just beginning. Trust me," Carla said.

"I don't know a single phone number. What am I gonna do?" I sobbed.

Carla walked into the room. "Did you set the account up online by any chance?" she asked.

"You know what? I did."

We hopped on her computer, and I retrieved my contact list from my cell phone. I printed it out and used Carla's phone to call Ivee.

"Hey, girl! I almost didn't answer," she said. "What's up with your phone? We've been trying to call you."

"It's a mess. I was wondering if you could come and pick me up. I'll tell you all about it. Oh, and I'm not at my house. Kevin put me out. I'm at Carla's. She lives four houses down, across the street."

"He *what*? What the hell is happening to us all? What do you mean, your husband put you out?" Ivee screamed.

"Please, come get me. We can talk about it when I see you. I need to call Peta. How long 'til you get here?" I asked.

"Give me an hour."

"Okay, thanks."

When I finally got her off the phone, Peta was next on my list. I dialed her number and listened to a similar greeting.

"Hey, what's up with your phone? We've been trying to call you," she said.

"I know, I know. Kevin had it turned off. Trust me this has not been fun. I had to get online to find your numbers. Isn't it crazy how I don't have a single number memorized?"

By now, I had my flask and was sipping.

"Don't feel bad about that. You're not alone. It's like these smartphones have made us all dumber," she joked. "But seriously, why did Kevin cut off the phones? Don't tell me. He's trying to save money, right?"

"Peta. Kevin's not trying to save money. We got into it after he found out about Chandler and me," I admitted.

"What the…"

I took another swig from my flask.

"You mean the guy who, ummm," she stammered.

"Yes, the one I told you guys about. I've been screwing the man who was responsible for killing my very own sister," I said. Before she could fully absorb that, I continued, "Yeah, apparently Kevin put some spy devices in the house, in my car, and laid out all the evidence he had been stockpiling."

"You have got to be kidding me!"

"Oh, and did you know that a baby monitor can be used to spy on you? Trust, I learned the hard way," I said.

"I'm at Carla's, my neighbor's, house now. I've been staying here. Ivee is on her way to pick me up. The car was in his name, so he took that, turned off my phone, and changed the locks on the doors."

"This is too damn much!"

"Yeah, tell me about it. He won't let me see the boys and he barely let me get any of my clothes. Told me that he had bought the drawers on my behind and the shirt on my back, and I needed to leave it all there!"

"Please! Stop! I can't," Peta managed.

"Girl, it has been a complete nightmare."

"But you're, I mean you sound like it's really no big deal. I am stunned. Like my mouth is over here on the ground," Peta said.

"Yeah, this isn't the best thing, but the experience is teaching me a very valuable lesson. I put everything into that man. I have no credit cards in my own name, no car. I have absolutely nothing in my name. What kind of dumb-ass have I been over the last several years?"

"Oh my God, Darby, I'm so sorry," she said.

"Oh, don't be. There's no need for you to be sorry. Maybe this was the wake-up call I needed. Good grief, it's 2014! I've been living in the damn fifties, kinda like my own personal *Twilight Zone!*"

The doorbell rang.

"Oh, wait. That's Ivee. You know what? Let me call you back," I said.

"Wait, where are y'all going? Tell Ivee to bring you over here. You know you can stay with us for as long as you need."

"Thank you, honey, and I may really have to take you up on that offer."

"I wouldn't have it any other way."

I hung up with Peta, walked out of the room, and found Carla talking to Ivee. A thought ran through my mind at the sight of them. *What the hell would I do without my girls?*

6 MONTHS
LATER...

PETA

"Peta, I'm about to leave!" Darby yelled from the guest bedroom. I was getting out of the shower. Since she had moved in, she had literally redone the entire house and it looked great. The chick had mad skills. My bedroom's walls were a warm chestnut color with gold accents throughout.

"Okay, call me in a couple of hours!" I yelled back.

My life wasn't where I wanted it to be—in no way at all, but I was in a better place. Kendal was at school, but when she wasn't, she split her time between my house and her father's. With some of the insurance money I got, I hired a lawyer and let him handle the issue with Kyle and child support. It was still ongoing, but I finally felt like I had someone on my side.

As I dried myself in front of the massive, gold-trimmed, full-length mirror that leaned against one wall, I thought about how much I missed attention from a man. I didn't miss it so much, however, that I'd allow myself to fall back into the mess that was my love life over the past year. The whole two-lover dilemma was "so last year," as my daughter would say.

I finally told Gordon that he no longer needed to keep that body on reserve, and we agreed to go our separate ways. We didn't agree as much as the restraining order kept him five-hundred feet away. I was a little disappointed when I learned that he had someone on the side all along, but what could I say? So did I.

Business wasn't exactly back on track, but it was on its way. Pamela and I had made a truce when we decided the greater Houston area was big enough for two mobile boutique businesses. We agreed to split the city with her taking the Bay Area, and that was cool.

The phone rang. It was Kyle.

"Peta, you need to call your dog off," he said.

I wasn't in the mood for a fight, so I listened to what he had to say. But my lawyer had my best interest at heart, and he wasn't going anywhere until the issue was resolved.

"You still there?" Kyle asked. "Why don't I come over so we can work something out?"

"Kyle, I don't handle that kind of work anymore. You can work it out with my lawyer."

"Peta, you know my memory is starting to come back."

"Yeah, and?"

"Well, I'm starting to remember little things here and there, like I'm not sure if there ever was a burglar in your house that day," he said.

"Listen, Kyle, I'm glad you're getting better. I'm sure in due time everything will come back to you and you'll realize that the best way to call off my dog is for you to do the right thing. Now, I need to go and we'll talk later, okay?"

Instead of waiting for him to respond, I hung up. Kyle wasn't slick; he wanted to come over so he could try and rekindle those hot, sweaty talks we used to have. He'd be disappointed when he tried to bring a bottle over the next time. I'd slowed my drinking considerably. As a matter-of-fact, the ol' cocktail club wasn't what it used to be, and I was perfectly fine with that.

IVEE

Six months ago, it looked like my marriage was headed to divorce court. But as I stood in the newly rented space and watched the work my husband had just finished, I was glad we'd hung in there.

"What? Don't tell me you don't like this color," he said.

"No, it's good. You've done a great job!"

I looked at the paint color he had chosen for my wall, and told myself I'd have to get used to it. It had been Peta's idea that helped me start my own business. She was right. I didn't need to be under Geneva or anyone else.

Although I couldn't take Wayne's business away from Geneva, he did slide me several other clients.

Zion walked around and inspected his work. "Have I told you lately how proud I am of you?"

The look of sheer shock was plastered across my face.

"You? Proud?" I joked. "I remember how hot you were when you found out I'd been fired."

He walked closer to me. "No, I was hot over the DWI. From day one, Ivee, I told you, you were smarter than Geneva. You're more charismatic, not to mention way finer. I realized you had it in you before you did. So when you lost that job, I was hoping you'd see that you could make it on your own, and I'm glad you finally did, babe."

I wrapped my arms around him. "You're the best husband a girl could ever have."

"I've been trying to tell you that all along."

"We should have an open house, a little mixer, to let people know you're open for business," he suggested.

"I like that idea."

After a long and passionate kiss, he pulled back and stared deep into my eyes.

"I wasn't a good husband a few months back. I took that DWI too personally, and didn't treat it like what it was, a mistake. I never stopped loving you, but I'm sorry I treated you the way I did. You forgive me?"

"I'm still here, aren't I?"

We laughed.

DARBY

I was going on three solid months with no alcohol whatsoever! That was a major accomplishment for me, and I was proud of myself as I worked to put my life back together.

My new job didn't rake in the big bucks like I used to make with Carla, but it was honest, clean money. And I loved working with Peta.

The work on the mobile boutiques helped keep my mind off the divorce and custody battle. Kevin used every opportunity he could to tell me how he planned to ruin me for what I had done, and I struggled not to respond.

As I got out of my car, I opened the trunk and removed merchandise. I walked up to the Sugar Land truck and made my deliveries.

"Hey, ladies, how is everyone today?" I asked.

"Oh we're great, Darby. I'm so glad Peta finally has help, and the trucks are all back up and running. Things run much smoother now that we're not always running out of stuff," Sandy said.

"Great!"

I restocked the merchandise and pulled out my phone when it chirped. I noticed a missed call from my brother and a text message from Chandler.

Hey, sweetie, lunch today?

Of course. Finishing up. How about an hour?

Let me know where to meet you.

In the months that followed the fallout with Kevin, Chandler had been incredibly supportive. He even understood that I wanted to ease into our relationship and not jump right in. The most valuable thing we now shared was our goal to be successful in AA.

We saw each other about three times a week and were trying to give it a serious go. But I told him my priority was getting joint custody of my children. He helped me with a lawyer and a vehicle, and we were in a good place.

"Okay, ladies, that's it. I'll see you guys next week," I said as I exited the RV and went back to my car. Since I had another stop, I figured I'd return my brother's call.

That was the one area of my life that still needed work. But after my mother agreed to counseling, we'd been trying.

Since Kevin and I had separated, he'd been allowing my mother and brother to spend time with the boys, so that helped. They still didn't approve of my relationship with Chandler, and when I finally accepted the fact that they never would, I was able to approach counseling with an open mind. Attending AA with Chandler helped me see the possible benefits of discussing my struggles and being open to talking with someone. I was stunned when Roger and my mom agreed to go, too.

We all still had lots of work to do, but the fact that we were all willing was probably a good thing.

"Hey, Sissy," Roger greeted.

It had been a long time since I heard joy in his voice when he called. The sound alone told me we were all on the right path.

THE END

Women are more vulnerable than men to alcohol's effects, even after drinking smaller amounts. Heavy drinking can lead to increased risk of health problems such as liver disease, brain damage, and breast cancer. Women are as likely as men to recover from alcohol dependence, but women may have more difficulty gaining access to treatment.

If you or someone you know might have a problem with alcohol, please seek help. A good place to start is with your family doctor or a healthcare professional. Many people with alcohol problems are reluctant to discuss their drinking problems, even with a health-care professional, because of some common misconceptions about alcoholism and alcoholics.

Ask questions about possible treatment or referral options. Ultimately, you will be the one to elect your choice of treatment options.

READER'S GUIDE

1) Did Peta's refusal to get serious with Gordon have anything to do with lingering feelings for her ex husband Kyle?

2) What did you think of Kyle's relationship with his daughter?

3) Why do you think Darby drank so much?

4) Darby felt like she was judged for being a stay-at-home mom, why do you think people have the misconception that it's easy to stay at home?

5) What are your thoughts about Kevin and his penny-pinching ways?

6) Do you think Ivee's strong personality caused problems with her client and eventually her boss?

7) In the end Zion was supportive of his wife, but why do you think it took so long for him to make that clear?

8) How realistic was it when Peta's friends showed up at her door with groceries and things she needed?

9) Why do you think Darby fell for the man who killed her twin?

10) Was Carla wrong to expect Darby to help her with the extra client?

11) What did you make of Carla's comment that Darby should be okay having sex for money since she already does it for free?

12) Which character surprised you the most?

13) Which character did you identify with and why?

14) How could these characters not realize the impact alcohol was having on their lives?

15) Would Peta have done what she did to Kyle if she had been sober?

16) How does your alcohol consumption compare to the ladies in the club?

ABOUT THE AUTHOR

Pat Tucker's novel *Football Widows* is being made into a movie! By day, Pat Tucker works as a radio news director in Houston, Texas. By night, she is a talented writer with a knack for telling page-turning stories. A former TV news reporter, she draws on her background to craft stories readers will love. She is the author of seven novels and has participated in three anthologies, including *New York Times* bestselling author Zane's *Caramel Flava*. A graduate of San Jose State University, Pat is a member of the National and Houston Association of Black Journalists and Sigma Gamma Rho Sorority, Inc. She is married with two children.

FOOTBALL WIDOWS

BY PAT TUCKER

AVAILABLE FROM STREBOR BOOKS

ONE

"Ww-what was that?"

B.J.'s pretty features twisted into a frown, and a perfectly groomed eyebrow rose. She tilted her head ever so slightly, straining to hear. B.J. needed a visual to go along with the foreign sound. It was so faint; it could've been her mind playing tricks. She stepped into her home's foyer.

The cool, crisp air was a welcomed relief from the smoldering Los Angeles sun outside. Something wasn't right; she could sense it. *Maybe it's nothing*, she thought as she consciously stepped lightly on to the marble floor. In case someone was rummaging through her jewelry box, B.J. didn't want to announce her arrival. Stranger things had happened.

There it was again!

This time, her heart slammed into her ribcage and her eyes quickly darted around the room. This was no figment of her imagination. She was certain she had heard something. She searched for anything that might be out of place, but nothing appeared to be. Maybe she should've grabbed something she could use as a weapon. She quietly closed the door and reached for her cell phone, fully prepared to call for help if needed.

Where could the noises be coming from? The house was supposed to be empty. Her husband's car wasn't in the driveway; she assumed he was still at the Los Angeles Sea Lions training camp. Their two young kids were still away with their grandmother so the nanny had been given some time off. B.J. herself was supposed to be relaxing at a resort in Palm Springs.

But it was like some evil force was trying to keep B.J. from her much needed mini-vacation. She and the other NFL coaches' wives usually took a break before the hectic season began. But this year, things had started off on the wrong foot from the very beginning.

First, Ella Blu, the wife of one of B.J.'s husband's assistant coaches, and the last person still willing to take the trip, had backed out at the last minute. Ella said her husband, Melvin, had begged her to stay home. Since they were having problems, B.J. figured she'd let Ella slide.

Determined to salvage the trip, however, she decided to head out alone. But then, as B.J. drove down I-10, her tire blew out. When her husband didn't answer his cell, she was forced to wait nearly two hours for the AAA tow truck driver to come and fix the flat. Once on the road again, it was nearly an hour before she realized she didn't have any of the paperwork needed to get into the exclusive resort. She reluctantly turned around and headed back home.

By the time she pulled up to her Brentwood home, she wasn't sure if she even had the energy to venture back out today.

There it was again, that sound. Something told B.J. not to call out as she had started to do when she first heard the faint noise. She placed her designer Hobo on the bottom stair and followed the noises around the cascading staircase and toward the back of the house where the master bedroom was located. The sounds, although still faint, were becoming clearer.

Her steps suddenly became heavy, each more challenging than the one before. By the time she made it toward the hallway that led to her bedroom, B.J. experienced a sudden surge of adrenaline. She could feel a lone trickle of sweat running down her back. Her heartbeat began to race, and her throat suddenly went dry, but still, she cautiously padded toward the bedroom.

"What the hell..." she murmured, struggling to believe her ears.

By the time B.J. reached the door and clutched the doorknob, there was no denying those were sounds of passion that filled the air.

B.J. felt her face burn, and the vein on the side of her neck begin to throb. She swallowed back tears that felt like broken glass gliding down her tightening throat, but she managed a rugged deep breath, then blew it out.

When she finally mustered up the strength to push the door open, her eyes instantly locked on those of a naked young woman who was riding her husband atop her king-sized bed. It felt as if the air had been sucked out of the room as she stood trying to process what she was looking at. B.J.'s mouth fell open, but she was too irate to utter a single word.

"OHMYGOD!" the woman cried and froze mid-stride.

At first B.J.'s own voice seemed trapped in her throat. Her eyes narrowed to slits and tears started to burn in their corners.

"I can't believe this shit!" she spat, finally finding her voice.

"Oh, Jesus!" She heard Taylor, her husband, before she could actually see him.

"Don't call on Jesus now, you bastard!" Sheer venom dripped from B.J.'s words. "And you!" she hissed toward the woman.

Suddenly, it was like a scene from a movie; everything seemed to be moving in slow motion. Taylor bolted upright and inadvertently shoved the woman to the floor. She tumbled down and quickly began to scramble for cover.

B.J. stood, still trying to comprehend the scene that played out before her eyes. As the wife of an NFL head coach, she'd been through quite a bit over the years, but nothing could've prepared her for the heart-wrenching situation she had stumbled onto. Her husband had brought another woman into their bed.

"I can, um, I can explain!" Taylor stammered as he also tried to find cover.

"In our home? In our bed? How could you?!" B.J. shrieked, utterly disgusted. "And of all people for you to stab me in the back with!"

Beside herself, B.J. grabbed the antique vase and flung it toward the headboard.

"You sick bastard!" she screamed. "And you, you backstabbing bitch!"

Taylor ducked and the vase smashed into the wall.

"Wait, B.J., hold on a sec," he managed to get out. "Ella, get dressed and get out!" he instructed the woman. "Hurry!" he added.

By now, Ella had found her clothes. But she was huddled in a corner crying and shaking as she tried to get dressed.

"I'm so sorry, B.J. I'm so sorry." She sobbed.

"You're sorry!" B.J. screamed and lunged toward her. But Ella was way on the other side of the room.

B.J. was frantically looking around the room as if trying to find something else to throw at her husband. But this gave Taylor time to scramble up from the bed and tackle his wife before she could find another weapon. He cradled her body as she struggled to break free.

Ella quickly got up, stepped over them, and hurried out of the room as B.J. and Taylor continued to wrestle on the floor.